On Herring Cove Road
Mr. Rosen and His 43Lb Anxiety

A Novel

**BOOK 1
OF THE HERRING COVE ROAD SERIES**

MICHAEL KROFT

This is a work of fiction. The characters and incidents are products of the author's imagination or are used fictitiously and not to be construed as real. Any resemblance to actual persons, living or deceased, is entirely coincidental.

© 2014, 2023 by Michael Kroft
All rights reserved.

Third Edition

All rights reserved. No part of this novel/book may be used or reproduced in any manner whatsoever, including by translation, without written permission, except in the case of brief quotations embodied in critical articles and reviews. All adaptations of the Work for film, theatre, television, and radio are strictly prohibited.

CHAPTER 1
Thursday Morning, July 8, 1976

He was comfortable. The first hour of his morning was his most comfortable time of the day. It wasn't that he was a morning person. He wasn't, and he also wasn't a day or an evening one. He simply appreciated his morning routine. At six-thirty, with his full head of black wavy hair lightly greased back, dressed in black dress pants, a white dress shirt, and a loose black tie flung over his shoulder, Mr. Rosen descended the stairs. Always in black and white, he didn't always dress the same. No, sometimes he would be wild and wear a white short-sleeved dress shirt. After the stairs, he made a left U-turn, passed the dining room to enter the kitchen, and after kissing and hugging his wife of forty-one years, the two sat across from each other at the small but heavy oak table.

He always sat on the same wooden chair of twenty-eight years with the right side of the seat badly scratched up from the small set of keys that over the last thirty years he had kept secured in his back pocket. Though the keys have changed over time, their scratching had continued daily and by this time had carved in the seat a shallow pocket of their own so deep that without the keys in his pocket, the chair would be uncomfortable to sit on.

Compared to his chair, his wife's was immaculate. Every morning it was polished by one of her many green nightgowns, some solid and others floral. That morning it was floral, and she would change and fix her disorderly medium-length white hair only after her husband had left for work. Until then, they ate their breakfast of porridge and toast while listening to the news from the living room's floor-model radio/record player.

While his wife stirred her porridge before taking a spoonful, Mr. Rosen mechanically dipped his spoon into his bowl, watching the level drop with each mouthful. Mrs. Rosen ate at her usual slow speed, but Mr. Rosen ate slowly out of boredom. He was satisfied with his breakfast, but that morning would've preferred bacon and eggs. It had been over a year since his wife had made that occasional breakfast, and only once since then had she offered him eggs without the bacon. He turned it down since that would be like eating dry toast. He could eat bacon alone, but not eggs alone. Eggs need bacon, not the other way around.

His wife's sudden anti-bacon position was the first sign, and six months later came the second: she decided they would attend synagogue on the high holidays. Mrs. Rosen was transforming into a practicing Jew, and Mr. Rosen was expecting her soon to suggest they attend the synagogue weekly.

The old man said nothing about the change in his wife's religious attitude. Even though it worried him, he went along with it just as he went along with everything else she had decided. He worried not because he had no desire to be among a group of people where he had to be on his guard against someone's attempt to start a conversation before or after the service, but because of the reason or reasons for the change. He had heard of seniors, who after becoming bored and/or lonely and/or began fearing the closeness of death, turning or returning to religion, but he had never expected the change in his wife, especially since he thought it was only for Christians.

Mr. Rosen laid down his spoon, used a white cloth napkin to wipe his mouth and brush his black chevron mustache, which appeared to support his large hawk nose, and in his habitual stone face and his refined British accent, the sort expected from a

Cambridge graduate, said, "Thank you, Ruthy. That was splendid."

"Av, you'd be welcome if you'd eat that last piece of toast there," his wife said in her just as refined accent as she slid the small plate with the half-piece of toast a couple of inches closer to him.

He wasn't sure if she had ended her request with *there* or *dear*. If she had said *there*, she was teasing him, but if she had said *dear*, she was serious. Both had grown slightly deaf over the years, and if he asked for clarification, it could turn into a sort of comedy routine, so he decided she had said *there* and replied, "Ruthy, I am more than full... and I expect the birds would appreciate it more."

His wife smiled. "All that butter for the little birds? It'll give them tiny heart attacks."

"Ok, I shall place it in the napkin and eat it on my way to work."

Mrs. Rosen dropped her spoon into her bowl and wiped her mouth with her napkin, which from Mr. Rosen's angle seemed to remove her smile too. "No, you won't, Avriel Rosen. I know you won't eat it, and I know I'll never see that napkin again," she said before pulling the plate back toward her. "Perhaps I'll try to persuade the squirrels to take it. Some of those little critters could use heart attacks. Have you seen the numbers raiding the bird feeders? They're out of control! If any of those furry-tailed rats get rabies, this street is done for!"

Mr. Rosen sat perplexed before he cracked a slight smile reserved exclusively for his wife and followed it up with a reserved belly laugh.

"Avriel Rosen, the squirrel situation is no laughing matter!"

He checked his laugh. "Ruthy, I was not laughing at you. I was laughing at myself. I thought I heard you say, 'If the squirrels get rabbis, this street is done for.'"

Mrs. Rosen's dark-gray eyebrows tilted inward as she stared at her husband for a second before laughing, or *glaughing* as he liked to call it since it was as loud as a laugh but sounded more like a giggle. Reaching across the table, she affectionately squeezed his large, thin hand.

He returned the squeeze, broke a rare smile, and added, "I wonder what our neighbor would do if the squirrels converted."

Her second laugh was louder, making his smile grow larger.

Proud to still make her laugh, Mr. Rosen forced his eyes from his wife and glanced up toward the wooden-framed clock on the kitchen wall behind her. He would've looked at his leather-strapped watch, but without his reading glasses, its thin arms were useless. He wore it more out of habit than practicality. As his smile dropped, he released her hand and said, "Well, it is time." Standing up from the table, he rinsed his plate and coffee cup under the tap and placed them neatly in the sink. Then walking into the adjacent dining room, he asked, "Ruthy, have you finished with all the stores?"

"Yes, dear," she answered, clanging the remaining dishes as she cleared the table.

Mr. Rosen picked up the five-inch pile of manila folders from the dining room table, packed them into his thick black briefcase, and, using some force, closed it. He knew the giant electronic calculator, the small box of pens and pencils, and the smaller box of pins resting on the table — his wife never trusted paper clips — would soon disappear to a location he had yet to discover, though he had never had a reason to search for them. And as he did every weekday morning, he walked to the front entrance closet, placed the briefcase on the floor, took out his black blazer, and put it on. With his briefcase in hand, he opened the front door, bent down to pick up the *Chronicle Herald* newspaper, and turned around to find his wife slightly out of breath with a small brown bag in her hand.

Trading the bag for the newspaper, the old woman struggled to catch her breath. "Now... now don't forget... about tonight. It's... Thursday."

"I will remember. I should be here by four-thirty."

Pulling his tie out from between the back of his shoulder and the blazer, she adjusted it and patted his thin chest at about her head height. "Ok, dear... just to remind you, I... I'll call you at four."

With his hands full, he bent down and swung his long arms around her, giving her a soft hug and a quick kiss, and then with her breathing almost back to normal, they wished each other a good day and she closed the door behind him.

He never brought attention to his wife's struggle for air, but it worried him. He worried about her constant struggle after exerting herself, worried about the decline in her quality of life, which she always downplayed, and he worried about her attempts to hide her struggles so he wouldn't worry. He worried that one day he would see her confined to the bed with an oxygen mask strapped to her face and oxygen tanks standing permanently beside it. He seldom worried about what would come after that because he refused to think about it, and the few times he did so, he distracted himself from it by reflecting on their shared past.

The Rosens never discussed death. To them, it was as taboo a subject as sex, though more inevitable. Until the discovery of his wife's heart problem, Mr. Rosen was comfortable with the high probability of him passing away before her. She could function without him. She had always been an independent, outgoing people person who could make friends easily if she tried, and he was the only reason she didn't. He, on the other hand, couldn't live without her. He was not a people person, kept himself securely protected behind a shell of introversion, and had become mentally and perhaps even physically dependent on her. So dependent that if one were to ask him where in their new home she kept the cutlery, he would have to think about it and might guess the top kitchen drawer. He would be wrong. The cutlery was in the second drawer.

Since she spent most of her time at home and had more time to cook meals, she found it more convenient to keep her cooking utensils in the top drawer.

For the last twenty-two months, the deterioration of his wife's heart — their doctor called it cardiomyopathy — had been slowly progressing.

When first informed of his wife's condition, Mr. Rosen hid his panic well but insisted that she stay home and from there do only, if she felt she must, the bookkeeping. He had surprised both her and himself with his insistence since it was the first time he had insisted on her doing anything.

After eight months of staying home, his wife decided they needed a smaller house. He reluctantly agreed and suggested they avoid one with stairs by purchasing a bungalow, but his wife felt a house that small would be inadequate for all their things. Then he suggested they get a housekeeper, but his wife said she could still use the exercise of cleaning and gardening, but on a smaller scale. In the end, they sold their much larger home and moved to the smaller two-story home on Gilmore Street, which his wife took upon herself to pick out.

Mr. Rosen didn't immediately question his wife's decisions. He had learned to wait and after he had given it some thought, he would find she was right.

His wife was his paragon. In the past, when she had decided they would make a dramatic change in their life, which wasn't often, she had never been wrong. When he returned from the war as a noticeably broken man, his wife suggested, as a needed change, they move to Canada. She was right. When they had the means and the opportunity to purchase an established drugstore, she pushed her reluctant husband to do it, and she was right. When their first store was doing well, she suggested they open another location, and she was right again. Moreover, after the seventh location was operating smoothly and making a profit, Mr. Rosen tried beating her to the punch by suggesting they open another, but she surprised him by disagreeing, telling him they had enough locations. Once again, she was right, though he didn't know it at the time.

The only decision Mr. Rosen wasn't confident with was the one to move to Gilmore Street, not so much the house, but the location. On Jubilee Road, where they had lived in tranquility for almost twenty years, the couple never saw their neighbors. The houses were separated from one another by almost three hundred and sixty degrees of trees, *almost* because the tree lines were only broken by the long driveways. And Gilmore was dramatically different from Jubilee. There was no isolation. The houses lining it were a spitting distance from one another, and Mr. Rosen didn't have to perform a survey to be confident that in that lower/middle-class neighborhood, his wife and he were the only Jews. With their telling last name and his stereotypical Jewish face, he was certain his neighbors had realized it and, even with the lack of space between the homes, kept their distance because of it. That was fine with him, but he knew his wife would've liked more contact with them and believed the main reason she had picked that neighborhood was to make friends.

Mr. and Mrs. Rosen had differing opinions of their neighbors. Mrs. Rosen didn't believe they were bigots, except perhaps for those on their immediate right, but thought the issues were that they had no children, were old enough to be the parents of most of the other parents on the street, and their British accents made them appear as foreigners and perhaps even snobbish. Having little to nothing in common with the other families made for distant relations, at least initially.

He fought to get his keys from his back pocket. Unlocking the door, he got into the oversized four-door Cadillac, placed his briefcase flat on the passenger side of the bench seat, and laid his lunch bag on his lap.

Rubbing his hands over his face, he yawned. He hadn't yet adjusted to his earlier schedule of leaving at seven-thirty instead of nine. That early in the morning was only necessary because it reduced the chances of coming across and exchanging insincere salutations with his bigoted next-door neighbor and his blond-haired, blue-eyed son who had recently started summer vacation and several times in the morning had greeted him as Mr. Jew. After being surprised the first time it happened, he learned to expect the greeting and retaliated by calling the child a goy boy, but only in his mind, since his wife didn't appreciate that sort of talk.

He picked up the lunch bag and searched inside for the small piece of colored paper containing a note with writing so small he started keeping a pair of reading glasses in the glove box for just that occasion. Since confining herself to the home, each morning Mrs. Rosen added small messages to his lunches. Sometimes they were romantic, sometimes reminders, and at other times, amusing. That morning, he found the usual roast beef sandwich wrapped in wax paper, but instead of finding a note, he found the last piece of buttered toast. He cracked a slight smile, closed the bag, and squeezed it between the briefcase and the backrest. Turning on the ignition, he put the engine in reverse, looked over his shoulder, and cautiously backed out of the driveway.

Mr. Rosen had never enjoyed driving, but with his wife no longer working with him in their main office above their seventh and final drugstore, he had learned to appreciate it. It had become the perfect place for his mental adjustment between home and work. His car was his acclimatizer, compressing him on the way to work and decompressing him on the way back, every weekday except Thursday afternoons.

CHAPTER 2
Thursday Afternoon

Waiting at the top of Gilmore Street, almost twenty feet from where it connected with Herring Cove Road behind him and forty feet from the steep drop-off ahead, and dressed in pressed beige shorts and a white *Keep On Truckin'* T-shirt, a nine-year-old boy who could easily be mistaken for a small seven-year-old, causing his father sometimes to refer to him as the runt of a litter of one, sat awkwardly on the bike's small seat. Even with the bike's owner lowering its seat until it could go no further, it was still impossible for the child to sit with his toes on the pavement, so the tip of his right high-top sneaker rested on the edge of the sidewalk as he struggled to keep the bike upright.

Looking past the road's drop-off toward the four older boys' tiny figures lining the sidewalk much further down the street, the child's current fear rose to a new level. They were so far away and so small. The road was so steep and so long.

His heart pounded in his chest. Sweat slowly slid down his brow, and his hands would've been shaking if not for their intense grip on the black rubber-wrapped handlebars. The slight wind brushing across his face and lightly playing with his straight blond hair didn't comfort him in the least, and the sun shining into the corner of his right eye seemed to taunt him.

Minutes before, while walking the bike up the steep sidewalk, he realized how grave a mistake he made by agreeing to take part in the competition and his fear grew. He wanted to back down but couldn't. It was the first time the older kids let him join in on something and he had to go along; otherwise, he would continue to be just another little kid on the street. And to add to the pressure, he felt he had to win. He had to impress the older kids, so they'd include him in their other activities.

To add to his fear, it was his very first time on a ten-speed bike, and it was almost a year since he was on any at all. At the end of the previous summer, a delivery truck had crushed his cherished red banana-seat bike, which he had named Flamer. He only ran into his house for a minute, leaving Flamer resting half on the road and half on the sidewalk, when a truck backed over it, crushing its back wheel and pedals. The boy's heart was crushed much like the bike and it was crushed further when his father refused to get him another until he had learned to be more responsible. Having no idea when that would be since he wasn't sure when he would've learned it, he asked his father and was sent to his room.

Anxiously waiting for the all-clear signal from Robby, who was the farthest away and standing at the first intersection, the child looked for the thin white chalk line dissecting the street, but from that distance, it was impossible to see. It could be somewhere between the second and third boy, but he couldn't be sure.

Then he decided to focus on the instructions Robby had given him: *Go as fast as you can, and when you reach the chalk line, squeeze the right brake and skid until you stop. It has to be the right break or you could flip over headfirst. The skid's only measured from the line, so brake as close as you can to it, but not after it, or you're disqualified.*

He felt a slight sting on his left forearm, and just as he realized it was a raindrop, Robby's shouting reached him. "All clear! Go, Dewey, go!" As the boy closest to the bottom of the hill echoed Robby, Dewey pushed off from the curb with the tip of his sneaker and with the other foot tried to force down the pedal. The bike moved slowly, too slowly. It was in its tenth gear. To add more force to the pedals, he stood up to use his body weight. The pedals turned slightly faster, and the bike picked up speed, closing in on the drop-off. Then worried he'd fail to get enough speed to create the longest skid mark, he pushed his fear aside and pulled up on the handlebars while pushing down on the pedals.

As the bike began its descent, he sat on the seat, leaned forward to grab the handlebars where they ended in a semi-loop, and pedaled with all his might. He ignored the oncoming wind moaning in his ears. He ignored the stinging raindrops, ignored his drumming heart, the sweat entering his eyes, the wind in his face, and ignored the sun's attempt to distract him. He focused his entire being on reaching the bottom as fast as possible.

Before he knew it, he completed the descent, and any anxiety he had had since starting the plunge had evaporated. The worst was over. It was straight through to the chalk line.

Continuing to pedal, his legs began to burn as he noticed the normally dark-gray asphalt was then glimmering black, and as he passed the first boy, the rain became fierce.

With the combination of his speed, the rain in his eyes, and the wet asphalt, Dewey failed to see the chalk line. What he saw instead was Robby further down the road, frantically waving his arms above his head as he screamed, "STOP! STOP! CAR! CAR!" As Dewey flew past the second boy and glimpsed his horrified expression, he stopped pedaling and squeezed the right brake lever. The back wheel locked, but the bike kept going. Then squeezing the lever until it touched the handlebar, he kept sliding and passed the third boy with the same horrified expression as the last.

Then Dewey saw it.

Creeping out of the intersection and directly into his path was his neighbor's car.

Panicking, he squeezed the left brake, too.

He kept sliding.

**

It was four-ten and ten minutes earlier, Mr. Rosen had received his wife's call. After hanging up, he hurried to finish his daily orders, which he had taken his time doing, and placed them quickly but neatly on his overbearing mahogany desk to be phoned in the next day by the store manager. Taking off the black-framed reading glasses that made him look like Groucho Marx (or a grumpy Groucho Marx as he had once overheard one employee telling another), and placing them in the middle drawer of the desk, he stood up and grabbed his blazer from the back of the chair. Then silently waving goodbye to the staff he spotted along the way, he left the office and rushed down the stairs to the pharmacy level and then down another set of stairs to the dark receiving area where the wishes for a good evening followed him as far as the metal door that rudely clanged as it locked itself behind him.

With the heat hitting him in the face, dust entering his nose and irritating his eyes, and the wind playing with his tie and blazer, he hurried to his car, which he habitually parked further down the gravel alley to make room for the morning delivery trucks, and halfway there, when he realized he had forgotten his briefcase, he stopped and thought about what he needed to bring home to his wife, and for a second time, the dust hit his eyes, reminding him it was Thursday's Stock Dinner, so she wouldn't be able to do anything if she had to.

In his car, safe from the wind, he backed out and drove to the alley's exit, where he made a left onto Queen Street, stopped at the red light, and then, after rolling down his window and adjusting his sun visor, the light changed and he made a left onto Spring Garden Road, or Skin Garden Road as his young male staff liked to call it during the summer months when the women wore fewer clothes. Mr. Rosen became agitated when he saw the next set of lights turn yellow, and as the drivers ahead sped up to beat them, he failed to keep up, and just as the lights changed and the car in front passed through the intersection, he had to brake.

Knowing he wouldn't make it home by four-thirty, he hoped it would be closer to four forty-five than five. His wife wouldn't be impressed if he arrived home around five, especially after calling him at four. She preferred sitting at their table no later than five-thirty.

Thursday's dinner, or Stock Dinner as Mrs. Rosen preferred to call it, began as her birthday dinner. On a Thursday almost twelve and a half years earlier, the couple took a table for the first time at a posh and perhaps pretentious restaurant called Morgan's with its dim lighting from the hanging oil lanterns, its windowless walls, and its two-dimensional staff dressed in black and seemingly unable to smile, all suggesting *Adults Only/Privacy Assured*. Being an almost perfect place for Mr. Rosen, it wasn't so much for his wife.

Before then, Mrs. Rosen had developed a habit of eavesdropping on the surrounding conversations, occasionally hushing her husband when he distracted her from some interesting subject. However, the conversations at Morgan's weren't what she was accustomed to. There was no one sharing the latest gossip and giggling or exclaiming after each disclosure. No married couples were squabbling over the many things married couples squabble over. There were no couples on their first dates wearing their best image and trying to make themselves seem interesting. Nor were there any married men out with their obvious mistresses trying to be discreet while dropping sexual innuendos as they anxiously waited for the end of the meal, hoping their date wouldn't cause further delays by ordering another drink. Instead, all around the Rosens were the dull business conversations of dull business people.

Initially, it appeared the night of eavesdropping would be a disappointment, but as the tables finished their main meals and the drinks were being vigorously ingested, the diners, full and loosened up, came alive and spoke with some volume as they began bragging about their latest financial ventures, including their current hot stocks and speculation on up-and-coming ones. This slightly interested Mrs. Rosen. A year earlier, the Rosens had started trading stocks, or to be more accurate, Mrs. Rosen had started trading stocks, getting her advice from the financial section of the newspaper or from her broker, whom, to the broker's discontent, she called Gerry rather than Gerald.

The Rosens' stocks were nothing that required constant care, and Mrs. Rosen once joked to her husband that watching their value change was much like watching a hundred-yard dash by snails; over a few days, there was almost no progress. They owned stock that changed value slowly, very slowly, and the old woman was content with that since she would never take risks with her limited knowledge of the market. Understanding only the simpler concepts of the stock market, she didn't bother educating herself on the riskier trading options like short selling, puts, and calls. No, she would leave those to the major players, like the Rothschilds, Rockefellers, and Vanderbilts.

That first night at Morgan's and more out of boredom than interest, Mrs. Rosen mentally recorded the gist of some conversations around them and that following morning acted on the newly gained information by conservatively purchasing the 'hot' stocks she could recall from the evening before, and to her amusement, the value of those stocks rose much faster than those she had previously purchased, making the tickled old woman decide they would eat dinner at Morgan's every Thursday night.

Most Stock Dinners were informative, but there were the occasional times when one seemed as if it was going to be a bust: there would be little or no sharing of stock information. Whenever this occurred, Mrs. Rosen, hoping to plant the seed of conversation at the surrounding tables, would intentionally raise her voice as she told her disinterested husband about her recent stock activity. Sometimes it worked, sometimes it didn't.

Knowing what every Thursday evening had in store for him, Mr. Rosen was mentally prepared beforehand and sometimes even tried to assist his wife in mentally recording the information, but his less-than-perfect hearing made it difficult, causing him to be fascinated by how his wife with her less-than-perfect hearing could eavesdrop from six to ten feet away on multiple conversations, with her hearing only occasionally failing her. On the first occasion it did, she walked over and asked the man two tables down if he could repeat the name of the stock he had mentioned, but instead of doing so, he rudely ignored her while changing the subject... and after that, she never interrupted anyone again.

With Mrs. Rosen's newfound source of stock information, she lost belief in the adage *buy low, sell high* and came to believe there were two simple rules: one, sell the stock for more than she had bought it for, and two, never look back at it unless she planned to buy to it again.

The stock market didn't interest Mr. Rosen. To him, with his zero understanding of it, it was gambling. He never even understood how a stock split could raise the price of the stock. Why would splitting a stock, then valued at one hundred dollars, into two stocks, then valued at fifty dollars, cause its price to jump up? And with his lack of understanding, he preferred not to know how much stock they had, but what he did know was that over the last thirteen years, his wife had invested her weekly salary into the stock market, and he knew too that they were making a profit because at the end of each year since first dining at Morgan's, his wife divided thousands of dollars among several charities, including Christian and Jewish organizations.

Because of her yearly donations, almost monthly, the Rosens received invitations to charity dinners. Mr. Rosen knew his wife would've liked to have gone to several, but she would never force him into a situation where he was in a room full of sociable strangers for several hours and she would never consider going alone. With the changes his wife had made in their lives, she never tried to force him to change. She never forced friends on him, never forced him into large tight crowds, and she had always tolerated the protective emotional covering he habitually wore outside of their home. She never once pushed him to leave his comfort zone for anything other than an absolute necessity.

Having the green light, Mr. Rosen drove to the end of the next block where the almost fifty-year-old Lord Nelson Hotel stood at the right corner with its several stories of plain red-bricked exterior concealing its elegant interior, and where ahead at the next corner was the Halifax Public Gardens with its colorful flowers attempting to escape through its black iron fence that he thought looked rather uninviting but perhaps existed to keep in the larger birds, like its several resident swans. Getting the flashing green, he turned right onto Bell Road, passed between the hotel and the Gardens, and came to a red at the Sackville Street intersection where he expected a long delay caused by the oncoming turners getting the flashing green first.

He pulled out a comb from the glove box, used the rear-view mirror to repair his hair from the earlier wind damage, and noticed a middle-aged driver behind him with his index finger buried in his nose. The driver must be confusing anonymity for invisibility, thought Mr. Rosen. Perhaps if drivers were required to display a large photo of their face on the driver's side door, with their name boldly printed above it, they would be more conscientious and even more cautious and courteous, or The Three C's as his wife liked to refer to them.

Fighting against looking into the rear-view mirror just as he would fight against looking at a bad road accident that both fascinated him and disturbed him, he look ahead to the opposite end of the intersection where two rows of waiting cars faced him and noticed the driver of the car on the inside lane frantically waving his arms about before grabbing a newspaper and swinging it just as frantically. Slightly amused but not amused enough, he found himself drawn to a young, attractive dark-haired woman waiting in the car beside the seemingly insane man. With the woman signaling to turn right as a seemingly endless line of cars passed by, the driver directly behind her laid on his horn for a couple of seconds, causing her to roll down her window, stick out her hand, and nonchalantly flip the bird. The gesture enraged the honker so much that he got out of his car, and just as he was reaching her driver's side door, the green light flashed and she made her turn. What a jerk, Mr. Rosen thought as he watched the man walk back to his car while the drivers waiting behind him pressed down on their horns, and after yelling something through the honking, he flipped them the bird before getting into his car and, with squealing tires, speeding off to the right.

A quick tap on the horn from the *boogerman* behind him brought Mr. Rosen back to his driving, and he moved forward through the intersection, comforted by the knowledge that he would make the next two green lights at the Summer and Robie Street intersections.

With all the honking Mr. Rosen had just witnessed, the last honk stood out as polite and he instantly knew they intended it for him. When he and his wife had gone looking for a new car the year before, the salesperson from the third dealership they had visited had told his wife that a black Cadillac, besides being the safest car on the market, was sure to command respect. Because of its intimidating darkness that overshadowed most other cars with its assumption of aggression, no one messed with a driver of a black Cadillac. Those two points and only those two points drove his wife to select that car, and soon after their purchase, Mr. Rosen began noticing the quick, polite honks and soon after that, began assuming they were aimed at him.

He passed on his right the ancient fortress high on top of Citadel Hill, looking out over the older portion of the city, and on his left, passed a horse riding club and then the back of the Nova Scotia Museum. Reaching the high school on his right, he made the green at Summer Street, passed The Halifax Commons' several vast fields of mowed grass, and relaxed, but only for a moment. With the traffic ahead of him slowing almost to a stop, a frustrated Mr. Rosen followed the line of vehicles as they navigated past a stalled car with steam escaping from its open hood.

Finally reaching the Robie Street intersection, Mr. Rosen got the green again and passed the point where Bell Road ended and Quinpool Road began, where, if maintaining an average speed of thirty-four miles an hour, he would make all seven green lights.

After passing several blocks of smaller houses converted into retail stores, the residential houses became bigger, the area became greener, and it soon allowed for the view down in the distance of a dozen small sailboats floating in the Northwest Arm, but the view only lasted seconds before the road descended and then swerved to the right, where a stone wall separating the cars from the boats guided him the hundred or so feet to the Armdale Rotary.

He looked at his watch, failed to make out the time, and became even more anxious. Since the dinner was the only thing his wife had to look forward to in the week, it wasn't so much the act of being late that bothered him as it was what his wife wouldn't say.

Swinging three-quarters around the rotary, he took the exit for Herring Cove Road, the area's major artery passing through several subdivisions before reaching Halifax County five miles away, passed the mob of swimmers at Chocolate Lake on his right, and with the single lane clear, he applied more gas than needed to begin the steep incline, where the green oxidized copper rooftops of the older houses sitting at the foot of the cliff on his left floated by rapidly, and on his right, just past the ditch, the intimidating wall of stone with streams of water flowing down against it blurred into an even color of brownish-gray.

The growing scream of a siren followed by the flashing lights in his rear-view mirror caused his heart to race faster, and taking a deep breath, he slowed down and pulled over to the side of the road to wait for the police car to stop behind him, but it sped by. Seconds later, another tore past and a few seconds after that, a speeding ambulance followed. Taking another deep breath, he waited until the vehicles disappeared over the hill before pulling out and continuing up the incline at the posted speed of thirty miles an hour.

As the road evened out, the new Cowie Hill subdivision, a steep hillside of townhouses, replaced the wall of rock on his right.

Mr. Rosen detested townhouses. He was familiar with them. He had once lived in similar structures, but at the time, he was a student and sharing a place with a couple of friends. Tranquility wasn't desired then; in fact, it was detested. At this point in his life, though, he couldn't imagine having to share a wall on either side of him.

As he passed Cowie Hill and then Punch Bowl Pond, a small body of water about a hundred feet long, thirty feet wide, and surrounded by clusters of cattail, Mr. Rosen's mind flashed back to the young woman with the *bird*. Did her looks motivate him to watch her? Two drivers were facing him, yet his eyes went to the woman instead of staying on the man fighting with what must have been a flying insect and should've been amusing to watch to its conclusion. Then a wave of shame passed over him, and he tried to justify himself by wondering if she had reminded him of his wife. Her reaction to the aggressive man's honking would've been similar, but different. She never would've flipped the bird. No, most likely she would've waved a friendly hello from the driver's seat as if responding to a friendly honk. Of course, since his wife didn't drive, Mr. Rosen was just presuming.

Focused back on his driving, he realized he had just passed Gilmore Street, and with his heart racing again, he slowed down, signaled, and took the next left to drive down a steep hill, passing on both sides an assortment of houses with well-maintained lawns. Stopping at a four-way stop, he rolled up the window and turned on the windshield wipers, which complained with moans as they cleared away the bit of drizzle. Making another left, he drove a short block before reaching another four-way stop, where he would make his final left turn onto Gilmore Street.

There was no traffic at the intersection, but there was a boy standing on the left corner with his back to him partially blocking the old man's view of the left side of the street and curiously waving his arms as if doing jumping jacks without the jumping.

With the wipers' moans suddenly replaced by a downpour beating against the car and the rush of rain hampering his view through the side windows, Mr. Rosen slowly moved the car ahead.

**

Dewey expected to see his life flash in front of his eyes just as he had heard happens in a life-threatening situation, but maybe it was because of his lack of years that, instead, he experienced everything in slow motion.

The bike seemed to inch toward the car that seemed to be motionless, and just as its front tire was about to make contact with the vehicle's rear fender, the small boy released his hold on the handlebars and shot his legs straight up and over them. As the bike's front wheel was crushed, its back wheel left the ground and the small rider was catapulted over the trunk of the car. With a crash, the bike flipped over the trunk, and even through the muffling effect of the rain, the sound of metal slamming against metal was loud enough to signal the street's residents to the accident.

Dewey's flight seemed to take minutes before he made the skin-scraping impact he had resigned himself to accept, and for twelve feet, he flipped and rolled like a rag doll before coming to a stop face up with all four appendages spread out as if frozen while making snow angels in the pavement.

After the crippled bike came to a rest beside him, there was a moment of silence as the small group of boys spaced out along the sidewalk took in what they had just witnessed.

Then one yelled, "Dewey!"

Another exclaimed, "Oh my God!"

Robby screamed, "My bike! My bike!"

And the last yelled, "Let's get out of here!"

Through the rain streaming down the driver's side window, Mr. Rosen had seen a quick flash of white, blue, and pink before feeling and hearing the crash against his car. Quickly collecting himself, he put the car in park and rushed out to discover what had happened.

With several soaked boys running away in both directions of the sidewalk, he saw on the other side of his car, about twenty feet away at the other end of the intersection, a boy lying face-up on the street next to a bent bike, and faster than expected for a man of his age, Mr. Rosen ran to him. Taking off his blazer and placing it over the small body to shield it from what was left of the sun shower, he kneeled next to the unconscious child and asked, "Boy? Can you hear me, boy?"

Releasing a groan, Dewey opened his eyes and tried to understand why he was looking up at the sky, and when he tried to sit up, a sharp pain in his right forearm and another in his left shoulder caused him to collapse, and then seeing the cold face of the old man staring down at him, he began to cry softly.

"Try not to move, boy. We will get help soon," Mr. Rosen said, before Mr. Smith, a husky man in his thirties who lived across the street from the Rosens, tossed the bike onto the front lawn of the nearest house and kneeled next to the old man. Becoming aware of the man's presence, Mr. Rosen calmly asked, "Sir, would you call an ambulance, please?"

Mr. Smith placed his hand on Mr. Rosen's shoulder. "I just did, Mr. Rosen. How's Dewey?"

Not noticing the hand touching his shoulder or the use of his name, Mr. Rosen softly squeezed the boy's limbs. "No obvious bends where there are no joints, but he could have fractures. His breathing appears to be fine, but we should not move him ourselves."

Neither noticed the spectators who had shown up, but both heard Dewey's mother. The young and thin blonde woman in jeans and a dark blouse rushed toward them, screaming her son's name while her normally pretty face held an expression of terror. As Mr. Smith went to intercept her, Mr. Rosen yelled sternly over the ambulance's siren in the distance, "The boy is going to be alright!" He wasn't trying to be stern. He hadn't yelled in over thirty years, and that was just how it came out.

While waiting for her husband on their covered porch, Mrs. Rosen witnessed the accident. Through the heavy rain and from the opposite direction than she had expected, she saw their Cadillac making a left onto Gilmore. She heard the shout of the boy at the intersection, glimpsed a child on a bike zoom past her house, witnessed the dramatic collision with her husband's car, and lastly, saw the boys lining the sidewalk rush off.

She arrived at the scene a few seconds after Dewey's mother, who almost collided with the slow-moving woman.

In a slightly damp light-green dress and standing at the edge of the road away from her neighbors, the old woman tried to catch her breath while repeatedly switching from fear for the boy to amazement regarding her husband, whom in the last thirty years she had never once seen drop his introverted shell in public.

As the sirens neared and like a flock of birds startled out of a tree and then, as if thinking as one, immediately returning to it, the spectators standing on the road moved out of the way of the arriving ambulance and police car, and then as the vehicles stopped, returned to where they had stood seconds before.

Becoming conscious of the surrounding crowd, Dewey tried but failed to stop his tears. He tried to speak but was too shocked to form words, and when he looked up at the old man looking down at him, he immediately wanted his mother.

Mr. Rosen only moved away from the boy when the two ambulance attendants demanded he did, and after handing his blazer back to him, they quickly examined the boy before gently (painfully to Dewey) moving his small body onto a gurney, fastening him down, elevating it to its full height, and sliding him into the back of the ambulance.

Dewey was slightly pacified when his mother joined him and both were soon sped off.

With the ambulance gone, the police about to leave, and the street clearing of its concerned neighbors, Mrs. Rosen joined her husband on the street where she embraced him for several seconds before he drove her the short distance home.

The sun had quickly evaporated the evidence of the shower, and the only evidence of the accident was a twisted bike resting on a pristine front lawn.

CHAPTER 3
Thursday Evening

Wearing the same clothes as earlier that afternoon, the Rosens held hands as they passed through the automatic glass doors of the IWK Children's Hospital, and with his blank expression, the expression that was effective at keeping people at a distance, Mr. Rosen intentionally kept his pace slow so his wife could keep up without losing her breath.

As the couple passed those on the several rows of chrome chairs taking up half of the Emergency Department's waiting room, Mrs. Rosen ignored the room's sights, sounds, and smells that were making her husband slightly nauseous. Some adults and children sat sleeping with their heads hanging forward, back, and to the sides. Some children were sobbing while others were silently staring at nothing, and some had obvious issues, like sloppily bandaged lacerations, while those of others weren't so obvious.

The two made their way to the reception counter where Mrs. Rosen asked the receptionist on the other side of the glass window where they could find Dewey Dixon.

The receptionist, a slim woman in her mid-thirties with her long hair held away from her face by hair clips, glanced at her clipboard and asked, "Dwight Dixon?"

"Yes, Dwight. Excuse me."

"Well, the little fella was here about an hour ago, but he's been moved to the third floor. Let me find the room." Picking up the phone, she dialed, and while waiting, asked, "Are you his grandparents?"

Mrs. Rosen only smiled and nodded.

"Hello, Bev? Hi, could you tell me which room the Dixon boy's in? Uh-huh, ok. Can he receive visitors? Uh-huh, uh-huh, ok. Great. Thanks, hun." Hanging up the phone, she said, "He's on the third floor, in room three-twelve. He's only waiting on some results, so you can go right on up."

"Thank you very much, dear," Mrs. Rosen said while her husband, whose blank expression had gone unnoticed since it was appropriate for the place, nodded his head.

"You're welcome," replied the receptionist with a slight smile. "The elevators are further down to the left. Have a better evening."

The two followed the instructions, and before Mr. Rosen could press the button to beckon the elevator, with a loud ding and then a low grind, its door slowly slid open. Stepping to the side, the Rosens waited for it to empty before they entered and Mr. Rosen pressed the large, round white button with a black number three, and as its door groaned to a close, his wife gently squeezed his hand. Looking down at her, his expression softened when she gave him a sympathetic smile.

The elevator dinged once for the second floor, again for the third, and then, with a subtle shake, it stopped and forced its door open.

Stepping out and searching the beige walls for a sign directing them toward the room, Mrs. Rosen gave a tug on her husband's arm and led him down the hallway on the left, and as they passed several staff and visitors, he kept his eyes on the floor to avoid any accidental glimpses through any of the rooms' opened doors. He had no desire to discover the source of the moans and crying.

The last place he wanted to be was at the hospital, and he was only there because of his wife's suggestion, and neither knew what sort of reception the Dixons would give them. Would they be bitter, indifferent, or cross toward his wife and him? They certainly wouldn't be in a welcoming mood, but then who would be when meeting the person who had put them in the hospital?

He wanted to rush through the hallway and get it over with, but then, realizing his destination would be worse than where he was, he slowed his pace so much that his wife had to slow hers even more. "There's a lot of beige here. There must've been a sale on beige paint," she said, attempting to distract his mind, and then finally reaching the room, which was too soon for him, she knocked on its half-opened door.

"Come in," came a woman's soft voice from the other side.

Gently pulling her husband behind her, Mrs. Rosen pushed the door open the rest of the way and entered to find Dewey's mother standing alone in the large beige room furnished with two beds against opposite walls and a metal nightstand beside each. One bed was empty while the one next to her held a sleeping child with its yellow sheets pulled up to his neck. The yellow privacy curtains attached to the ceiling tracks over each bed were pulled back to allow the large floor fan standing in one corner to circulate air, and at the far end of the room beyond the large window occupying the top half of the wall were the tops of trees standing in the groomed green space at the front of the building.

The young mother's face revealed her surprise. "Oh... hello... uh... Mrs. Rosen, Mr. Rosen," she whispered uneasily before gesturing to the chrome chair beside her son's bed. "Please, Mrs. Rosen, sit here."

After Mrs. Rosen silently directed her husband to grab two more chrome chairs beside the vacant bed, she whispered, "No thank you, Mrs. Dixon. Please sit. Avriel will bring chairs."

Relieved that Mr. Dixon wasn't there, Mr. Rosen grabbed the chairs by the top of their backrests and placed them next to the one already there.

Blushing, Dewey's mother sat her thin frame in her chair and brushed her long blonde hair out of her face, and as Mrs. Rosen took the chair next to her, it hissed as air escaped its rubber-covered padding. "How... how is the poor thing?"

"Oh, it's nothing life-threatening. The worst is only a fractured arm, which the doctor cast up. He fixed his dislocated shoulder and addressed the cuts and scrapes, too. In a month, he'll be as good as new. You two really didn't have to come down here. Mr. Rosen, Dewey made sure I knew the accident wasn't your fault and we're both awfully sorry for all the fuss he caused."

"It's no fuss at all," Mrs. Rosen said, speaking for her husband. "We were told you're waiting on more tests... the test results."

"Yes, that's true," she nodded. "We're waiting for the X-rays of his head and chest to come back, but after that, we're free to go if nothing else is wrong, knock on wood," Mrs. Dixon said, tapping the top of the metal nightstand. "It's going to be several days in bed for Dewey so his cuts and scrapes can heal prop—"

"Mommy?" said the drowsy nine-year-old. "Mommy?"

Obviously faking excitement, Mrs. Dixon said, "Honey, you have guests! You've only been here for a little over two hours and you already have guests!"

Leaving her chair, she reached down and turned the crank on the bed's side, and as its top half slowly bent upward, it forced her son to sit up and reveal the bandages on his forehead and right cheek.

It surprised Dewey to see the old couple, and seeing no reason for them to be there unless they came to scold him for crashing Robby's bike into their car, which would be a long way to go just for that, he figured they must have been passing by when they noticed his mother, and he said, "Uh... hi, Mr. and Mrs. Jew."

While his wife smiled and said, "Hello, Dewey," as if the child had said nothing out of the ordinary, Mr. Rosen pushed his back against the chair as if trying to vanish into it. *Goy boy!*

Mrs. Dixon's jaw dropped. Her pale complexion turned scarlet red, and it took her a couple of seconds before she could speak. "Dewey, what... what did you say?!" she demanded. "Why would you call the Rosens Jews?" Then her expression changed as if suddenly realizing she didn't want to know the answer.

"Rosens? They're the Jews," Dewey informed his mother before looking to the Rosens for confirmation. "You're the Jews, right?"

"Dwight Paul Dixon!" exclaimed his mother.

Dewey immediately knew he had said something very wrong. His mother addressed him as Dewey when she was content with him, addressed him as Dwight Dixon when she was being stern, and only addressed him as Dwight Paul Dixon when she was furious with him. He had no memory of ever hearing his full name at a reasonable volume or tone, and if someone was to ask him for it, he might just shout it out angrily. The last time his mother used his full name was the summer before when she discovered he had used all of her new tube of lipstick. He was out of red crayons.

Not understanding how he could've gotten the old couple's last name wrong and with tears building in his eyes for upsetting his mother, Dewey tried to get the words out as he explained, "Daddy... Daddy talks about the Bradleys, the Campbells, the Smiths, and the Pattersons and... and sometimes he talks about the Jews, the Jews next door. If they're the Rosens, then you have to tell Daddy too!"

As his wife struggled to hold back her laugh, Mr. Rosen relieved the pressure against his backrest.

"Forget what Daddy says or knows! They're the Rosens, and you'll address them as Mr. and Mrs. Rosen from now on!"

"Ok," Dewy nodded, confused.

Then, relieved, Mrs. Dixon looked down past the bed at nothing in particular and whispered to no one specific, "Thank God. I thought he'd been bigotized."

"Bigotized?" Mrs. Rosen asked.

Turning to the Rosens, Dewey's mother forced herself to say, "Oh, it's... it's just jargon somebody I know uses when someone doesn't agree with him. If you don't agree with him on say... Black people, he'll say you've been blackidized." Then embarrassed by her explanation, she put out her arms as if she was on display. "Tah-dah! Meet the redneck Dixons!"

Having been enlightened, Mr. Rosen traded his habitual blank expression for a sympathetic one. Through a misunderstanding, he had rudely ignored the greetings of an innocent child, certainly hurting his feelings, and the presence of him and his wife had just caused the mother and son's current embarrassment. "No worries, Mrs. Dixon," he said, surprising and then shocking his wife as he stood up and stepped in front of her to stand next to the young woman, placed his hand on her thin arm, and whispered, "From the mouth of babes, yes?" And after she replied with an awkward nod of her head, he turned his attention to Dewey. "Well, boy, you are correct... in one sense. We are the Jews, just as you are the Christians, but we are also the Rosens. I am... I am Mr. Rosen, and behind me is my lovely and empathetic wife, Mrs. Rosen."

Thinking it strange the old man would call his wife pathetic, Dewey nervously looked at his wife, pulled his left hand out from under the sheet, and waved it to her.

Glossy-eyed and at an unusual loss for words, Mrs. Rosen just smiled and waved back, and as Mrs. Dixon sat down to give the man more room, she missed Mrs. Rosen's discreet wiping of an eye.

Mr. Rosen continued. "We are the Jewish couple next door to you, and I will say it is a pleasure finally to make your acquaintance. I would shake your hand but... but I think it is out of commission."

Dewey, not understanding the term *Jewish* but guessing correctly that it was related to the word *Jew*, stared at the man for a second. "Sir... Mr. Rosen, it's nice to meet you," he said, trying to sound mature as he stuck out his small right arm.

Mr. Rosen took the small fingers sticking out from the cast, gave them a gentle wiggle, and said, "That is a rather weak handshake, boy, but under the circumstances, it is understandable." Then, with Dewey smiling and his mother relaxing and breaking a smile, he said, "This place reminds me of a similar experience I had myself. Now, do not take me as a person who has a story for everything. I do not, and I think those folks with all their stories can be... well... annoying at times. My story, my one story, has to do with the first time I recall being in a hospital... as a patient, that is. My bed was in a much larger room than this one, with perhaps twenty other patients. It was an incredibly loud room with much groaning and moaning, and some people were even screaming. I would have to say it was not nearly as pleasant as the place you have here," he said before clearing his throat. "Well... well, when I was there, I met a Russian gentleman—"

"You met a Russian, seriously?" Dewey asked. "Seriously?"

"That is correct. The first one I came across at the time. He was in the bed beside me and it turned out spoke English quite well, surprisingly well. He was a nice sort, and we attempted to talk to each other through the noise. I told him my name, and he gave me his. I missed his name the first time, but being the smart fellow he is... or was..." Clearing his throat again, he fought off his stage fright and continued in his monotone voice. "He repeated his name, saying, 'My name is Christian.' Well, let me tell you, Christian and I would talk for hours, telling jokes, comparing stories, and that sort of thing. If it were not for him, my time there would have been rather unbearable.

"Now, I am not sure how many times I selfishly woke him by hitting his bed and asking, 'Christian, are you up?' but it was many and he would wake up to let me talk until his ears were bleeding... well not bleeding... not literally, figuratively... an expression. Sometimes when one is in bed too long, one can get so bored that when a chance presents itself to talk, one forgets to let the other person speak. Anyway, they discharged me before Christian and as we were saying our farewells, he shook my hand and asked me, 'Why do you call me Christian? I do not call you Jew.' Well, let me tell you, I simply stood there stunned until he laughed and said, 'My name is Pyotr. It is Christian. It is a Christian name.'

"I do not expect I have to tell you that I was embarrassed to the extreme, probably the most up to that point in my life, and I found myself apologizing repeatedly until Pyotr told me he understood it was an honest mistake but found it so amusing he let me continue calling him by his religion.

"Well, with that cleared up, we shook hands and said our goodbyes, and he joked, saying, 'Avriel, you are a Jew, but I still like you,' and as I was leaving, he yelled out, 'I made a rhyme! I think I will write a poem just for you, starting with that.' Well, I had to leave to make the truck and as I walk down the corridor, I could hear him shouting,

'Avriel, you are a Jew,
But, I still like you!
You make me smile,
And bust a gut,
Even as I lay here
With a bullet in my butt.'"

Of the three laughing, Dewey was the last to stop. Mrs. Rosen's laugh caused him to laugh even more.

"It is strange how I still remember that, but perhaps that last part was not suitable for here," said Mr. Rosen, pausing for a moment. "It turned out that Pyotr, which I would learn later is Peter in English, understood my mistake but never corrected me. It amused him. You see, he had originally said something like, 'Call me Pyotr.' But with all the noise, I missed that and only heard the second part, 'My name is Christian,' causing me to believe his name was Christian... like Christian Jones, if you will. Now someone else might not have understood my error, thought I did not like Christians, and got upset with me. So, you see, boy, you and your father are not the only ones to make that mistake, but I hope we are the few who have."

Feeling better about his confusion with their names, Dewey asked, "Why were you in the hospital?"

With Mr. Rosen stiffening up in response to the boy's question, Mrs. Dixon cut in, "Honey, that's a personal question. Mr. Rosen may not want to talk about it."

Mrs. Rosen smiled. "Oh, it's fine. Dear, show Dewey your scars."

With a wave of anxiety splashing over him, Mr. Rosen looked at his smiling wife, looked at an excited Dewey, looked back at his then nodding wife, and took a large breath before lifting his right shoe onto the side of the bed, and as he pulled up his pant leg and pushed down his dress sock, he forced out, "I received a pair of scars."

"Wow!" Dewey exclaimed. "Two scars! How? How'd you get them?"

"I stumbled onto something rather sharp. It went straight through."

As Dewey went to touch the scars, Mr. Rosen quickly pulled up his sock, dropped his foot from the bed, and wiped the bed clean before sitting in his chair.

Dewey asked, "What went—"

"Let me show you Evel Knievel's wounds," Mrs. Dixon said, changing the subject for her uncomfortable neighbor as she stood up.

When the Rosens joined her, she gently pulled down the bedsheet to expose Dewey's light-blue hospital gown and the bandages on both of his knees, and with Dewey successfully holding back any sign of pain, she slowly peeled off the tape from one side of each bandage to reveal the wounds on his forehead and cheek and the wide scrapes on both knees. They finished by looking under the bandage on his left elbow to count the stitches, with Dewey making a mental note that there were twelve.

"Well, boy, you are looking at, perhaps, five days in bed," Mr. Rosen said, "and those bandages will have to be changed daily."

Then stunning her husband, Mrs. Rosen added, "And it's lucky for you that you have an army medic from the war living next door to you."

"Who?" Dewey asked excitedly before it occurred to him and he looked at Mr. Rosen. "You? You were in the war?"

"That's correct," Mrs. Rosen answered for her husband.

"Which one?" Dewey asked.

"Which one?" Mrs. Rosen asked back and then laughed. "Why the second, of course."

Dewey thought for a moment. "But..." he said before deciding it was better to say nothing.

"But what?" pushed the old woman.

"Uh," Dewey said, embarrassed to reveal his thought but feeling pressured to do so, "He's... Mr. Rosen, you're too old to be a soldier in the Second World War."

The two women laughed and Mr. Rosen even cracked a slight smile that he quickly hid so as not to invite any further discussion on the topic.

Not understanding what was so funny, Dewey threw a puzzled look at the old man, who shrugged his shoulders and pretended not to understand too.

After the three returned to their seats and Mrs. Dixon apologized again for the accident ruining whatever plans the Rosens might've had that evening, Mrs. Rosen told her they didn't have any plans and added that it was the most excitement they had in a very long time.

Then, with the two women becoming more comfortable with each other, they talked while both Mr. Rosen, with his protective covering firmly back in place, and Dewey, trying to fight off sleep, listened. The little boy had learned from his father that when adults talked, he was to be seen but not heard, and preferably not seen too.

The women talked about the weather, their neighbors on Gilmore Street, and Dewey's hobbies and school, with him interjecting when he couldn't control himself, and after a little over an hour of talking, Mrs. Rosen decided to go for drinks and asked what they would like. Dewey asked for a Coke, Mr. Rosen would take a coffee and Mrs. Dixon didn't want anything but offered to go with her to the cafeteria, which Mrs. Rosen welcomed as long as she didn't mind walking at a snail's pace.

As they were leaving, Mrs. Rosen stopped at the door and turned back to her husband. "Av, while we're gone, don't be *Jewidizing* the boy, and there better not be a bris performed in here if you know what's good for you."

With the smiling women gone, Dewey looked over at an agitated Mr. Rosen and whispered, "What's a bris?"

"A... a Jewish ceremony... of sorts."

"Neat. A ceremony for what? What do they do? Is it like a party?"

A wave of extreme discomfort splashed over the man. It certainly wasn't appropriate for him to tell the boy what they did at a bris, and more so when it would probably involve more questions. *What's a foreskin? Why do we have them? Why do you take yours off? Can you take mine off too?* The answers weren't his place to give, so he replied in a cold voice that he hoped would close the door on any further conversation. "We celebrate the *henway*."

"What's a henway?"

"Approximately six and a half pounds fully grown."

"Huh? A henway's *approximintly* six and a half pounds fully grown?" Dewey asked and then realizing that Mr. Rosen had set him up for a joke, laughed and forgot his original question.

After Dewey calmed down, neither knew what to say to the other, so both looked straight ahead in silence. Minutes later, after Dewey yawned and Mr. Rosen followed it up with one of his own, Dewey was sleeping, and Mr. Rosen, who had tried to fight off doing the same, was snoring so loudly in the chair that a nurse came by and closed the door.

**

As they waited for the elevator, the two women heard the laughter of a child that was so out of place that it puzzled Mrs. Rosen.

"That's Dewey's laugh. Your husband must be funny."

"He can be," replied Mrs. Rosen, downplaying how proud she was of her husband at that moment.

Soon the elevator arrived and strained to open its door, and as they walked in, Mrs. Rosen asked, "Mrs. Dixon, before we go to the cafeteria, would you like to make a quick trip to the Maternity Ward?"

"Sure, I haven't been there since Dewey was born. I wonder if all the same babies are still there."

Mrs. Rosen laughed, and as the door closed, Mrs. Dixon pressed the second-floor button and laughed too, not because of her joke but because Mrs. Rosen's laugh was addictive.

After the elevator dinged and stopped with a light bounce, both women slowly exited to the left. Both knew exactly where they were going. Walking at Mrs. Rosen's snail's pace down a pink hallway with a large mural of teddy bears, geese, and cherubs, they came to an intersection, turned right, continued past an even larger mural of nursery rhyme characters, and arrived at a large observation window at the dimly lit end of the hall.

An older couple stood in front of the window, holding hands and whispering to one another while occasionally waving to get the attention of a specific baby. Past the couple, a gray-bearded man with his short, chubby body stuffed unevenly into a dark-gray polyester three-piece suit seemed to be there to fill the area with smoke from his oversized cigar.

Stopping at the side of the window, the two women look in at the newborns.

Organized in three rows and tightly wrapped in blankets, the babies rested in small padded plastic boxes. Most were asleep, but those awake moved with small motions and occasionally returned the gaze of the observers.

After a few minutes of looking at the newborns, Mrs. Rosen whispered, "It always fascinates me how much they all look like little Winston Churchills."

"It's true," Mrs. Dixon grinned. "I've never noticed that before."

Several minutes later, the older couple left, and the two neighbors took their spot to watch a young nurse enter the room, gently pick up a baby, and exit where she had entered.

"Ya pretty ladies shoppin' fer a kid er ya?" joked the older man, who appeared at Mrs. Rosen's side.

"No, we're just window shopping," answered Mrs. Rosen, continuing to admire the infants.

"Er ya 'ere fer yer grandchild den?"

"We are," Mrs. Rosen said, continuing to look at the children.

"Well den, which'ne is 'e dere?"

"The one on the left."

"Ah, da one wid da green blanky dere?"

"No, the second row."

"Ah, da one dere wid da pink blanky."

"No, the one on Pinky's right."

"Ah, da black... da black baby!?"

"That's him," Mrs. Rosen smiled, finally looking at the confused man. "That's my little grandson, Johnny. Isn't he just the cutest little thing?"

As Mrs. Dixon grinned while holding back a giggle, the nonplussed man huffed and walked away, and as he neared the corridor, sped up and disappeared around the corner, leaving a wake of smoke.

"You almost made that man drop dead," Mrs. Dixon said through her grin.

"Well, if he must be fresh, he'll have to be slightly more tolerant and open-minded. It should increase his chances," Mrs. Rosen grinned. "Come, Mrs. Dixon, let's get those drinks."

"Please, call me Lisa."

"I will if you'd call me Ruth."

CHAPTER 4
Dewey

With his bedroom washed in a yellow glow from his Batman nightlight, Dewey rested on his back staring up at his model F-4E Phantom jet fighter hanging from the ceiling and brought to life by the cool breeze coming in through his opened bedroom window overlooking his moonlit backyard.

An hour earlier, they had arrived home and his mother quickly, but gently, helped him into his Spiderman pajamas and then into bed where he tried several times to sleep, but because of the day's events, his normal method of falling asleep by thinking about what he did earlier that day only kept him awake, and it didn't help that he had slept at the hospital. And to make matters worse, because of his scrapes, stitches, cast, and still aching shoulder, he couldn't roll over onto his side. He could only rest flat on his back, which was his worst position for sleeping.

Then, frustrated by his failure to sleep, he resorted to his old method: counting sheep while imagining them jumping over a white picket fence. But as his mind wandered back to the events of the day, he lost count and had to start over, and after three restarts, he gave up on the sheep and turned his mind to the Rosens, whom he thought were a nice couple, though they seemed to be the opposite of one another. On the drive back from the hospital, the old woman talked almost nonstop about her gardening, pausing only occasionally to let his mother speak, but the old man didn't speak at all, not one word. Dewey liked Mrs. Rosen, but he wasn't sure about her husband. It seemed to the boy there were two people within the old man: a cold, seemingly mean one and a funny, seemingly nice one.

Turning his mind to the accident, he was thrilled to receive his first and, hopefully, last cast and stitches to show off to whomever he could, but the payment for it was the destruction of Robby's bike and a bunch of cuts that would confine him to his bed for several days and probably didn't include any bragging rights. The bike may have scratched and dented Mr. Rosen's car too, but he couldn't be sure. When they left the hospital, it was too dark to notice any damage to the black vehicle. And then there were the not-so-obvious costs, like the humiliation of screwing up the first time and probably last time the older kids included him in something and the weeks of frustration caused by the limitations of his cast, which was sure to cancel the rest of the summer's weekends of playing catch with his father.

For the last two summers, he and his father spent a couple of hours each weekend at a baseball diamond. This year they started in early June, almost two weeks before the summer break. Usually, they threw the ball back and forth, slowly growing the distance between them to develop Dewey's throwing arm, but if they met up with another boy, Dewey's father would lend him his giant glove and bat the ball out to the two of them. Sometimes the children they met were Dewey's age, making the event even more fun for him since outside of school he had no friends to play with. His classmates either lived too far away for him to travel to by himself or lived closer, but on the other side of Herring Cove Road, which he wasn't allowed to cross by himself, and on his street, there were no boys his age. He didn't enjoy playing with the younger ones, and the older ones felt the same way.

Then it hit him that the cast wouldn't interfere with everything. He and his mother could still go to the matinee at the Hyland

Cinema just across from the Armdale Rotary, and as a bonus, they would go by bus.

Occasionally, to give his wife some downtime, his father would also take him to the cinema, but the one on the lower level of the Spryfield Mall, which was in the opposite direction of the Hyland Cinema and just across from King's Bar. Dewey wasn't as fond of that cinema. It meant that on their way there, his father would stop at the bar to talk to his friends, leaving Dewey to wait in the car for maybe twenty minutes, and the wait always caused the anticipation to build up so much that the movie couldn't live up to it.

As Dewey stared up at the ceiling, yet another cost came to him. He would get a scolding from his father, actually two of them. His father's scolding always came in sets of two. The first always caused the boy to cry, and the crying caused a second. His mother could get angry, but she rarely scolded him, and if she did, it was mild compared to his father's.

Dewey was certain that if his father had been there when they returned from the hospital, he would've gotten his scoldings then and he worried he still could that night when his father arrived home. Maybe, he thought, if he fell asleep before his father came home, he could postpone the pair until the next day, when he would be better prepared and maybe not cry, making it just one.

Dewey wasn't sure how much time he had before his father came home. He only knew he came home from his weekly night out at King's Bar after he had gone to bed, which should've been at least an hour ago. Dewey didn't know exactly what a bar was but had overheard it spoken about by his parents — his mother in the negative and his father in the positive. Dewey knew he couldn't go into it, knew his father's friends were there, and he had often wondered what they did there. He knew it involved drinking beer, but they had to do something more because that would be too boring. Did they watch TV? Did they play board games, do arts and crafts or play war?

Often on his father's return, Dewey would wake up. Normally, he woke to his father's yelling, but at other times, it was the banging or groaning, and it was the groans that concerned him the most. It sounded like someone was in pain, and it was then that he would find himself desperate to fall back to sleep, knowing that in the morning, all would be fine.

Sometime around one in the morning, he woke to his father's loud, slurring voice. Dewey tried to move, but it hurt too much and he wondered if that was what it felt like to be paralyzed, or as his father called it, a vegetable. *What's the worst thing about eating vegetables? Their wheelchairs.* Dewey never understood the joke, even after his father explained it. Why would someone want to eat another person who couldn't move and why would someone want to eat the wheelchair too?

Dewey listened to his father complaining about the small plot of grass in front of their house being too long, his mother telling him the mower's blades still needed sharpening, and then his father complaining about how everything always came back to him. Then he heard his father stumbling around and banging into things: a kitchen chair, twice the hallway table, and lastly the floor lamp in their bedroom. There was a loud crash of metal and glass, and then silence.

Relieved there was no groaning or scolding, Dewey closed his eyes and fell back to sleep.

A few hours later, the sun shining through the bedroom window woke him. He went to move but winced and groaned. He would never have imagined that the pain would've gotten worse, but it had. Deciding to stay as he was, he tried to eavesdrop on his parents in the kitchen, but couldn't make out anything.

Then, anxiously waiting for his father to come in and give him his scoldings, Dewey was surprised to hear him leave the house. And a few minutes later, his bedroom door opened and his mother walked in wearing her regular pink cotton robe and matching slippers and carrying a tray holding a bowl of cereal, a glass of orange juice, and two pieces of buttered toast. "Good morning, Honey."

"Hi, Mommy."

She set the tray on his lap and as she gently helped him sit up in the bed, causing him to groan, she asked, "How was your sleep?"

"It took a while, but when it happened, it was ok."

Placing the two pillows behind his back, she said, "Sounds like you're in pain."

"My body hurts. It hurts to move my arms and legs, even just a little... but I can take it."

"Ok, that's normal. Your muscles went through quite a strain yesterday. Do you want an aspirin?"

"Yup... Yes," he said, correcting himself before she could.

"Ok, I'll get one for you, but the more you move, the faster the pain will go away. You've got to get the blood running through your muscles. Eat with slow movements and you'll soon find yourself moving faster with less pain. Ok, I'll go and get your aspirin. Oh, and your vitamins. I forgot about your vitamins." Turning to leave, she paused before turning back toward him with wide eyes. "Oh, and I just remembered the Rosens are dropping by this morning to change your bandages. I have to hurry!" Leaving, she said, "Call me if you need anything else."

Finished with his breakfast, Dewey used the last of the milk in the bowl to take the aspirin and the couple of Flintstones Vitamins that his mother had set beside him on the bed, and knowing he preferred two different characters, she had taken the time that morning to choose Barney Rubble and Dino.

Dewey placed the tray with its plastic Tupperware dishes on the side of the bed. For as far back as he could remember, he had to use Tupperware dishes. No one else did, just him. His parents used white ceramic ones, but he had to use plastic ones. He hated using them, and when he complained about them, his father told him that the day he stopped using them would be the day he was no longer a child, and when he asked when that would be, his father sent him to his room.

Painfully, he placed the pillows back in their proper places and laid himself down on his back, turning his head slightly to stare at his goldfish, J.C., doing a slow backstroke in the small fishbowl resting on his desk.

Bored, Dewey glanced around his room. He liked his room — his domain. He liked having his smaller toy jets sitting on the two shelves across from the bed and his larger one hanging from the ceiling. He liked his books alphabetically ordered by title and standing upright on the single shelf above his desk. He especially liked his *Hardy Boys* books, which he had read at least twice. He enjoyed reading them a second time almost as much as the first since it gave him a second chance to spot the clues leading to the guilty party. Dewey also liked his toys neatly stored away in the large white wooden toy box beneath the window, and he liked his superhero posters hanging on the walls. The posters his father had put up with the staples that silently frustrated his mother because of the tiny holes they put in the walls: eight staples in a poster, sixteen tiny holes, except for the poster that had once fallen from the wall. That one caused thirty-two holes.

Dewey appreciated everything in his room, but not his room. He didn't like the colors: light pink on two opposite walls and baby blue on the others. The colors were there for as long as he could remember, and he felt he had outgrown them, but he was too afraid to ask his father to change them out of fear of being sent to his room.

Dewey had dozed off when he heard a knock on the front door and a few seconds later, heard his mother exchanging greetings with Mrs. Rosen, and by the old woman's laugh, he guessed they had gone into the living room. Knowing he wouldn't make out anything from there, he let himself fall asleep.

"Wake up, Honey. You have visitors. Shake off the sleepies and say hello to Mr. and Mrs. Rosen."

Dewey opened his eyes, painfully lifted his head, and looked around his room. Holding a large dark-green purse on her lap, Mrs. Rosen sat on a chrome kitchen chair to the left of his black cast iron footboard. Across from her, at the opposite end of the footboard, his mother sat on his wooden desk chair, and standing at the right side of the bed next to another kitchen chair was the seemingly gigantic Mr. Rosen wearing what looked like the same clothes and expression as the day before. On the desk behind the old man was a small stack of bandages next to a plastic bag.

Becoming self-conscious, Dewey wondered how long they had been in his room while he slept, which must have been a deep sleep since the wooden tray of Tupperware dishes had disappeared and they had added two more chairs to his room. Trying to move, he felt more pain and decided he wasn't in the mood for company, especially company that intended to force him to move. "Hi," he said, reluctantly.

As his mother went to assist him in sitting up, Mrs. Rosen asked, "How are you this morning, Dewey?"

"I'm good, Mrs. Rosen. How are you both this morning?" he replied, trying to sound *adultish* while having to hide the pain from his mother moving him.

"We're good, thank you. Avriel is going to change your bandages while mummy and I watch."

Hearing Mrs. Rosen say, "mummy," caused a delayed laugh.

Because of her accent, Dewey found the word funny and in his head, or he thought it was in his head since sometimes he said things aloud by mistake, he repeated how she had said the word and laughed. Startling the adults and embarrassing himself, he stopped.

"Well, his stomach muscles are fine," observed Mr. Rosen in his monotone voice.

They weren't. It hurt when he laughed.

Sitting down on the kitchen chair at the right of the bed, Mr. Rosen pulled out a small glass canister from the plastic bag, and unscrewed its top, revealing a strong sour-smelling white cream. "Now I need you to turn your head toward me. This may sting a little, but you will have to stay still so as not to disturb the wound anymore than we must."

"Ok," Dewey said, dreading the coming sting and hoping he'd show no reaction to it.

Then a little frightened when Mr. Rosen's large hands came toward his head, he tried to relax when the old man began removing the tape from one side of his forehead's bandage, and after slowly peeling off the bandage that was stuck to the wound, causing only a slight sting where he expected a larger one, the old man scooped out some cream with his fingers and gently rubbed it on the wound. It was cold, but there was almost no pain. "Did that hurt?"

"Yes, but just a little."

"Good. I-I mean to say it is good that it was only a little."

After using one of the clean cotton bandages to wipe the cream from his fingers and then placing it cream-side down over the wound, he pulled off several pieces of tape that he had earlier stuck onto the headboard and attached them to the edges of the bandage. Then, with the bandage on the forehead changed, he moved on to Dewey's cheek, and like a barber, he turned the boy's head slightly to access the wound.

Dewey tried not to move his mouth too much as he said proudly, "I figured out how you were in the war."

"Is that so?" Mr. Rosen asked, feeling even more uncomfortable.

"The war was a long time ago, and you were younger then."

"That... that is correct. I was in my twenties."

"Did you see any action?"

"Action?" Mr. Rosen asked, well aware of what the boy meant but trying to delay the conversation.

"Did you get any Krauts?"

Both Mrs. Dixon and Mrs. Rosen listened intently but for different reasons. Mrs. Dixon had never witnessed Dewey attempting to have a conversation with another adult outside of the family, and Mrs. Rosen had never witnessed her husband having a conversation with a child since before the war.

Mr. Rosen threw a desperate glance at his wife. "By... by Krauts, do you mean sauerkraut?"

Dewey smiled. "German soldiers. Did you get some?"

"Did I get some? Well, if you mean kill some... well... I was a medic... so I was not supposed to fight." Giving his wife a second glance, he added, "And by the Geneva Convention, I was not supposed to be shot at either."

"Geneva Convention?"

"Where the countries created the rules of war. Keep your face turned for a few seconds more, please. There are rules of war that each country is supposed to follow."

"Did the Krauts?"

"By Krauts do you mean—"

"The German soldiers. Did they follow them?"

"Not always, but I am not certain we always did, either. There, now for the left elbow," he said before picking up the remaining bandages and the canister of opened cream and walking around to the other side of the bed. Passing by his wife, he gave her a third desperate glance before bending down to change the bandage over the stitched-up elbow.

"Oh," Mrs. Rosen said, to her husband's relief, "I brought you something. If you're going to be in bed, you may want something to read." Reaching into her purse, she pulled out a faded paperback novel. "I brought you *The Adventures of Huckleberry Finn*," she said, reaching across and handing the book to Mrs. Dixon, who placed it on Dewey's desk. "It's about a little boy close to your age growing up in The South over a hundred years ago."

"Thank you," Dewey said, not understanding what *The South* meant.

Finished with the elbow, Mr. Rosen moved down the bed and pulled back the bedsheet. When he lifted the first pajama leg, Dewey giggled, and when he lifted the second, Dewey laughed.

"That tickled," the little patient said to the confused man. "The... the henway tickled."

"What's a *henway*?" his mother asked.

"About six pounds all grown up," Dewey said and then laughed.

After the women laughed and Mr. Rosen cracked a smile, Mrs. Rosen's smile suddenly vanished. "Oh, my! Dear, I think your goldfish has kicked the bucket! This hasn't been a good week for you. No, not at all."

With Mr. Rosen stopping what he was doing to look toward the goldfish bowl on Dewey's small desk, a grinning Mrs. Dixon stood up and tapped on the bowl, causing the small fish to flip itself over and dash around. "No, he's just fat. J.C. will turn over again when he slows down."

"Well, I'll be! I've never seen such a thing before. Avriel, have you ever seen that before?"

"No... no, never, and that is a different name for a fish."

Mrs. Dixon tossed a puzzled look at the old man before she realized what he meant and laughed. "J.C.'s short for Jacques

Cousteau, the ocean explorer... not Jesus Christ."

It was the first time Dewey saw the connection, and he laughed too.

The old man was soon finished with the knees, and to Dewey's giggles, he lowered each leg of his pajamas. Walking over to the desk, he put the top back on the canister, placed it in the bag with the rolls of tape and clean bandages, and left the bag on the desk for Mrs. Dixon to use over the weekend.

After Mrs. Dixon had discarded the dirty bandages and directed Mr. Rosen to the bathroom so he could wash his hands, the old man headed to the office, and after saying their goodbyes to Dewey, the two women headed to the living room, leaving him alone with J.C., who had returned to his backstroke.

It was around six-thirty when Mrs. Dixon woke her son for supper. "Good morning, Sleepyhead."

Having fallen asleep in the sitting position with Lego pieces covering his bed and a partially built Lego airplane in his hand, Dewey's neck hurt when he raised it to watch her brush aside some of the Lego pieces and lay the tray holding a Tupperware bowl of spaghetti with meatballs and a Tupperware cup of milk next to him. "Daddy's home, Honey."

Suddenly, a palm of apprehension slapped him fully awake, and with his heart then racing, he was at a loss for words.

"He'll be in to see you after supper. He's very proud of you trying to climb that tree in the backyard, but he's not too happy with you falling," Mrs. Dixon winked at her son. "He says you're just like he was at your age," she said, before patting his feet through the blanket and leaving his room.

Dewy got the hint and calmed down. It wasn't the first time his mother had lied for him.

After finishing his supper, Dewey had to wait only a few minutes before his father was standing at his door in his work clothes of blue denim pants and a matching shirt. The dried sweat stains under his arms weren't as noticeable as the smell, and the bangs of his medium-length blond hair stood at attention from the repeated wiping of his forehead.

"Hey there, Spiderman!"

"Hi, Daddy," Dewey said with a nervous smile.

Walking in, Mr. Dixon stood tall frame near the kitchen chair that had remained on the right side of the bed since that morning. "So yer mom tells me ya were climbin' the tree this mornin'. Let's see yer cast there," he said as he reached out and roughly took Dewey's casted arm in his large hands. "Oh, nice! That there's a good one, and it's a virgin!" Dropping the casted arm, he grabbed a black marker from off his son's desk and added, "And I'll be the first ta sign'er!" Then, after using his teeth to pull the top off the marker, he wrote on the cast, *Dewy #1 son! Love DAD*, and drew a small tree with a tiny stick figure falling from it. Placing the top back onto the marker, he said, "There, now whens ya get this off, ya'll always remembers how ya got 'er. Ya know ya get ta keep 'er, eh?"

Dewey didn't know that, but he nodded he did, and it pleased him to know it.

"Daddy, do you want to see my stitches?"

"Sure do. Where're they? Under the bed? In the closet?"

Laughing, Dewey held up his left arm. "No, on this elbow!"

Walking around the bed, Dewey's father didn't seem to give any thought to the two chairs at the foot of it, but when he lifted Dewey's elbow, he frowned and said, "Yer lyin'," causing Dewey to panic. "Yer lyin', cause all I sees is a bandage. Nope, no stitches at all there. No, nothin'."

With his heart calming down, Dewey said, "Maybe they're under the bandage?"

After Mr. Dixon roughly removed one side of the bandage's tape, he feigned his surprise. "Oh, so there they are! There looks like ya have... you have one, two, three, four, five... twelve, twelve stitches and a future battle scar, too."

"That's right," Dewey said, genuinely proud.

After his father used more force than necessary to press the bandage's loose tape back onto the elbow, he teased him about how girls liked men with scars and how his girlfriend should be impressed. He knew Dewey didn't have a girlfriend and knew Dewey thought girls were strange, and he expected him to protest the teasing, but, instead, he just smiled.

"Ok, I'm goin' ta leave ya alone now. Get some rest and if ya need anythin', yell ta yer mom," he said as he picked up the tray of Tupperware dishes and left the room.

Relaxed and proud, Dewey slowly laid himself down, causing some Lego pieces to tumble to the floor.

CHAPTER 5
The Little Guest

That Saturday and Sunday Mrs. Dixon had changed her son's bandages just as she had seen Mr. Rosen do it, and the following Monday morning after Dewey had eaten his breakfast and his father had left for work, the Rosens returned to inspect the wounds, but instead of changing the bandages, Mr. Rosen removed them all in just minutes, leaving little time for any interaction with the boy. Hearing that the wounds were healing well and that there was no chance of infection, Dewey was eager to leave his bed, which by then he considered a prison that allowed daily visits that his mother took advantage of, but not so much his father. But then, to the little boy's disappointment, Mr. Rosen suggested he stay in bed for another day so the soft scabs could harden, and after the man said goodbye and left for work, his wife again stayed with Mrs. Dixon.

The two women could've easily spent the entire day talking and laughing with one another and only ended their conversations after almost an hour, with each assuming they were taking too much of the other's time.

Dewey woke the next morning more than ready to leave his bed. He had spent four days confined to it and for as far back as he could remember, that was a record.

Over that time, he had learned that the boredom from doing very little would tire him out, and he tried to fight it by making various creations with his Lego until he felt he had exhausted all possible ideas with his limited supply of pieces and turned his attention to his metal Hot Wheels cars and the two-story parking garage he had made two months earlier from a cardboard box his mother had discarded.

He was proud of his parking garage. He had cut three sides of a rectangle into the top of the box and bent it in to form a ramp for rooftop parking, and he had cut several small, rectangular windows in three sides to give light to the first level, but when his mother discovered he retrieved the box from the garbage, she made him promise not to play with it outside, with the threat that if he did, it would go back to where he had found it. Dewey didn't want his garage in the garbage, so he only played with it inside until his mother surprised him one morning by painting it black and releasing him from her threat. The paint hid any sign of the women's hygiene product label.

When bored with both his Lego and Hot Wheels, Dewey acted out war scenarios with his twelve-inch G.I. Joe action figure, but with only one, the fun was lacking and again he wished he had several more.

Dewey received his first and only G.I. Joe with its rubber kung-fu grip hands two Christmases back and had asked for another for his birthday and again the following Christmas. Even though it was on the top of his list both times, to his disappointment, he never got another. His father, not telling Dewey directly, thought dolls were for girls, and his wife couldn't convince him otherwise. "Just cause they're called action figures," he reasoned, "don't change the fact that they's still dolls!" Out of fear of his son turning into a *sissy*, his father demanded Dewey never receive another, and he didn't.

On his third day of confinement, his mother had moved the twelve-inch black and white television from hers to Dewey's bedroom, and when he requested it, she would change its channel.

Dewey was initially thrilled to watch television from his bed, but the thrill quickly wore off. Except for the lunchtime cartoons, he found the daytime shows only added to his boredom.

The best boredom fighter by far was *The Adventures of Huckleberry Finn*. He had tried reading it but found it too difficult, making it slow going, so on that Friday evening, he had asked his mother to read it to him, and she did, reading it with liveliness and changing her voice for each character. She enjoyed reading it, and Dewey enjoyed listening to her. He enjoyed it so much that she could've read the Bible to him and he would've been engrossed in it. Not understanding some words, he refused to interrupt her for an explanation, choosing to save his questions until the end of the session when mother and son could spend an additional half-hour discussing what she had just read.

When Dewey was the most bored, he reread parts of the book aloud to himself, trying to change the voices as his mother did, and sometimes he made himself laugh when he mixed up the voices of the characters.

Then finally no longer confined to the bed and not wanting to see another Lego piece or Hot Wheel car again, Dewey wanted to be out of the house where he might have a chance to show off his cast, and that early afternoon, he began begging his mother to let him go outside. He figured that if he asked enough times, she would either give in or address him as Dwight Dixon, ending his requests for the rest of the day.

More out of pity than frustration, his mother gave in on the third request and helped him into his red raincoat and matching rubber boots that went almost up to his knees, and since they made him feel like a firefighter, he enjoyed wearing them, but that day with a tightly taped garbage bag protecting his cast, he felt more like a wounded one. And just before he left the house, his mother made him promise to keep his hood up, and as an added protection against the rain, she handed him his small yellow umbrella, which he took reluctantly since he had never seen a firefighter carrying an umbrella.

After being outside for ten minutes and having walked up and down the block several times with no one passing by to show off his cast, Dewey struggled to come up with something to do in the light rain. He considered going door-to-door to show it off, just as he had done on his fourth birthday when he snuck out of the house to knock on the doors of the neighboring houses. When the knock was answered, he held up four fingers and screamed, "I'M *FWOR TODAY!*" He had made it as far as the ninth house down the street before Mrs. O'Brien brought him home to his upset mother. He figured it would be silly for him to do it at nine years old, but if he did, he told himself, he would skip Mrs. O'Brien's house.

Growing desperate to do something, he walked up to the top of the street, dropped a leaf into the water flowing against the curb, and enjoying his return to mobility, he walked fast enough to keep up with it as it floated down and into a drain at the bottom of the street. Then deciding to do something less physical, he placed his umbrella on the sidewalk, dropped a leaf in a puddle, and from several feet away and with his awkward left arm, tossed pebbles at it. With each pebble he threw, he tried to make the whistle sound of falling bombs, but it sounded more like air escaping from a balloon.

After five minutes of bombarding the leaf, his name was called from the direction of his house, and expecting his time outside was about to end and hoping the umbrella wasn't spotted on the ground, he quickly picked it up and turned around to find Mrs. Rosen standing on her covered porch. Relieved it wasn't his mother and hoping the old woman wouldn't tell her what he was doing, he walked over to hear her better.

"I see you escaped your confinement," smiled the old woman, who had been amused by watching him play.

"Yup... yes, Mrs. Rosen."

"And have you had a chance to read the book I gave you?"

"Yes, I finished it yesterday," Dewey said, not wanting to admit that his mother had to read it to him.

"Great! Would you like to read another? We've many here and they're just collecting dust, so if you'd like, you may come in and take a look."

"Sure."

More interested in seeing what was in their house rather than looking through their books, Dewey walked up onto the porch and followed the woman in while hoping to see some war stuff, like a uniform, rifle, helmet, and maybe even medals.

"Take your boots off here, please," she said, pointing to the mat before taking his umbrella and helping him remove his raincoat from over his plastic-wrapped cast.

And while she crouched down and helped him remove his boots, he sat on the mat with his back to the door, looking around. Directly in front of them was a straight staircase where on its wall to the left and following the steps upward hung three framed paintings of tranquil street scenes. Along the hallway to the right was an entrance where he could see a large and old-looking wooden dinner table surrounded by six matching chairs. And on the wall just past the dining room entrance was a large group of framed black and white portraits of varying sizes that ended at another entrance that Dewey assumed correctly was to the kitchen.

With his boots off, Dewey stood up and followed the heavy-breathing woman left into the living room that took up almost half of the main floor, and instead of seeing the war stuff he had hoped for, Dewey saw lots of tall bookcases packed with spines of books and the occasional knickknack, photograph, or heavy bookend. There were so many bookcases that he immediately thought of the mystery movies where there was usually a hidden passage behind one of them, and for a second, he wondered whether there was one there.

The only bookcase-free zones in the long room were the large windows at each end, and beneath the front one stood a floor-model radio/record player with the bottom two shelves of the bookcase to the left of it containing record albums. Along the long windowless wall, pushed up against several bookcases, was a Victorian-style sofa in almost pristine condition, with a brown leather armchair at each end, and in front of the sofa and chairs was an old wooden coffee table. If not for the furniture, the room would have looked like part of the Halifax Public Library.

Dewey couldn't help but compare their living room to his, which was about half the size and had only one bookshelf of photos and knickknacks. Besides having a smaller record player on a metal stand, his parents also had a floor-model television, a modern sofa and its matching loveseat, and one wall was almost hidden by his mother's assortment of plants hanging from the ceiling or sitting on plant stands of various sizes. With not a single plant in the Rosens' living room, he wondered if one of the Rosens was allergic to them, just as he heard some people were to dogs and cats. He considered asking the old woman but then worried it might be too personal a question.

Mrs. Rosen watched Dewey take everything in and, when she was satisfied he had finished, led him toward the armchair to the right of the sofa. "Here's where your books are hiding. Dear, if you'd help me move this chair, we could start going through them." After they slid the armchair out from the bookcases, Mrs. Rosen, slightly out of breath, sat on the floor between the chair and bookcase, and Dewey joined her. "Now... these two shelves... on the bottom here... should hold some treasures."

As she pulled out books, making one pile with some, a second with others, and returning some to the shelves, Dewey tried to look helpful by pulling out several books from a shelf and pretending to give them a curious look before putting them back. He noticed that many of the books had small print and he knew that small print meant a tough book since they always had big words. Picking up three hardcover books from one of Mrs. Rosen's piles, he read their titles: *The Wizard of Oz, Gulliver's Travels,* and *Alice in Wonderland.* The first book was thicker than what he was accustomed to, the second sounded boring, and the last book he figured was for girls.

"Dewey, do you like reading?"

"Yup... yes, we've only got two channels," he replied matter-of-factly while placing the three books back on their pile.

"Two channels?"

"On the TV. Other kids have cable, but we just got two channels. There's really three, but the third is French and I don't know French. There isn't a lot to watch, so I read."

Mrs. Rosen smiled. "We don't even have one channel."

"What happened? Your TV broke?"

"Can't break what you don't have," she said, continuing to smile.

"You don't have a TV?"

"No, we've never had one. We'd have little time to watch it and if we did, we'd rather read."

"Then what do you watch at supper?"

Mrs. Rosen laughed and placed her hand on Dewey's shoulder. "Dewey, you can make me laugh so easily."

With Dewey not understanding what was funny, Mrs. Rosen put the conversation back on track by asking her little friend what sort of books he liked and was happy to learn he liked mystery and adventure books, like the one she gave him, but was disappointed when he let it slip that he didn't understand some of its words. Then wondering if she was giving him books beyond his reading level, she asked him about the books he read and was surprised by the unfamiliar titles, like *The Hardy Boys, Encyclopedia Brown,* and *The Adventures of Pippi Longstocking.*

Confusing Dewey, Mrs. Rosen frowned and started placing the

books back on the shelves. "Dewey, you'll have to excuse me. I'm rarely around young gentlemen, and I think I may be out of my competence. These books aren't right for you. No, not right at all, and I'll have to see what Mr. Rosen knows about the subject," meaning she would send him reluctantly to the bookstore to get some advice, "and together, we'll get the right books for you. Are you ok with that? I hope I haven't disappointed you."

"No. I mean, I'm not disappointed," he assured her.

After he helped her place the books back on the shelves, they pushed the chair back to its original position, and Dewy joined her on the sofa where she took a moment to catch her breath before asking, "Dewey, would you... like to stay for supper? If you'd like... I could call your mother and ask her."

"Sure, Mrs. Rosen," replied Dewey, wondering why the old woman was so out of breath.

"Ok... I'll call her now... and be right back," she said before slowly making her way to the kitchen.

The Rosens didn't have a phone in the living room and that might've surprised Dewey if he wasn't so preoccupied with the meal. He had agreed to supper before finding out what it was, and he was panicking. *What if they're having cow's tongue?* Would Mrs. Rosen make him something different, just as his mother does? *What if it's corned beef and cabbage?* Would they make him sit at the table until he finished it? Then trying to take his mind off the meal to come, he looked back at the titles of the books on a bookcase behind him, and with some titles having the word *History* and others the word *Biography*, he wondered what *biography* meant and wondered why someone would voluntarily read history books. *What if it's corn chowder? Mommy doesn't make it for me because it makes me gag, but Mrs. Rosen doesn't know that!*

The old woman interrupted the boy's panic when she returned and confirmed that his mother had given permission.

"We should probably remove your cast's protection," she said as she sat next to him and began carefully removing the garbage bag. "What would you like to eat? Since you're the guest, you get to decide."

"How about cheeseburgers?" Dewey asked, relieved.

"How are you with just burgers?" she asked bashfully.

"Sure. You're out of cheese. That's ok."

Finished removing the bag, she said, "It's... it's not that we're out of cheese. Being Jewish, we can't mix dairy and meat."

Not understanding what she was saying, Dewey just stared at her. *What's dairy? And if cheese has something to do with it, why would it be a bad thing? Everybody likes cheese!* He didn't know anyone who didn't like cheese. He could understand if Jews had a problem with fish; he hated fish.

Seeing the child's blank look, Mrs. Rosen added, "Being Jewish is like being a Christian, but different. We have a different set of rules to follow. In this case, it's the Kashrut laws." And with his blank look continuing, the little old woman regretted not letting the conversation end with the assumption she was out of cheese.

"Ok, no–cheese burgers are great with me," Dewey said while hoping the explanations would stop since he was confused enough as it was.

"No cheeseburgers?" Mrs. Rosen asked, staring at the boy for a moment, and then realizing what he meant, said, "Yes. Great, let's have those. Ok, it's almost four-twenty and Avriel will be here around five-thirty, so I better start preparing. But first I have to make another phone call."

After bunching up the garbage bag into a tight ball, she left her little neighbor alone in the living room for a second time.

**

Hanging up the phone, Mr. Rosen could feel the perspiration beginning to accumulate on his forehead, and he had to loosen his tie and unfasten the top button of his shirt.

Without his wife saying it, he knew exactly who their guest was. There was only one little guest whom he could think of and he cringed at the thought of having to spend supper and who knows how long afterward with him, but it wasn't that he disliked the child. It was only that children were alien to him and he had little idea of how to interact with them. He normally closed up around adults, and he expected the same thing to happen with the child. He expected too that his wife would avoid causing him any discomfort by not leaving them alone together and by taking control of the conversations.

Mr. Rosen leaned back in his desk chair and took a deep breath. He would have to prepare himself to talk to a salesperson. A salesperson whom he expected to be pushy, forcing more on him than he intended to buy, and buy it all he would if only just to get out of there.

**

Just before six and satisfied with having found a helpful salesperson who offered only what he needed, Mr. Rosen came through the door carrying his briefcase, a bag of buns, and a plastic bag boldly marked Colby's Toys. Setting his briefcase down at the door, he removed his shoes and nodded to the young boy sitting on the sofa and looking over at him with an opened book on his lap, and before Dewey could return the silent greeting, Mr. Rosen went into the kitchen where his wife had finished cutting up lettuce, onions, tomatoes, and pickles. Setting the bags on the counter, he kissed the top of her head.

"Thank you for picking up the game," she said, gently squeezing his hand. "I trust your day was uneventful."

"It was," he nodded, "until now."

At one time, when she started staying home, she would have asked him how his day had been, but after constantly receiving his habitual response of, "As good as it could be," she had stopped asking.

Helping him take off his jacket, she placed it on the back of a kitchen chair, and when she removed his tie, she was surprised to find the top button of his dress shirt undone, and giving him a sympathetic smile, she said, "Now, Av, unless we're planning to eat the game, you should take it into the living room."

Forcing himself through the shock of her leaving him alone with the boy, he nodded his head, took the game out of its bag, and with a gentle push from her, reluctantly left to join Dewey.

When he entered the living room, Dewey was sitting without the book.

"Hello, Mr. Rosen."

"Hello, boy. How are you today?"

"Great. You?"

"As good as I can be."

"How was your day?"

"As good as it could be... and... and yours?"

"Great."

"Good. I... I picked up this game," he said as he handed the board game to Dewey and sat down in an armchair next to the sofa. "The salesman said it is one of the most popular. Have you heard of it?"

"You got Trouble! Sure, it's a neat game! I saw the commercials on TV!"

"Would you like to play it after supper?"

"Sure!"

Then an idea came to him and he took advantage of the opportunity to delay the uncomfortable silence soon to come between him and the boy by asking, "Would you be so kind as to open it and set it up on the coffee table?"

"Sure!"

The uncomfortable old man watched as the boy excitedly removed the plastic wrapping from the box, pulled off its top, removed an instruction booklet and a square plastic board with small holes around its edges and a transparent plastic dome in its center, and then used his teeth to tear open a plastic bag containing four different colored sets of hollow plastic pegs. Finding he enjoyed watching the child attack the box, he joked to himself that he should buy more just to watch him go at them.

"Have you played the game?" Mr. Rosen asked. "Do you know how to play it?"

"Nope... no, but they give you the instructions on TV. They're really easy."

"Great. We should probably wait until after supper so you can explain them to Mrs. Rosen and me."

"Mrs. Rosen and I," Dewey impulsively corrected the old man, just as his mother would correct him.

"What is that?"

"It's Mrs. Rosen and I, not Mrs. Rosen and me," Dewey explained shyly.

Mr. Rosen was confused until he realized what the boy meant. For a second, he considered correcting the boy's confusion with pronouns, and then the next second decided against it. "Right... good, thank you."

Then, with the board game set up on the coffee table, both sat silently looking at it, occasionally glancing at each other before again looking at it.

Mr. Rosen would've considered pulling out a book and rereading it until supper, but he knew his wife wouldn't approve, so, instead, he began searching for something to say and found it. *Questions! Questions are simple!* He only had to ask questions, and the boy would do all the talking. The trick, so the question couldn't be asked back, is to ask a question not related to an opinion or experience, and if he did it right, he could ask questions until supper without having to answer a single one. Then clearing his throat, he said, "That board is different. Why is it plastic?"

"It needs to have holes for the pegs... the playing pieces."

"I see. Why are the pegs different colors?"

"Each person gets a different color, so we know who is who. I can be red, you can be blue and Mrs. Rosen can be... she can be—"

"Green... she likes green."

"Sure, she can be green. We'll leave the yellow off the board."

"Do we use cards to play?"

"No, we use dice, but we have to get a six before we start moving. Nobody starts until they get a six."

"I see. Do you like board games?" Mr. Rosen asked and then realized he had asked for an opinion. *Bloody hell!*

"Yup, yes. Do you?"

"Yes. What is that plastic dome in the center used for?"

"It's the dice shaker. It holds the dice so you don't lose it."

Mr. Rosen was considering correcting the boy's use of the word *dice* for the single die in the dome when Dewey leaned into the coffee table, pressed down on the dome, and the sudden snap and then the die violently bouncing around within it distracted him.

"It rolls the dice for you... and it's fun to pop. Wanna... want to try?"

"Yes... yes, I would."

Unaware of his guard slightly dropping, the old man moved over to the sofa to sit next to the little boy, pushed down on the dome and with a child-like fascination, watched as it snapped back and the die bounced about. Pushing it again, he cracked a smile, surprising Dewey, who smiled too.

From the living room's far entrance, Mrs. Rosen had to fight back her urge to laugh, and when she got control of herself, said, "The burgers are ready, gentlemen."

Dewey and Mr. Rosen followed her into the dining room where a white tablecloth covered the dinner table and three spots on one end had been set with china plates on brown cloth placemats. To the right of the placemats were glasses of what looked like lemonade and to the left, brown folded napkins and a set of cutlery.

In the middle of the set portion of the table was a rectangular plate with burger patties on one end and buns on the other and beside it was a long plate of sliced vegetables, a glass bottle of ketchup, and glass containers of mustard and relish.

While Mrs. Rosen pulled out a chair for Dewey before taking the chair on the end, the old man sat down across from him and said, "Well, you must be a very special guest. Mrs. Rosen never brings out the tablecloth and good dishes for me."

With Dewey smiling shyly to the compliment before following the Rosens by placing his napkin on his lap, Mrs. Rosen asked him if he liked lemonade, and when he told her he did, she told him to make a hamburger just as he would like it.

For the next thirty-five minutes, all ate in silence until they finished almost at the same time, with Mrs. Rosen eating one burger, Dewey eating two, and Mr. Rosen eating three, and when Mr. Rosen took his cloth napkin and wiped his mouth, Dewey copied him and thought it strange how the old man seemed to like hamburgers as much as he did. He didn't seem like the type to like fun food as his mother called it, and when his wife returned the condiments to the kitchen where she would prepare the desserts, Mr. Rosen confirmed it by leaning across the table and whispering, "You should come over more often so we can have hamburgers again," but left out that the only thing he liked more than hamburgers were cheeseburgers.

"It's often, not *ofen*," Dewey corrected him while exaggerating the T's sound.

Again, Mr. Rosen considered correcting the boy's correction but decided against it as quickly as he had considered it. "Right... thank you."

In twenty minutes, they finished with their fruit cocktails and settled into the living room with Mrs. Rosen and Dewey sharing the sofa and Mr. Rosen pulling up an armchair for better reach of the dome, and during Dewey's explanation of the rules, Mrs. Rosen gently interrupted him twice to remind him that since the dome holds only one, he should use its singular form, *die*.

Then, when they were ready to play, Dewey failed to pop his six. Mrs. Rosen was next and laughed when she popped the dome for the first time. Finally, after going around popping the dome three times, Mrs. Rosen was the first to pop a six and start.

In the beginning, they played the game slowly, each being courteous to the others, but as the game progressed, they were soon popping the plastic dome and moving their pegs across the board at a faster pace, with Mrs. Rosen and Dewey laughing or groaning as they got their pieces closer to the end or were forced back to the start. Then twenty minutes into the game and as all were getting tired of repeatedly leaning into the coffee table, Mr. Rosen, who had been playing silently, left his chair to sit on the floor, and Mrs. Rosen and Dewey soon joined him.

After Dewy won their first game and did a victory run from the living room to the hall and back while using his throat to poorly mimic the sound of the crowd's applause, Mr. Rosen revealed his competitive nature. Each time he forced one of Dewey's pegs back to the starting position, he would say, "And this little *peggy* cried, 'Wee, wee, wee!' all the way home," and when Dewey did the same to Mr. Rosen's pegs, he said, "Sooo Sooorrryyy, Mr. Rooosssen," and added a giggle to the sting.

Two hours later and to the disappointment of the old man and the little boy, who had by then gotten used to her laugh, Mrs. Rosen decided it was time to call it an evening, and in the end, Mr. Rosen and Dewey each won one game, and since they were so focused on the other's pegs, purposely leaving Mrs. Rosen's alone if they could, she won two.

While Dewey stood at the door in his rubber boots and raincoat, Mr. Rosen bent down to shake his small left hand, but with Dewey not seeing it coming, he had to take the boy's left hand to shake it. "Well, boy, it was fun hav—"

"Av, he isn't a dog. His name is Dewey, and, Dewey, his name is Avriel. Now say goodnight again, gentlemen, and, Dewey, I'll see you soon," Mrs. Rosen said before leaning down and giving the little boy a light hug while being careful not to put pressure on his wounds.

"Thanks for the no-cheese burgers, Mrs. Rosen. They were great," Dewey said, confusing the old man.

"Dewey, it was my pleasure."

"Goodnight, Dewey," Mr. Rosen said. "It was fun. Now, do you know your way home?"

Dewey laughed. "Yup, I'm pretty sure I do. Goodnight, Mr. Ro... Avriel and Mrs. Rosen."

After Mrs. Rosen handed Dewey his small umbrella and opened the door for him, she and her husband held hands as they followed him out onto the porch and watched him run across the lawn, around the back of the two cars, and into his house.

It had stopped raining.

**

With their backs to the front door, Mr. and Mrs. Dixon sat on their sofa watching television. Both heard the door open and together they said, "Hi, Dewey."

"Hi, Mommy! Hi, Daddy!"

Dewey dropped the umbrella at the entrance, took off his raincoat, and then sat down to struggle with his boots, and when they were off and scattered about with his raincoat and umbrella, he ran into the living room and jumped up onto the sofa between his mother and father, who had just made room for him.

"Hey, Dewey, yer mother tells me ya had supper at a friend's."

"Yup, we ate no-cheese burgers and played Trouble!"

"Yes, not yup," his mother corrected him.

"Which friend's this?" Mr. Dixon asked, causing his wife's heart to skip a beat.

"Avriel," Dewey replied.

Releasing her nervous energy through a laugh that got her husband's attention, Mrs. Dixon said, "I-I find the name funny. Isn't it the funniest name?"

CHAPTER 6
Changes

After nine in the evening, if one were to stand on the sidewalk in front of the Rosens' closed second-floor bedroom window, one would almost be certain to hear a low rumbling coming from within. Both of the Rosens snored obstreperously, and when their timing was off, it could easily be mistaken for a competition. With neither's snoring waking the other, both slept deeply.

Without the help of the alarm clock, Mrs. Rosen woke at her usual time of five, and she would be joined almost an hour and a half later by her showered, shaved, and dressed husband, who would've woken to the clock's alarm. Wearing her favorite solid dark-green nightgown, she swung her short legs over the side of their king-size bed and slowly made her way around it, following the narrow path created by the overbearing antique furniture surrounding it, and a few minutes later, with several file folders in hand, she descended the stairs, placing both feet on each step before taking the next.

Normally, she wouldn't have given the slightest glance at the photos on the wall to the left of the dining room, but the files slipped out of her nervous hand, and after slowly picking them up, she stood and stared at her husband's face, but then realize it wasn't a photo of him. It was one of her father. He had the cold look that she remembered well, appearing as if he was posing for a photo during the nineteenth century: holding a blank expression so as not to blur the image during its long exposure. Mistaking one for the other startled her. Strangely, she had never noticed the outward similarity between her husband and her father. She had never once compared the two. Her father was a man who took few opportunities to laugh, in or out of the home, spoke little unless he was in a situation where he had to, and rarely smiled. To anyone not knowing each as she did, which was everyone, one would appear much like the other, and though she had never accepted her father's temperament, she accepted her husband's. It was easier to accept when she knew the cause.

When the Rosens had first met over forty years earlier, they were similar in most respects. The couple shared similar views on religion, the same sense of humor, the same work etiquette, and the same outlook on life. Both were well-read, intelligent, and enjoyed being around people, and people enjoyed being around them. They were easygoing and outgoing, and neither one smoked nor drank in excess.

**

The youngest of five sons of a middle-class non-orthodox Rabbi, Avriel Allen Rosen was born in Brackley, England, a small market town in rural Northamptonshire resting almost in the middle of the country. His mother was a French immigrant whose family arrived in England when she was in her early teens, and even though she didn't live to see Avriel's sixth birthday, he still had strong memories of her. He remembered having his first taste of tea with her as they sat on their front steps. He remembered her calling him Av, the only one in the family to do so, and he remembered well her pretty face with its high cheekbones, large eyes, thin lips, and small nose. Avriel got his looks from his father, who was an easygoing, optimistic man who believed almost every problem would eventually work itself out on its own and handled his children as he would handle the members of his synagogue, giving advice while keeping an emotional distance. Not being one to push his sons in any direction, he left them to make their own choices as long as they didn't conflict with their religion, and to a certain point, he was relaxed with that.

In the fall of 1931, Avriel left his family to study pharmacology at Cambridge University, and just as in high school, he proved to be an excellent student who could balance the challenges of university with his social life, including sports in which he excelled. He made friends easily and soon developed a reputation as a practical joker, making it an unofficial honor to be the victim of one of his pranks, with even the targets of his most embarrassing ones happily granting their forgiveness either immediately or shortly after.

The only daughter of a humorless and strict London merchant and his overly affectionate, colorful, and empathetic wife, Ruth Abigail Goldman was a big-city girl who after graduating from her all-girls school, went against her father's wish for her to marry and start a family by attending women's college to study bookkeeping. And it was while she was studying at the college when her mother died.

Almost a year after her mother's death, her father married a friend of the family who was just as humorless as him and whom Ruth thought of as the wicked stepmother, and not getting along with either of them and while her father was trying to marry her off, she left home for Cambridge, where she started a bookkeeping career with a company called Rothman and Tourney Construction.

One cold and wet evening on November 18th, 1933, like most Saturday nights on Cambridge's Regent Street, music mixed with laughter and shouting resonated down its cobblestones.

While the copper ceiling of Dirk's Pub helped to amplify the tinny sound of Irving Berlin's *Puttin' on the Ritz* playing on the large polished gramophone behind the large center bar, a crowd took up all the seating and most of the floor space within its dark wood-paneled walls.

Perspiring from the heat of the bodies crowded along the mahogany bar, a clean-shaven young man dressed in a brown two-piece suit and waiting to order drinks found himself almost elbow to shoulder with a pretty young woman dressed in a pink sweater and black skirt, and boldly tapping her shoulder, he said loud enough to be heard over the music, "I like your sweater."

Turning her head, the woman had to look up to see his face, which was an immediate turnoff since the first thing she saw was into his nostrils. "You like pink, do you?" she asked facetiously.

After he held up four fingers to the bartender, he said, "On you, not so much on me."

"Oh, that's nice to know. Do they sell men's clothes where you bought that suit?" she asked as her nincompoop alarm started lightly ringing.

For a second, the young man was at a loss for words, and then finding them, he said innocently, "I'm... I'm not sure. I'd assume so."

Ending the conversation with a patronizing nod, she turned back to the bar, and with his drinks arriving, he paid for them, and before she could order hers, asked if she would hold one of his for a moment. Out of habit, she obliged, and with his drink in her hand, she watched him carry his three drinks into the crowd.

After waiting a couple of minutes, she questioned what she was doing and looked around for the tall, skinny young man with deep nostrils. Spotting his head sticking out above the crowd some distance away and appearing as if he had forgotten about her holding his drink, she made her way toward him, and after taking almost a minute to navigate around the human obstacles, she tapped him on the back of his shoulder.

"Yes?" he asked, turning around and smiling.

"Excuse me, but how much longer would you like me to hold this drink? Perhaps you'd like to take your time drinking it while I wait for the empty glass, too?"

"You don't like bitters?"

"No, I don't."

"Pardon my mistake," he said, taking the ale from her and guzzling it down to the cheers of his friends, and after throwing a cocky smile back at them, he handed the empty glass to her. "But, Bridget, don't say I don't do you any favors."

Reflexively taking it, she became frustrated with herself. "My name isn't Bridget! It's Ruth!" she said, and then realizing she had fallen for another of his tricks, she kicked the trickster's shin, and as he yelped and hopped melodramatically on his good leg while his friends laughed, clapped, and demanded she punish him further, she turned and made her way back to the bar.

Still steaming from being tricked twice, or three times if she counted accepting the empty glass, she stood at the bar directly in the line of fire of the gramophone and waited to order her drink. Then, in the mirror behind the glass shelves holding the bottles of liquor, she saw the top of the young man's head sticking out of the crowd, making its way toward her. It reached her just as the bartender took her order.

Towering behind her shoulder, he raised his voice over the music. "I'm sorry for that. I expected you to drink the bitter. I was trying to be mysterious by walking away. What can I say? I'm a nincompoop."

"Excuse me, I couldn't hear you."

"That's because the gramophone is right there," he almost shouted. "I said I'm sorry. I was trying to be mysterious. I'm a nincompoop."

"I'm sorry. Could you repeat the last part once more?"

Just as the music ended, the pub filled with, "I'M A NINCOMPOOP!"

For the first time that night, the pub went completely silent before filling with laughter and clapping.

Smiling, the young man turned toward the crowd behind him, stretched out his arms, and bowed twice, and as he turned back to Ruth, the clapping stopped and the bartender, who was enjoying the moment, brought her two drinks and waved off her money.

Ruth turned to the showman, who was still smiling at her setup. "Hold this ale for a moment, if you will."

Instinctively taking it, he watched her walk away with her shandy, before following her to her group of girlfriends huddled directly in the opposite corner of the pub from his group, who had heard his declaration and not wanting to miss the show, soon joined them.

"Does this drink mean you've forgiven me?" he asked.

Ruth looked at her friends. "Girls, should I forgive this... uh... gentleman who's confessed to being a nincompoop?" And after they replied in the negative, some shouting and others shaking their heads, she turned back to him. "There you have it. The jury says you're not to be forgiven. Just because you're aware you're a nincompoop doesn't make you any less of one."

"Yes, that's true, but perhaps, my lady, I could earn your forgiveness? I... I could get down on one knee and beg. If you'd like, you could even throw a drink in my face, or you could even... even kick me in the buttocks with those heavy boots."

"No, I expect you'd enjoy that far too much. Do you drink Shandies?"

"No, but I would if that's what it'll take."

"That's certainly what it'll take," she said before turning her back to him, reaching down for a second, and facing him again with her boot in her hand. "Hold this if you would." After the young man guzzled the ale, handed the empty glass back to a friend, and took the boot, she held her drink over it, paused to give him a chance to back out, and was unpleasantly surprised when realizing what she intended to do, he just smiled. And to the laughs of the two groups and dreading having to wear it with its beer-soaked fur lining, she reluctantly poured the drink into the boot. "Now, if you would drink this... this shandy, all shall be forgiven."

As both groups chanted, "Drink! Drink! Drink!" he smirked and raised the back of the boot to his lips, turned it up, and guzzled down the liquid, with a bit leaking out from the corners of his mouth. With the boot almost upside-down and for dramatic effect, he held it several inches above his head to catch the last few drops, and as the two groups cheered, clapped, and laughed, he wiped his mouth with his sleeve and released a large burp, causing more laughter. Then dropping to one knee, he held the boot up with both hands, much like a knight would hold his sword up to his king.

Taking back her boot and hiding her discomfort as she placed her foot into it, Ruth asked, "And what may I call you, sir?"

"You may call me Avriel, my lady."

It took a lot of persuading, but by the end of the night, Avriel had got an appointment for their first date, though Ruth refused to call it that. And as he expected, she wasn't like any girl he had ever met. She didn't seem to want or need a man. She was independent, intelligent, witty, opinionated, and outspoken, but only showed the last two qualities on the occasions when she strongly disagreed with someone.

After their first few months together, Avriel admitted his love to her, and for a couple of months after that, he had to put up with her telling him, "I like you very much." It would take her that long to admit to herself that she loved the nincompoop. Then that fall after Avriel got his pharmacology degree, his father married them, and a month after that, the newlyweds moved to London where Avriel worked as an assistant pharmacist and Ruth as a bookkeeper.

The two were as happy as they could hope to be and wanted

nothing more than a child, and after two years of trying, they were overjoyed to discover she was pregnant, but tragically disappointed when she miscarried two months later. They continued trying and thirteen months later, met with another miscarriage. And then, to their great disappointment, their doctor told Ruth she couldn't carry a child to term, and with only one option available, they started talking about adopting, but soon postponed the idea.

The whole of Europe's future was in question. Germany was making aggressive gestures toward England's allies, and even though England was in denial at the prospects of war, there was still a large question mark hanging over the country. Then in September 1939, Britain declared war on Germany, which had just attacked Poland after annexing Austria and Czechoslovakia and forcibly regaining two territories from France.

Ruth naively hoped it would be a short war and felt Avriel should wait before enlisting, but by June of the next year, there was little sign of it ending, and pressure was growing on Avriel to join the war effort — women on the street were even accosting him for being dressed as a civilian — so the couple decided he would enlist before being conscripted, and because of his education, he spent three months training as a medical officer before leaving England.

It would be the first time since they were married that they would be separated from each other for more than a day and the first time each would fear for the other's safety.

With Avriel gone, a melancholic Ruth tried to distract herself from worrying about him by focusing all of her energy on her job, taking on project after project no matter how large or small, and with the growing shortage of men within her company not slowing down, she soon became the Acting Operations Manager. Outside of work, she distracted herself by joining several war-effort groups, and outside of those, she took to reading anything unrelated to the war as a temporary escape from reality.

Each longing for the other, Ruth and Avriel wrote almost daily, but because of the postal delays, their letters arrived two to three weeks later in bundles. In Ruth's letters, she detailed her day, told about the rumors she was hearing, gave news on what was happening within the families of each, detailed her thoughts for their future after the war, and often repeated herself by telling Avriel how much she loved him, missed him and worried about him. Many times, Ruth's letters would go to five or six pages, and by the time Avriel received her bundle, it was the size of a short book.

Since he usually only had time to write a page or two daily, Avriel would describe his love and longing for Ruth, the places he had *visited*, and the sites he had seen, as long as he felt they wouldn't cause her alarm. Making light of his experiences, he probably confused the Censorship Bureau by writing as if a tourist, adding several comical observations and regularly using euphemisms, like his habitual use of unfinished for destroyed.

March 11, 1941

Dear Ruthy,

It's now been sixty-two days since I last saw your beautiful face looking back at me while I stood anxiously on the ship's deck. Even from that distance, you could reduce my anxieties.

I continue to keep your image in my mind as a pacifier. It helped last night when the last two days of tranquility were suddenly ended by a sudden and fierce storm. My fellow tourists and I were caught out in the open among the lightning strikes, with one fellow being sent into the air, but luckily, as if a miracle, when he landed, had only scratches on him. We were able to find refuge in an unfinished church and ended up huddling together in a corner under its partially completed roof.

The next morning, we woke just as the sun was coming up. It was as if not a creature but us existed — there was not a sound.

When we packed up to continue our cross-country trek, one of us noticed Murray, the same Murray from my letter almost two weeks back. He was standing quietly in the corner we had all huddled into the night before. It turned out he hadn't woken with the rest of us. He had slept standing up the entire night! We knew he could sleep anywhere, at any time, and through anything, but to sleep standing up was new. He only fell over when we woke him.

We are heading out in a few minutes, so please forgive the shortness of this letter. I will write again at our next rest stop.

Your loving nincompoop, who misses you dearly,

Avriel

PS, I have to make a confession. Yesterday, when we had the unusual luxury of a cooked breakfast before making our way into the storm, I tried bacon and ham and enjoyed them both, though the guilt seemed to work against my digestion. Please do not tell father, yours or mine.

Avriel had left out that he had tried bacon and ham several times and would try them again many times after that. His fellow tourists had made it a routine to give him a portion of one or the other of theirs, if for no other reason than it amused them to watch the Jew eat bacon and ham with such passion. What bacon Avriel didn't finish, he stuffed in his pocket for later, referring to it as his pork jerky.

In May 1941, Germany ended its bombing campaign on London with one last horrific run lasting for three weeks and surpassing all previous bombings in combined explosive power, but lucky for Ruth, the bombs somehow spared her apartment complex, only breaking its taped windows and damaging its brick exterior, but her company wasn't so lucky and had to close for a period to recover.

While waiting to return to work, she kept herself busy by helping each day with the cleanup of the streets' debris, usually involving throwing bricks in a cart that the men would wheel off, and soon she was used to discovering bodies, which the men retrieved and carted off too, but she never got used to the smell, the smell that warned her when she should expect to find one. For a short time, the work made her feel useful and reminded her that her problems were minor compared to those of others, others related to the discovered corpses, living in the destroyed buildings, or owning the destroyed shops.

The chaos caused by the bombings delayed Ruth's letters, and a concerned Avriel only received her much larger bundle in late July. With the fighting becoming more intense, he only had time to read his wife's letters while on the march, literally. He had no idea of the intensity of the bombing of Britain and only found out about it after the fact through her letters.

Avriel was living a nightmare. All around him was death and destruction, and even those who were far away from him and should've been secure at home were at great risk of harm and even death. With his loved ones short of food and without electricity and running water, the world had turned completely upside down and there was little to nothing he could do but wait for it to upright itself.

For the first time, Avriel felt helpless and the only things keeping his mind from the dangers at home were the dangers in front of him. Most of the time, he never knew where they stood in the fighting: at one moment, it seemed they were surrounding the enemy, and at another, surrounded by the enemy. And often he would go days without a full meal and even longer without a full sleep, making him believe his battalion was doing all the fighting.

**

As the delays between Avriel's letters became longer and his bundles became smaller, Ruth had to force herself to keep her spirit up.

She had weathered more than four years separated from her husband before the rumors spread that Germany would soon collapse, and two weeks after receiving what would be his final bundle of letters, the most recent letter dated two months earlier, Germany did.

With Victory in Europe Day celebrations going on around her, Ruth isolated herself in her apartment and ignored the door when her neighbors knocked, hoping to include her in their festivities. Not being able to celebrate without her husband, she anxiously waited for his next bundle of letters, expecting it to be the final one telling her he was on his way home, but it never came.

The European war had been over for two weeks, and Ruth still had received nothing from her husband. Wondering if it was all just God's joke, she slid into a deep depression. God denied her a child and now He was denying her a husband, a husband who had fought through the war only to die at its end. Then with her spirit broken, Ruth waited for the telegram bringing her news of his death.

It was almost two weeks later, on a Saturday midafternoon, when Ruth received a light knock on her door. Expecting it to be the official notice forcing her to join England's many widows, she slowly opened it and found herself looking at the chest of a man whom she didn't immediately recognize. Dressed handsomely in his officer's uniform, the man stood blank-faced with arms by his sides and a duffle bag at his feet.

With a scream, she embraced him, and he slowly embraced her, and the two stood holding each other as her tears soaked his biceps.

When the tenants on her floor heard her scream, they opened their doors to peek out, and seeing the embraced couple in the hall, they quietly closed them.

Neither Ruth nor Avriel spoke a word. Neither could nor felt they had to, and they spent the next couple of hours in silence, dressed and embraced on their bed with the duffle bag in the building's hallway. Eventually, both fell into the most secure and comfortable sleep either had had in years, sleeping for almost ten hours while occasionally waking up to stare at the other snoring.

Ruth soon discovered that Avriel had returned a noticeably different man, and she couldn't help but feel he had left a part of himself on the other side of the channel. He didn't smile his full-teeth smile and hardly spoke more than a few words at a time, and with her doing all the talking, she could only hope he was listening.

Avriel had lost his motivation to do anything, including showering. He ate when Ruth placed food in front of him, sat with her while she listened to the radio, and cleaned around the house when she did. Sometimes he dusted the same thing for several minutes before she noticed and directed him to dust something else. And when their neighbors visited, he would sit quietly and inhospitably on the sofa. Every visitor noticed, but none brought attention to it.

For several days, Ruth waited patiently for Avriel to decide to shower and shave, but when his body odor became too intense, she had to ask him to. With a simple nod of his head, he did as he was asked and when he returned, had the beginning of a thick mustache much like that of Ruth's father. She disliked it, but she accepted it.

As the weeks passed, Ruth began losing hope in her husband

returning to his old self, and even though it scared her, she tried to force herself to accept it, but still, she couldn't help fantasizing about him snapping back and would be pacified for a time if she could just get a glimpse of the man she had married. Then on a night in August, she got it.

After having tried to get Avriel to waltz to a swing song on the radio, their song, *Puttin' on the Ritz*, only to be disappointed by his new touch and feel, she was adjusting the tuner to the news when she passed a football match. As his new placid self sat on the sofa staring ahead at the wall across from him, Avriel surprised her by softly asking if she would go back to the football match, which she did, and as both sat listening, he began to mumble to himself, becoming louder and louder over the next half an hour until he was soon cheering on one team and damning the other. Astonished, Ruth sat beside him as he bounced up and down on their sofa, seemingly oblivious to her, but when the match ended, to her disappointment, he returned to his placid state.

Fascinated by the football match's effect on Avriel, Ruth began searching *The Daily Telegraph* for the scheduled matches, tuning into them and then sitting beside him as he returned to his old self. Sometimes at the end of a broadcast, he would even stand up, lift her to her feet, and plant a kiss on her lips, and occasionally, he would remain his old self for a short time afterward, and they would hold hands and talk until something she said or something in his head caused him to snap back to his postwar state.

The football matches' effect on Avriel caused Ruth to believe that there was a cure for his current state, and by knowing the cause, she hoped to find a more permanent solution than having to tune into *The Old Avriel Show* for a few hours each weekend during football season. She was realistic enough to understand that even if she could heal his mental wounds, he would still have permanent mental scars. He may never be the same man he was before the war, but he could be better than he was when returning from it.

Determined to find out what had caused or could have caused her husband's state, early on Sunday morning while Avriel slept, she searched through his many letters for his army mates' first names. She remembered reading about a Murray, a Jenkins, and a Harrington but couldn't remember one first name. Then later that week, after finding the first name to go with Jenkins, she went down to the war office to confirm he had survived. To her relief, Corporal Timothy Jenkins, who had spent much time with Avriel after 1943, was alive, and after many rewrites, she sent him a letter explaining Avriel's state of mind and asking for a description of the events that could've led to it.

Two weeks later — it seemed like months to Ruth — she received a short reply.

September 24, 1945

Dear Mrs. Rosen,

I'm saddened to receive your letter regarding your husband's state. I knew Rosen was a changed man but didn't comprehend to what extent, but regarding your request for the details that may have led to his current state, I must decline as I feel it's only Rosen's place to do so. I can only say that your husband is a great man and was appreciated by all those around him. He made life bearable for many of us. I'm sure that in his own time, he'll snap out of it and return to his resilient self. Until then, please be patient with your husband. He may not say it, but I know he needs your support, just as all of us now back at home need the emotional support of our loved ones.

I do appreciate your concern but have to ask you not to write to me again as it brings back memories I'm not prepared to deal with at this time. The war is behind me, and I very much want to leave it there.

Sincerely,

Timothy Kenneth Jenkins

Ruth would respect Mr. Jenkins' request not to write to him again, and that following Sunday morning, she put together several small meals for Avriel and took the almost hour-long train ride to Mr. Jenkins' home.

Sitting alone on a bench at the back of the passenger car with the constant clicking of its steel wheels passing along the sections of the rail, Ruth's mind raced. How would she approach Mr. Jenkins? What would she say to get him to talk? She could call him from the station and let him know she was coming, or she could show up at his door without any advanced warning. If she called first, she expected the same response as the letter and it would be giving him a chance to flee. If she showed up at his door, she might be able to trick her way into his house and then tell him who she was and why she was there, or maybe she could just be upfront with him and hope for the best. And then it occurred to her that she might not be able to handle the information she needed. Since Mr. Jenkins wanted to keep it to himself, something horrific must have happened. Could it involve Avriel doing something extreme? Could he have committed an awful crime? Could she handle learning her husband did something so extremely out of character? Then worried about finding what she was seeking, she considered going back home, but after silently crying for ten minutes, she pulled herself together and convinced herself she had to go forward and accept the incident or incidents.

Leaving the train station and forgetting her umbrella on the train, Ruth entered the first waiting taxi in the line, and arriving at the address ten minutes later, she paid the driver and asked him to wait with his meter clicking away.

Mr. Jenkins, a thin, prematurely balding man who was only five-foot-four and no older than thirty, answered the door of his small cottage home and asked, "Yes? Can I help you?"

"You most certainly can," Ruth responded, boldly putting on a strong front through the rain. "My name is Ruth Rosen."

The man's friendly face was replaced by a stunned one and then a moment later replaced by a stern one. "Mrs. Rosen, I thought my letter made it clear I wasn't to be... to be bothered again!"

"Well, yes, you asked me not to write, so I came in person," Ruth said, trying desperately to justify herself.

"Must I have stated for you not to visit too? I'm sorry you wasted your time and money coming here! Good day, Mrs. Rosen!"

When Mr. Jenkins went to close the door, Ruth shot her small foot between it and the frame, and as a sharp pain streaked through it, she said in a voice louder than she was accustomed to, "Sir, if you have information that'll help me understand my husband's problem, I'll not leave here without it! Even if you were in Russia, I'd be at your door and wouldn't be leaving until I've heard what I need to hear! And if I must, I'll send the taxi away and wait here for as long as it takes you to prepare yourself to tell me! You'll see me each time you leave and return!"

The seconds it took the gentleman to respond felt like minutes to Ruth. Even with the cupboards and icebox full of food, Avriel might starve to death if she were forced to carry out her threat.

Softening his voice, Mr. Jenkins said, "Well, Mrs. Rosen, seeing how often Rosen proudly described you, I expect you're not making an empty threat." Taking a deep breath, he glanced at the waiting taxi and then back at the soaked woman. "If you promise to leave when I've had enough and never return for seconds, I'll disclose what I can, though I make no promises to the fullness of the disclosure."

"It's a promise! After today, you'll not see me again, Mr. Jenkins!" Ruth blurted out as she tried to push aside her fear of the ominous implication of his use of the word *disclosure*.

After Mr. Jenkins led the limping woman into his living room without either realizing she was making small puddles through his home, he brought her a glass of water and a towel and told her that before February 1945, all seemed well with Avriel. He told her about how they had become inseparable, relying on each other as confidants and co-conspirators, and he began to smile and laugh as he recalled some anecdotes of their first year together. One involved them convincing a young recruit that Germany was using poisonous gas and because they hadn't yet received their gas masks, they had to keep a cloth on them at all times because a urine-soaked cloth held over the face would neutralize the gas and save their lives, which it actually would with chlorine gas. Believing them, the cautious recruit then carried a cloth on him at all times.

"We let him go on for a couple of days before we snuck up on him while he slept and shouted, 'Gas! Gas!' And in a flash, the chap was up, grabbed his cloth out of his pocket, and right in front of us, relieved himself on it. Then he put it to his face and took several large breaths! He breathed like that for a bit before catching on that we had both put down our dry cloths and were breaking our guts. Thundering, how we laughed! Little things like that kept us amused, kept us going."

The man was enjoying the good memories and probably would've gone on avoiding the reason for her being there if she hadn't gently pushed him for the relevant information, causing him to lose his smile, his eyes to lose their glow, and her to become a little frightened and suspect he might forcibly remove her from his house, but he didn't.

"Well... ok... I... I suppose Rosen's first serious moment, the first noticeable change in him, came when we met up with the

Russians. I think it was the end of February. We couldn't help but witness the crimes they were committing and... and we were helpless to do anything about it. They were outright murdering Germans... soldiers and civilians. At one point, Rosen told me those brutalities were eating at his soul. Those were his exact words, 'eating at my soul.' I remember because it made me stop and listen. He had to say them twice because my mind refused to make sense of them coming from him. He never seemed to let anything bother him. Maybe they did before I met him, but if they did, I'm sure he learned to deal with them by then. I mean, he was the one who kept me sane several times. Let me tell you about the time I was... no, no, sorry, this is about Rosen. Ok... where... where was I?"

"He said, 'Eating at my soul.' That's where you ended."

"Right... ok, well, after that comment, I was worried for him, but, you know, soon afterward he seemed to have gotten it together again." Mr. Jenkins looked to the floor and was silent for a moment before saying, "Then, maybe a month later, we were assigned to the Eleventh Armored Division, part of the forces to enter Homburg. After a bit, we came across a concentration camp, Belsen they called it, and it was the strangest thing: we didn't have to fight to clear out the Germans. Before we went in, our side negotiated terms with the SS bastards, agreeing to allow most to leave before we even entered. And here's where it gets disturbing," he warned. "As soon as we neared the wired fence, we saw thousands of starving inmates lining the other side all huddled together. Truly... they were walking skeletons. And when we entered the camp, we discovered thousands of rotting corpses piled high out in the open." Mr. Jenkins' voice changed to a whisper. "It was a ghastly sight." Then he cleared his throat and asked, "Would... would you like some more water?"

Ruth didn't, but she handed her glass to him anyway, said, "Yes, please. Thank you," and watched him walk to the kitchen, and a after minute, he returned with the glass of water and a dry forehead.

"I remember the numbers... the estimates. There were over fifty thousand alive and over ten thousand corpses out in the open. I'm sure I don't have to say we were horrified by the discovery. Never had any of us seen anything like that, never, and who would've ever imagined it? Yet, we let the criminals go!" he said with his voice getting louder. "The Nazi bastards walked right out of the camp, going on their merry way!"

Taking a moment to calm down, he continued, "It was horrible. Some of the walking skeletons were so starved you couldn't tell if they were men or women, just skeletons barely alive. And then, like a miracle, one with a small bundle came up to us pleading for milk. A baby there in a place like that! Who would've believed it possible? Right? Right? And then, when Rosen looked inside the bundle, it had been dead for days!" Again, Mr. Jenkins took a moment to calm down. "Anyway, we learned it was a slave labor camp. It killed its prisoners through work and starvation.

"I don't need to tell you it had a major impact on us, but even more so on Rosen. He stopped joking around, but then who could after that? But he hardly talked too, which was strange for him. I don't have to tell you he's a talker, right... or he was.

"Anyway, while they brought doctors in to rehabilitate the prisoners back to health, we, Rosen and I, were ordered to stay there to assist. Our first task was to take an inventory of those still living, and for the first few days while the dead were being buried in mass graves, we walked through the mud of blood, feces, and things I can't even mention and witnessed things I never imagined possible. Once, we came across a large group of prisoners who had somehow found the energy to tear apart one of their own with their bare hands. We were told later it was a kapo. Uh... a kapo is German for a prisoner who acts as a guard for the Germans.

"I'm sure a lot of us changed that first week — Rosen certainly did. From the second day there, he wore that same strange expression. I can still remember it. It was so strange on him: a cold, lifeless expression, which was so unlike him. He hardly talked or ate, and he used to clean his plate no matter what was on it, but there... there, he hardly touched his food, not even bacon." Mr. Jenkins broke a distant smile. "The bacon that attracted dogs. He once had three dogs follow him around for almost half a day until he gave in and fed them the bacon he was saving in his pocket."

Catching himself digressing, he lost his smile and continued, "I think we all have a breaking point, and I think Rosen's was the news that there were more camps like Belsen, even larger ones. We heard rumors of death camps set up to murder Jews just for being Jews. Rumor had it they murdered somewhere between four and five million. I'm... I'm sorry. I'm sure you already heard about that.

"Anyway... let me tell you, that was it for Rosen. He closed up. I didn't hear it myself, mind you, but was told he'd been mumbling to himself incoherently. Then he refused to get up or even to talk to anyone, including me, and yet nothing was physically wrong with him. We began to worry he might try suicide, and... and soon after that, he was sent to a hospital.

"Rosen was a popular fellow, and I can't tell you how upset we all were when he broke. He truly seemed like the last chap to do it. Before then, he was the one helping many of us cope. We figured if Rosen broke, more of us would follow... and some did. I know of one chap who was back there with us who just recently committed suici—" Mr. Jenkins paused for a moment before suddenly becoming agitated and raising his voice. "That's it! That's all I'll say about that! That's where my story ends! I'm not going into any more details! You get the situation! You get the picture! Your man's... your husband's a great fellow and I hope he snaps out of it, but that's all I'm saying, ever!"

Ruth stood up, thanked him, and left with a promise never to return.

Mr. Jenkins didn't walk her to the door. Even with her sore foot, she was moving too fast for him to catch up.

Three hours later, Ruth was on the train heading home. She tried, but she couldn't sleep. Her mind refused to shut off. Several times she went over what Mr. Jenkins had told her and still she couldn't figure out how to use the information to find a cure without somehow erasing that part of her husband's memory, but then she thought that since she couldn't erase his memory, maybe she could bring some prewar memories to the forefront of his mind by having his two surviving brothers visit — his father had passed away during the war — but then she gave up on that idea since they weren't very close, and even if they accepted the request, they most likely would just sit and silently stare at each other.

Then a few minutes later it occurred to her that a change of environment could help, an environment where there were few to no physical signs of the war — the fewer the signs, the fewer triggers that would cause Avriel to recall his terrible memories. Ruth considered Palestine, but it was still in its infancy with an uncertain future; she and her husband would be unaccustomed to its climate, and most likely, it would constantly remind them of Germany's attempt to exterminate the Jews. No, Avriel needed a place similar to Britain's culture and climate but much further away, and after considering several places, she decided on Halifax, Nova Scotia, which she had visited as a child. It had much the same climate as England and its people were easygoing, British friendly, and except for its naval port, it would show almost no signs of the war.

Even though Canada's immigration laws made it more than difficult for Jews to enter the country, being British-born Jews, they would have no problem immigrating. The only obstacle was the ocean voyage. Could Avriel handle it? Ruth would have to wait until after the next football match to ask him.

**

Pulling herself away from her father's portrait to enter the dining room, Ruth placed the small pile of folders on the dining room table next to a taller one and sat down to reflect on the coming discussions. If she could even call them discussions since she would talk and he would listen. Perhaps she should call them presentations or proposals. Whatever she should call them, she didn't look forward to them.

For the last few weeks, she had been busying herself with her plans, acting on them before she had discussed them with her husband, a first, and had only recently decided to discuss all the changes in one sitting. *Why create three separate stressful moments when instead it could be one large one and be done with?* And she had also decided the order to discuss them in, from the easiest to the most difficult, and from previous times, she had found that the morning was the best time for them. Avriel would be a little tired and less guarded, and during the day, he would mentally regurgitate what she had said and, by the evening, he would be more comfortable with the idea. And if he had questions, he would ask them during supper. Also that morning, she would give him a silent warning of what was to come so it won't be a surprising shock to him.

If one could call an occasional action over thirty years a routine, she had created a routine of making her husband his favorite breakfast of eggs, toast, hash browns, slices of ham and bacon, and a large glass of milk before discussing the dramatic changes soon to come in their lives, like the opening of another drugstore or the move to Gilmore Street, and from the mix of smells coming from the kitchen, he was sure to realize something was up and, maybe, mentally prepare himself for it before even sitting at the table.

At six-thirty, Avriel, wearing his usual black dress pants, white dress shirt, and a loose tie flung over his shoulder, made his way downstairs where his nose caught the party of smells coming from the kitchen, arousing him to where he had to swallow... before a sudden fear engulfed him. The smells and the fact that the radio was off meant only one thing: there would be a discussion. And there was the possibility of two: one he could handle and the other he couldn't, or wouldn't. With the fear continuing to engulf him, he had to force himself to walk, consciously placing one foot in front of the other.

Entering the kitchen, he kissed the top of Ruth's head and received a hug, or a squeeze as she liked to call it before she placed a long plate of toast, hash browns, and slices of cooked ham and bacon on the kitchen table, and as he sat down in his chair and took a shaky sip from his cup of coffee while eyeing the bacon and his glass of milk, Ruth placed a plate of two eggs sunny side up in front of him before sitting down with her plate of one egg over easy.

Staring at Ruth for a moment, he asked, "Is there a discussion com—"

"Yes. Dear... I need you to... to go to work... a little late today."

Noting that Ruth, without physically exerting herself, was having difficulty breathing, Avriel only nodded, and with his thoughts confirmed and his wife adding toast and hash browns to her plate while avoiding the bacon and ham, he added toast, hash browns, and several slices of bacon and ham to his plate, and asked, "Are you leaving me?"

Ruth almost choked on her coffee. "No! Why would you... you ask such a thing?"

"Well then, all is good," he said, and not getting the expected smile from her, he stuck his fork into his hash browns.

After a couple of minutes, Ruth noticed her husband's awkward attempt to eat and said, "It's quite... quite the opposite, dear. I'd like to... to discuss our retiring together."

Avriel knew Ruth had been thinking about their retirement. He knew the discussion was coming soon, and he needed little time for mental preparation. Relieved there wasn't the second subject, the one he was dreading, he asked, "Is that all? I thought perhaps it was about the possibility of the squirrels converting."

Appreciating his attempt to relax her, Ruth's smile caused him to smile.

After Avriel had finished eating and with food still on her plate, Ruth stood up, and leaving the dirty dishes on the table, took his hand and led him into the dining room where they sat down across from each other with the two piles of file folders between them.

"Dear, the bookkeeping is finished."

As she slid the larger pile of folders further down the table and out of the way, the number of different colored file folders in the small pile confused Avriel, and his blood pressure rose. *Three!*

Ruth picked up the top green folder and held it in front of her. "Now to start, this is my investment folder. To the disappointment of Gerry, I've moved most of our stocks into bonds," she said, surprising Avriel. "The stocks remaining are only of Maritime Telephone and Telegraph and a company called International Business Machines, a typewriter company. I expect good things in the future from both."

She slid the folder over to Avriel, who picked it up, opened it, casually scanned the papers, and understood nothing he was seeing until he came to the page summarizing the dollar value of the stock they owned in each company, making Ruth proud when she saw the subtle shock in his eyes.

"You did well, Ruthy, very well."

"*We* did well, Av."

Handing the folder back to his wife, who placed it further down the table, he asked, "Does this mean we are no longer having Stock Dinners? We are *not* going this evening?"

"Correct to both questions. It means we're all done with Morgan's. Now we can sample other restaurants. We can start living a little," she smiled. "I still want to eavesdrop but on much more interesting conversations."

"Great. That sounds great. Just for future reference, I was hoping to try that new burger restaurant further down Herring Cove Road, the one called Macdonald's," Avriel half-joked.

"Av, they're calling that kind of food *fast food*. Anything that travels through you that fast can't be very good for you."

"Right, but they do not take tips... so Thomas tells me," Avriel said and then joked, "Sort of goes with our Jewishness, does it not?"

Ruth feigned anger. "Avriel Rosen! Sometimes I think you're an anti-Semitic Jew! No, sir, that one won't be receiving a smile from me!" Then when Avriel cracked a smile, she did, too. "Ok... so we're going to spend tonight at home. I'll make a nice celebration dinner. Dear, could you pick up a bottle of wine on the way back this afternoon?"

"Of course," nodded Avriel, who dropped his smile when he saw her pick up the blue folder to reveal the pink one.

"Ok, now for your... our retirement, which I'm sure doesn't come as a surprise to you. Four years ago, when we were approached by Craig Frank, I made a mistake," she said, causing Avriel to immediately understand how she was planning their retirement. "I should have been thinking of our retirement, but I was comfortable with the way things were. Our health... my health was the furthest thing from my mind.

"Last week, I contacted him, and he's still very much interested, and I suspect he's now even more interested. He only opened one location here and I'm certain it's not doing so well," she smiled mischievously. "Lucky for us, this city might not have room for another chain of drugstores and ours may be the only fast way to move his chain east of Quebec. We haven't set an exact date yet, but he'll be coming by sometime next month to talk about the locations." Noticing Avriel's eyes registering surprise, a surprise due to the combination of her not asking his opinion before starting the process and the potential speed of the sale, she added, "I expect we shall get a third more than he had originally offered now that he knows how difficult it is to go in fresh. Dear, what do you think?"

"Well, as usual, Ruthy, you are correct," Avriel assured her. "Decades later and you still surprise me," he said as he reached over and gave her hand a gentle squeeze. "Ok, you handle the negotiations and just tell me where you need me to stand."

Smiling, she handed the blue file folder to Avriel, who opened it and pretended to give the communications between her and Mr. Frank an interested look. Closing it, he laid it perfectly on top of the thinner pink folder, covering it completely, and then, standing up, he pushed in his chair and left the room. Returning a minute later, he laid his briefcase on the table, opened it, picked up the pile of bookkeeping folders, and placed them inside of it.

Holding back a smile at her husband's desperate and pathetic attempt to avoid the last folder, Ruth cleared her throat and said, "Please sit a little longer, dear."

By his wife's serious tone, any question as to whether she had said *dear* or *there* wasn't there, and he remained standing while gripping the back of the chair in front of him with both hands.

As Ruth moved the blue folder to the green and picked up the pink one, Avriel gripped the back of the chair tighter.

"Av, we need to discuss this last item. As negative as it is, we should talk about this now. In this folder are all the arrangements made and paid for. All you'll need to do is call Rabbi Lavigne's number on the inside of the folder next to the number for

Parker's."

Noticing Avriel's straining fingers becoming pale and with her heart then pounding so hard that it worried her, she decided to ignore the details within the folder since he would only have to know them when the time came.

"They know what's to be done... and they'll work together to ensure it's... it's proper. It'll all be short. That's it. It's that simple. We're done."

Slightly dizzy, Ruth added the pink file to the other two.

As Avriel released his grip from the back of the chair, finding it painfully difficult to straighten his fingers, his wife slowly stood up and put her arms out, and after he walked around the table, they kissed and hugged.

Breaking their embrace, Ruth said, "Ok, Av, go grab your lunch on the counter and I'll meet you at the door."

After forcing his briefcase closed, he picked it up, headed into the kitchen for his usual paper bag, and met her at the door where they embraced again.

"Ok, Av, go to work before I decide to keep you home today."

With both having to force themselves to break their hold on the other, Ruth failed to notice that he had forgotten his blazer and instead of picking up the newspaper, he had stepped on it.

He leaned back in the driver's seat, and after taking a moment to collect himself, opened his lunch bag and saw a sandwich wrapped in wax paper and beside it, a pink note folded over. With his reading glasses retrieved from the glove compartment, he unfolded the tiny paper.

I am so very proud to call myself Mrs. Avriel Allen Rosen. So many years and yet my love for you continues to grow even stronger.

With his hands slightly shaking, he put the note in his shirt pocket, placed his reading glasses back in the glove compartment, and backed out of the driveway.

Avriel was well aware that the discussions' raison d'être was his wife preparing him for being alone, and the immediate change, the selling of their drugstores, wouldn't be difficult for him or the stores. His wife had made them so efficient, to the point where they were almost self-running, that he could leave tomorrow and they would operate fine.

Daily, he had a lot of free time, too much of it. The tasks he had required little time, and he only kept them to feel useful, and since Ruth had begun staying home, he spent more time in the receiving area. Instead of the thirty to forty minutes he would spend down there when she was working with him, he spent between two to three hours sitting on its counter while sharing several newspapers with Thomas who was the first in and the first out of the Spring Garden Road location each day.

Thomas was an unassuming man who was a little younger than Avriel but looked older because of his gray hair and gray facial stubble that grew longer throughout the week, only to start again as a five o'clock shadow the next Monday morning. He was rather introverted too, though less so than Avriel, and he appreciated working in the receiving area for its lack of personal interaction.

Like Avriel, Thomas too went to war, and by his job application, Avriel vaguely knew of his service, and Thomas too may have suspected Avriel of having been in the service, but neither had ever brought up the subject.

Thomas' experience overseas was different, but just as horrific as Avriel's. Thomas' Winnipeg Grenadiers was part of the first Canadian forces to see action in the Pacific War. In 1941, even though the soldiers lacked field experience, the Canadian government sent them to assist the British in defending Hong Kong against the Japanese invasion, and along with the British, they ended up surrendering on Christmas day. Thomas was lucky enough to survive both the failed defense of Hong Kong and the notorious Japanese POW camps, where he performed forced labor for almost four years while watching others around him die from exhaustion.

Changed by the experience, when he returned to Canada, Thomas moved to Halifax to put as much distance as possible between himself and the Pacific Ocean, and soon after arriving, he began working for the Rosens in their first drugstore, and as each new location opened and they moved their main office to it, the Rosens took him along.

Even though Thomas and Avriel hardly spoke and when they did the conversations were short and always about minor things, like the weather, Thomas was the only person whom Avriel was somewhat comfortable around and whom he considered a friend, and when their chain was sold, Avriel expected he would miss him.

Then, with his mind away from driving, Avriel drove twice around the Armdale Rotary before taking the Spring Garden Road exit.

CHAPTER 7
Making a Connection

In her pink bathrobe and holding a stainless steel lunchbox, Mrs. Dixon met her husband at the door.

Standing up from tying his work boots, Mr. Dixon took his lunchbox and asked, "What abouts this Avriel kid? Maybe ya can make arrangements with his mom fer sharin' the babysittin' so ya can both get a break in the day."

"I could do that."

"Good. Hey, what's this kid look like?"

"He's thin, tall, and with black hair."

"Oh, yeah? Black hair? Not a foreigner, I hopes."

"Yes, he's British."

"That's not really a foreigner. Has ya met 'is parents? Does they have the accent?"

"I think his parents passed away some time ago, but he has an accent. He lives with an older woman. She has the accent too," Mrs. Dixon said, enjoying the conversation.

"Cool. So you'll talk ta 'er and make arrangements fer sharin' the watchin' of Dewey and little orphan Avriel?"

"Sure. That's a great idea. I'll give her a call this morning."

"Hey, maybe I'll take 'em ta play catch when Dewey's cast's off."

"I think they'd both like that," she said, finally releasing the smile she had been holding back in fear of it turning into a laugh.

"Cool. So I'll see ya this evenin' then," he said, giving his wife a peck on the lips before leaving for work.

Later that afternoon, as Mrs. Dixon was enjoying the sun by sweeping her cement walkway, Mr. Smith approached her with a clipboard under his arm. As usual, he appeared to be a man on a mission.

"Hi, Rob. What's up?"

"Hey, Lisa. Fairview's string of break-ins is what's up. I've been thinking, and I think we should be prepared so it doesn't happen over here too, and the only way we're going to prevent it is if we look out for one another. I heard someplace in New York has set up something they call a Neighborhood Watch and I figure why not try it here too? So I'm going around seeing who wants to get involved and which hours they can put into it. We start watching at nine in the morning and end at nine at night, every day of the week. I'm asking everyone to take two slots of two hours if they can. I don't think four hours each will cover the time, but it's a start. We can probably begin by watching from our windows for now, and we'll work it out better as the program goes on. Oh, and, Lisa, I'll be holding a meeting at my place this Thursday night at seven-thirty to go over everything," he said, pausing for a moment to let her absorb what he had said. "So, what do you think? Are you interested?"

"Uh... that's a great idea. Can I take the first watch on Tuesday and Thursday mornings, at least until Dewey starts school again?"

Mr. Smith looked at his clipboard. "Sure. That's great." And then, pulling a pencil from behind his ear, said, "That means Mrs. Rosen will be watching at eleven. She's on board too and wants to follow your shift. So, Lisa, I'll see you at my place Thursday at seven-thirty?"

"For sure. What should I bring?" she asked, smiling at the man while finding it an interesting coincidence that he chose the one night Paul wouldn't be home.

"Just yourself... and Dewey, but if you want to bring some snacks, feel free. See you then and thanks," Mr. Smith said as he left, almost skipping to the next house.

**

Standing on the sidewalk in front of his house, he pulled back on his small balsa-wood glider, tightly stretching the thin rubber band attached to it and his thumb sticking out of his cast, and after releasing it into the sky, where it reached its maximum height of about twenty feet, he shaded his eyes with his good hand as he watched it slowly make larger and larger circles on its elegant glide toward the ground.

With incoherent shouting coming from up the street, Dewey turned to see Robby at the top of the hill running down the sidewalk toward him, and trying hard to keep up, two other boys followed behind him. As Robby closed in, Dewey stepped onto his front lawn to get out of the older boy's way, and as the glider flew in two more large circles and landed on the sidewalk, Robby, moving fast and breathing hard, stepped on it and knocked off its front wing. Three seconds later, Robby's friends, whom Dewey didn't recognize, ran by and further crushed it. Curious more than disappointed, he watched Robby turn left at the intersection and disappear and then watched his friends do the same.

With nothing more to distract him, Dewey picked up the pieces of the glider and brought them back to the steps of his house, where he sat to figure out if he could fix it. After a minute, he decided it was unfixable, but he wasn't upset. He would've been if he didn't have two more gliders still in their paper wrappers waiting for him to take the minute to put them together.

When the two boys, who had been following Robby, passed his house on their walk back toward Herring Cove Road, the taller redheaded boy said, "Hey, kid, sorry abouts yer plane there," and the second, a smaller blond-headed boy, nodded his head at him.

Surprised that they talked to him, Dewey said, "It's ok. I have more."

"Cool. Great cast ya gots there too," the redhead said as the second boy gave Dewey a thumbs-up, which Dewey returned as they passed the Rosens' house.

A minute later, Dewey's mother, who had seen her son's glider destroyed on its first flight, appeared dragging their push mower behind her. "Honey, do you want to try something different? I'm not sure if you can do it with just one arm, but you can try," she said, both surprising and exciting her son since it was a grown-up job that looked like fun.

Five minutes after she had shown him how to use it, Dewey was alone with the mower, and his mother was in the living room, watching him through the window as he pushed it across the grass with only his good hand.

After examining his first pass, he realized that to get it cutting evenly at the edges, he would have to get more momentum on the blades before he was on the grass and to do that, he would need to take a running start. So from the driveway, he pushed the mower as fast as he could toward the lawn and, when reaching it, put his chest against the mower's crossbar to give it the extra push it needed. And after examining his second attempt, he was impressed with his work.

In twenty-five minutes, he had finished cutting the small front lawn evenly and was about to put the mower away when he remembered he had to cut the grass separating his and the Rosens' driveways, and this time, he took his starting position from the middle of the quiet street and pushed the mower onto the thin strip of lawn, cutting it in one pass. And when he turned back to inspect his work, he found Ruth standing in her driveway with a glass of something yellow in one hand and a dry dishtowel in the other. "Dewey, that was fun to watch! I bet you could use a drink, though."

"Sure. Thanks, Mrs. Rosen," Dewey said proudly before taking the glass and trying not to drink the lemonade too fast. He was thirsty, but never realized it until the moment the liquid touched his lips.

Ruth took the empty glass and wiped his forehead with the dishtowel. "What a great job you did. I know it's hard work, but you make it look rather easy, even with only one arm. Dewey, how'd you like to earn fifty cents by cutting my lawn?"

"No, Mrs. Rosen, I'll do it for free because we're friends."

"I can't have you do that. Fifty cents is a small fee and if you charge nothing, you may end up doing all the lawns here for free. No, Dewey, you have to charge a token sum at the very minimum."

"A token sum?"

"An amount so small everyone can afford it, but knowing that they have to pay it, they only ask if they want the job done. With no token sum, people could ask you to do things on a whim. It's like the toll we pay every time we cross the bridge."

Dewey immediately understood the toll concept. Every time his family crossed the bridge between Halifax and Dartmouth, it was his job to roll down the back window and toss either a small metal token or fifteen cents into the large black funnel on the side of the tollbooth.

Her explanation persuade him to take the money, and when he told her he had to let his mother know, he was surprised to learn the old woman had already phoned her.

With the mowing paid for, Ruth tucked a portion of the towel into Dewey's front shorts pocket, patted him on the bottom, and returned to her home.

As the two coins jingled in his back pocket, Dewey began cutting the Rosens' front lawn, using his running starts from the driveway. Focused on his work, he failed to notice Ruth place two kitchen chairs on her porch, put a small foldout table between them, and set a glass pitcher of lemonade and three glasses on the table. Then after his mother came out and annoyed him by placing sunscreen on his face and the exposed portion of his legs and arms, making sure to avoid the scabs, she joined Ruth on her porch, and together the women sat and watched the little man cut the lawn, both amused by his running starts from the driveway.

"I so love watching young men at work!" Ruth joked.

"Then we should take these chairs up to Herring Cove Road. Some men are working on the road a block down the way," Mrs. Dixon joked back with a smile.

Talking and laughing, the two women continued watching Dewey cut Ruth's lawn.

Dewey was almost finished when Mr. Smith approached him, waved greetings to the women, and asked his small neighbor if he could mow his and the lawn of the Argyles, who were away on vacation and whose front lawn joined his, but before Dewey could agree, Ruth interjected, "For fifty cents."

Mrs. Dixon laughed.

Then, reminded of the monetary potential, Dewey said, "Sure, Mr. Smith, but it costs fifty cents."

"Each," added Ruth.

"Fifty cents each."

"Don't forget to say please," his mother reminded him.

"Please," Dewey said, becoming annoyed with the coaching.

"That's a bargain," said an amused Mr. Smith, who handed over a two-dollar bill. "That should about cover it. Keep the change, my good man," he said before holding out his right hand to shake, realizing the problem, and switching hands.

Trying to hide his excitement, Dewey vigorously shook Mr. Smith's hand before placing the bill in his back pocket and saying, "I'll be done here soon, and then I'll start on yours, Mr. Smith."

"Don't forget to say thank you," his mother reminded him.

"Thank you."

"No. Thank you," Mr. Smith said, waving goodbye to the women before returning to his home across the street.

Dewey was proud of himself. He was doing a job that was a lot of fun, and in his back pocket was the most money he had ever had.

After Mr. Smith moved his car onto the street so his little neighbor could take his running starts from his driveway, Dewy began his work, and thinking that if Mr. Smith had watched him working, then others were too, after every two or three passes with the mower, he pulled out the dishtowel from his pocket and wiped his forehead, sweat or none.

Before Dewey was done with Mr. Smith and the Argyles' front lawns, Mr. Campbell, the neighbor sharing a driveway with Mr. Smith, asked him if he could also mow his lawn, and Ruth and his mother were impressed when, without being able to hear what was said from across the street, they saw Mr. Campbell hand Dewey a bill and return to his home. They were sure Dewey said, "Fifty cents, *please*," and then, as he thanked him, he even offered out his left hand to shake.

Mrs. Dixon was happy for her son, but not as happy as Dewey when Mr. Campbell also told him to keep the change. The boy couldn't help but believe Mrs. Rosen was a genius.

It was close to five when Dewey, exhausted and sweaty, finished mowing the lawns, and the two women, after making plans to meet the next morning at Ruth's home, decided to call it a day.

Later, Dewey would notice a horizontal bruise along his chest, and he would be so proud of it, he would consider playing outside topless.

**

Dewey didn't want to be there, but he had no choice. He had only been there for fifteen minutes but it seemed like an hour since he had first sat on Carl Smith's recently tidied-up bedroom floor playing with one of the six-year-old child's rubber toy cars, which the child repeatedly crashed his car into. All Dewey wanted to do was drive the car around, maybe have a car chase, maybe use Carl's blocks to make a ramp or a bridge, or maybe just go home.

"Hi, Robby!" little Carl shouted.

Holding a paper plate of pastries while looking down on the two boys, Robby stood at the doorway in pressed pants and a polo shirt. "Hi, kiddies. Ignore me. Keep playing with your toys and pretend I'm not here."

Embarrassed, Dewey looked up and said, "Hi," before noticing both of Robby's eyes had wide, dark marks surrounding them. "What happened to your eyes? Hey, can I have one?"

"None of your business! And did you just ask me for a black eye?"

"No, one of the things on your plate."

"They're on the table. Get your own!"

"Ok," Dewey said, glad to have a reason to leave.

Getting to his feet, he squeezed between the doorframe and Robby, who laughed and said, "You know you're only a couple inches taller than Carl there, right?" And then fuming from the older boy's words, he walked down the hallway to the dining room to stand at the chairless dinner table with its assortment of desserts and sandwiches. Taking a paper plate, he peered into the living room where Mr. Smith, from somewhere behind the narrow dividing wall on the left, was addressing a group of people, most of whom Dewey recognized.

With Mr. Smith's daughter on her lap, his mother sat on the sofa under the front window. Next to his mother sat Mrs. Rosen, who smiled and waved to Dewey, who waved back. Sitting on the other side of Mrs. Rosen was Mrs. White. A thin old woman who lived at the top of the street and liked to yell out to anyone walking near the sidewalk's edge bordering her lawn, "Get off my grass, you!" Sitting alone and taking up two-thirds of the loveseat against the wall on the right was the very large Mrs. O'Brien in her yellow floral muumuu and three-inch yellow stilettos. Other women sat on kitchen chairs while others, mostly men, stood, and with a blue notebook in everyone's hand, it seemed to the boy that they were in some sort of class with Mr. Smith as the teacher.

Turning his attention back to the table of food, he chose a small pastry that looked like a half-sized Pillsbury crescent roll. Biting into it, it didn't taste as he expected. It was sweeter, but he liked it, and when Mrs. Rosen gestured to let him know she had made it, she lost her smile when he gave her a thumbs-up and recovered it when she realized it was a good thing. Then giving Mr. Smith her attention again, Dewey decided to eat at the table while listening to the man.

"We do nothing but observe. Under no circumstances, and I can't stress this enough, under no circumstances are we to confront the person... or persons, and we're not to call the police until we're certain of suspicious behavior or see an actual crime being committed. Mrs. O'Brien, please, please, no calling the police if someone parks in front of your house."

"What if my Robby gets assaulted again? I'll certainly call the police! Did you see his two black eyes?"

"Right, you should, but as a group, we're looking for suspicious people hanging around outside, standing or in a car for an extended period of time, let's say twenty minutes. We're primarily looking for car thieves and house thieves. I'm told by the police that those are the two most common crimes."

Mrs. White exclaimed, "What! People are stealing houses now?"

"No, Mrs. White, they break into houses and steal your things."

"Oh... now that makes more sense."

Seeing her son's pastry-filled cheeks stretched outward, Mrs. Dixon gave him a stern look and signaled that he had eaten enough.

Then all were distracted when Robby went to the door and quickly put on his shoes.

"So, in the front of your notebook, you'll find the shift schedules and phone numbers of the other members. In case you need to change—"

"Come on mom! I'm bored! Let's go!" Robby yelled before opening the door and leaving.

"Jesus Christ! Robby, I'm going to give you a third black eye!" Mrs. O'Brien yelled as she struggled to get out of the loveseat, balanced herself on her shoes, and much like a circus bear walking on two legs, made her way to the door to leave without a goodbye.

While most were distracted by the woman leaving, Dewey swallowed the pastries he had stuffed in his mouth and snuck two more, and when Mrs. Rosen, smiling as usual, gestured that he was being naughty, he played stupid by waving to her and giving her another thumbs-up.

**

Having found someone they could talk to, the two women spent most of their weekdays together, sometimes talking over coffee at one or the other's home, and sometimes taking a bus ride to a park where they would sit for hours talking while eating lunch. Several times they took the bus to the Spryfield Mall where they ate lunch and shopped for groceries, and they once took it downtown to walk along the harbor front while picking at pastries.

Dewey enjoyed the outings for the food, but that was about it. He would listen to the women's conversations, but they usually bored him unless they were about him.

Occasionally, Ruth would mention her husband and once got the boy's interest when she described the old man as a converted introvert and then went on for some time explaining the mindset of the extreme introverts, who were often misunderstood and mislabeled.

Avriel was content that his wife had found a good friend whom she could spend time with. He liked Mrs. Dixon. Though he didn't know her well, he liked her because his wife did, and it fascinated him how one-half of the Dixons could be a closed-minded bigot while the other half was open-minded and non-judgmental, and one morning over breakfast, he admitted his fascination by saying, "Mrs. Dixon is impressively tolerant with our being Jewish."

"Av, she's not tolerant at all," Ruth corrected him, causing his bushy eyebrows to rise. "She doesn't have a problem with us being Jewish to require any tolerance. And you could call her Lisa, not Mrs. Dixon. We are beyond formalities with her, dear."

**

On a Friday night, Avriel went to the garbage container, pressed down on its pedal to raise its lid, and was about to wipe the remaining food from his plate into it when he spotted an unopened envelope resting on top of the trash with the words *Friendly Reminder* printed on it. Hoping his wife wouldn't notice, he retrieved it, placed it in the front pocket of his dress pants, and later that night, slipped it into his almost empty briefcase.

That following Monday at the office, the first thing he did was open the envelope. Sitting down at his desk and putting on his reading glasses, he found his assumption was correct. The letter was regarding a charity's formal dinner for that coming Thursday night, and that evening after supper, he presented Ruth with three tickets to it.

"Avriel Rosen! Oh my! We're going to the dinner?" a shocked Ruth asked.

"Yes... well, they are for you, Lisa, and Dewey."

Then, only surprised, she said, "Oh, Av, that's so thoughtful of you! This is so wonderful! Thank you!"

"Thank the charity. Seeing how Lisa is free on Thursday nights, it was perfect timing on their part, and there may be some interesting conversations there, too," he half-joked before she hugged him, kissed him, and thanked him again for the tickets.

The next morning, as Ruth had coffee in her friend's living room while they shared their Neighborhood Watch duties by looking out the front window onto the street, she invited Mrs. Dixon to the dinner and was pleased when her neighbor excitedly accepted the invitation. And when Dewey came into the living room, curious about the excitement, Ruth told him about it too.

"What's a formal dinner?"

"Dear, that's where you dress up."

"Seriously?"

"Yes. Do you like dressing up?"

"I love dressing up!"

"And he has the cutest little three-piece suit he wore for his Summer Break concert. But I'm going to have to go shopping for something to wear myself."

Ruth's eyes lit up. "I have to find something too! This could be even more fun! We can do it together! Why not tomorrow morning? It's supposed to be sunny and while we go shopping, I'll have Avriel watch Dewey. He's been talking about painting the back fence and I'm sure he'd appreciate Dewey's help. This'll be so much fun! Dewey, would you like to help Avriel paint tomorrow?"

"Sure, but I never painted before."

"That's ok. It's easy, and if you're not sure about what you're doing, just have him show you."

The women had a plan, and Dewey had two apprehensions. He liked the idea of painting a fence, but except for the very short time at the hospital where they both slept, he had never spent time alone with the old man, and he liked the idea of dressing up but not dressing up in a suit.

The next morning, Avriel woke in a sweat and assumed he was coming down with something until he remembered he wouldn't be going to work that morning and why, and he began sweating more. Then that morning while shaving, he did something he hadn't done in years: nicked himself several times.

At nine, Mrs. Dixon and her apprehensive son arrived at the Rosens', where Ruth had coffee prepared, and only minutes earlier, her husband had gone out to the backyard to get ready to paint. To Dewey's delight, which temporarily distracted him from his apprehension, Ruth placed five dollars in his pocket for services to be rendered and then surprised the little painter with a new pair of small blue coveralls, a small pair of leather work boots, a pair of gardening gloves and an oversized painter's cap, all which her husband had reluctantly purchased the previous afternoon, and once Dewey had changed and the women made their comments on how cute he looked, he cautiously went out to join Avriel, who was wearing almost the identical outfit and had received the same *cute* comment from his wife.

"Hi, Avriel."

Stopping his painting, Avriel turned around. "Hello, boy... Dewey. Well... well, it looks like you are all set to paint."

"I am," Dewey said proudly.

"Ok, I stirred the other can of paint there and perhaps we may work on the same section together. You paint the bottom bit on my left while I paint from here up, and together we work to the right. Are you comfortable with that?" asked Avriel, who would've preferred Dewey to start on the other end of the fence, but his wife, guessing his preference, let him know hers.

"Sure, ok," Dewey nodded.

With the child sitting to the left of the old man as instructed, he dipped his brush into his can of paint, and both quietly painted.

Fearing Dewey would eventually want to talk, Avriel sped up his painting to try and create a distance between him and the boy, but that only caused Dewey to paint faster too, quickly sliding his bottom to his right as he went, and after several times trying, Avriel gave up on losing him.

After a few minutes and finding it easy to paint with his left hand while doing as his mother had asked, keeping the sleeve of his coveralls over the cast and out of the way of the wet paint, Dewey broke the silence. "I never apologized for calling you Mr. Jew, you know."

Avriel stopped painting and looked down at the little boy. "Apologize? There is no need."

"You apologized to Peter... Peter the Russian for calling him Christian, but I never apologized to you. Maybe I forgot to because the story was funny, but I should've. So I'm sorry."

"Oh... then I should apologize to you as well."

"To me? What for?"

"For calling you a goy boy."

"You did? Seriously? What's a goy boy?"

"I did... not out loud... in my head... before I realized you had confused my religion with my last name."

"But what's a goy boy?"

"Uh... right... well... goy means non-Jew, like a Christian. Sort of like how infidel can mean... can mean non-Christian... if a Christian uses it. So, I apologize as well."

Dewey smiled. "Apology accepted."

"Apology accepted, also," Avriel said, hoping they would then go back to silence.

"So you're Avriel the infidel and I'm Dewey the goy boy," Dewey laughed, causing the old man to crack a smile since, even for him, it was impossible not to break a smile when a child laughed.

"Right, but perhaps we should keep that to ourselves; otherwise, we may waste much time explaining it to others," Avriel said, returning to painting and hoping neither Mrs. Dixon nor his wife would learn what he had taught the boy that day.

"Sure," said Dewey, who also returned to painting.

They painted in silence for another ten minutes before Dewey broke it again. "You like painting fences?"

"No. Do you?"

"Yup... yes... so far. It's my first time."

Avriel looked down at Dewey and, testing the waters, said, "Really? With the way you are going, I thought you were a professional."

Dewey smiled as he continued to paint. "My daddy always says anything worth doing is worth doing right the first time."

"Your daddy is an intelligent man."

"Yup, he is."

A few minutes later, Dewey asked, "You like baseball?"

"I do, but I do not follow it. I like football also, or soccer as it is called here, but I do not follow that either, anymore." Then he offered, "I like boxing and used to do some in university."

"That's neat. I don't follow baseball either, but sometimes I play catch with my daddy. Hey, he told me he'll take you with us to play too when my cast comes off."

"Oh?" a confused Avriel asked. "That... that sounds like... like fun. Do you and he usually play catch with your friends?"

"No. I don't have any, not around here."

"Is that so?" Avriel asked, feeling bad for the boy.

"Yup," Dewy nodded. "They live mostly on the other side of Herring Cove Road, and my size doesn't help me make friends here, not with the older guys."

"Your size?"

"Yup. How old do you think I am?"

"Seven," Avriel said, expecting to be correct.

"Nope, nine. My daddy says I'm a runt, too short and thin for my age."

"Nine?" Avriel asked, finding it hard to accept.

"Ten in a few months," Dewey said. "My daddy says I should be almost a foot taller, but my mommy says I should be half a foot taller. What do you think?"

"Perhaps... perhaps somewhere in between, perhaps eight inches taller? I can't be certain about such things, but I expect you will fill out as you age, and I would also expect you to have a growth spurt coming," Avriel said. "And even if you remain shorter than average, there are many short men who have accomplished great things."

"Yeah?"

"Yes," Avriel nodded.

"Who?"

"Uh... there is... there is Winston Churchill."

"Never heard of him."

"There is Napoleon."

"Never heard of him, either."

"Uh... there is also Gandhi."

"Don't know him."

"And there is...," Avriel said as he searched for someone who the boy would have heard of. Then remembering something he had read recently in the entertainment section of the newspaper, he said, "There is Bruce Lee."

"Bruce Lee? He was short?" Dewey asked as he stopped painting to look up at Avriel.

"Yes, he was only, uh... four feet tall, I believe," Avriel lied.

"Really? I never saw his movies, not allowed to, but I think I would've heard if he was only four-feet tall. That's really, really small for a grownup."

"Four feet?" Avriel asked, after realizing he had overshot.

"Uh... I meant to say five. Yes, he was five feet tall."

"That makes more sense," Dewey nodded before continuing his painting. "He's a Kung Fu fighter, and maybe he learned it because he was small."

"Maybe," Avriel nodded.

"Were you small? Is that why you learned to box?"

"No, and I should admit I never actually learned to box, not officially. I only picked up what I had seen."

"Were you any good?"

"Any good at what?"

"At boxing."

"I was, but only because I was taller than most, taller and thinner... and I suppose I still am. They even had a name for me. I was Eleven-Foot-Pole Rosen."

"Huh, Eleven-Foot-Pole?"

"Yes. Have you heard the expression, *I would not touch that with a ten-foot pole?*" Avriel asked while looking down at Dewey, who looked up and shook his head. "Well, usually it means a person does not want to address something, and because I had... have long arms, an opponent once protested he could not touch me even if he had a ten-foot pole. Meaning, he could not reach me if he wanted to, even using a ten-foot pole. So after that, I was Eleven-Foot-Pole Rosen."

"Oh," Dewey said, still not understanding the name. "Does Mrs. Rosen like boxing too?"

"No, she feels it is barbaric."

"Barbaric? Like *Conan the Barbarian* barbaric?"

"I am not sure. Who is that?"

"He's in a comic book. Mommy says he's primitive."

"Oh, then I would say Ruthy... Mrs. Rosen would not like Conan either."

The time went by fast for both as they painted and talked, or more specifically, Dewey talked. He talked about his school, his books, and his classmates and then talked about his future career as a soldier.

Learning that Dewey wanted to be a soldier reminded Avriel of how the times had changed. As a youth, he and his friends wanted to be firefighters, police officers, and movie stars, and one friend, Tommy, wanted to be a milkman, but that was only so he could get free chocolate milk. Nobody even considered the army as an option.

As Dewey explained why he wanted to be a soldier and how he planned to become the world's most famous soldier, like G.I. Joe, the old man decided he needed either a change of topic or some quiet time and chose a change of topic that should give him some quiet time.

"Dewey, here is a riddle. If you can answer it in five guesses, I will give you five dollars."

Dewey's eyes lit up. "Five dollars! Seriously?"

"Yes, seriously, but you have to answer it in five guesses or fewer, so do give it much thought before answering. Are you ready?"

"Yes!"

"Then listen carefully...

B*rother nor sister have I none,*
But that man's father is my father's son.

Now, who is that man in relation to me? Ok, now to make sure you have it correct, repeat it back to me."

After Dewey repeated the riddle three times before getting it correct and Avriel reminded him again of the five-guess limit, they were silent for several minutes as they painted and the boy thought.

"Your mother!" Dewey suddenly exclaimed.

"What? No!"

Avriel made him repeat the riddle so he could see his error, and after a few more minutes, he guessed, "Your brother!"

"No. Remember, brother *nor* sister have I *none*. That is two guesses."

"Your step-brother!"

"No. Now that is three. You only have two guesses remaining."

"Your cousin!"

"No. Now you are not even thinking about it. Only one guess remaining, just one. Do you want to lose the chance for five dollars because you guessed from the top of your head rather than from inside it? Think about your next answer. Give it some thought. It is difficult, but you can solve it. You just have to give it some thought."

Releasing a frustrated huff, Dewey went back to painting and thinking about the answer. He repeated the riddle in his head several times, then repeated the first line several times, then the second line several times, and then, frustrated, asked in a defeatist tone, "Your son?"

"That is correct."

"Huh?"

"Ding, ding, the boy wins the prize!" Avriel joked while beginning to relax.

"Seriously?"

"Yes, that man would be my son, but tell me, how did you come up with that?"

Dewey answered shyly, "I guessed from the top of my head."

"Is that right? Well, since it is the correct answer in the allotted number of guesses, I suppose that is unimportant. Remind me to give you the money when we have lunch. Do you like baloney and mustard sandwiches?"

"Sure. I once tried baloney and mayonnaise, but it was gross."

"Then that is what we shall have, baloney and mustard, my favorite."

For the next thirty minutes, Dewey quietly painted as he added up his current accumulation of money and tried to decide if he should keep saving or spend it. If he were to spend it, what would he spend it on? If he continued to save, what would he save for and how much would he need to save? At one point, when wondering whether he had enough for another G.I. Joe or another Lego set, he startled the old man by whispering to himself, and Avriel decided then that the next time he wanted some quiet time, he would avoid the game and just give the child five dollars.

After three hours of painting, two lemonade breaks, and several bathroom breaks, they had painted just over half of the fence before it was time to eat.

In the house, Avriel gave an excited Dewey the five dollars and made the baloney and mustard sandwiches, and while eating, and not letting the food in his mouth impede his words, Dewey asked for financial help and was surprised to hear Avriel didn't know how much a G.I. Joe cost, or even what it was. Then Dewey spent the next ten minutes bringing Avriel up to date on the action figures and all the stuff available for them: the helicopter, the jeep, the tank, the large headquarters, and even a space capsule that included a spacesuit.

Avriel found himself amazed at the amount of equipment available for a doll that was twelve inches high, and he almost choked on his sandwich when the little boy suggested he buy one for himself so they could play with them together.

Finished eating, they continued their painting.

Then twenty minutes into it, Dewey asked, "When we're all done painting, can I see your war stuff?"

"Sorry? War stuff?"

"Yeah... yes. You were in the war. You were a doctor, right? So you must have war stuff, right?"

"Well... a medic... a medical officer. I helped to prepare soldiers... injured soldiers on the field for the doctors. But I have nothing from the war."

"Seriously? No uniform, gun, or even a helmet? You must've got a medal for those two scars on your leg," Dewey persisted.

"Well, I do recall getting a medal for those."

"Can I see it?"

"I do not have it. I got rid of it before the end of the war."

"Seriously?"

"Yes, seriously. I could not eat it... or use it to help me do my job. It had no use to me."

"You really got nothing from the war?"

"I have many scars."

"Right. I saw those," Dewey said with disappointment. "Ok, so what was it like?"

"Sorry?"

"What was it like fighting in the war?"

Then desperate to change the subject but not able to think of another that was fitting for a boy, Avriel mustered his mental strength and said, "Well... well, I expect that the things you have heard about the war do not come close to the actual thing. I mean to say the actual horrors."

"Horrors? How's that?"

"Well, in the heaviest fighting, I saw men vanish right in front of me... from the larger guns. I saw men, not so lucky men, die slowly, painfully slowly, crying out for their mothers as they bled. I saw men without limbs... and limbs without men."

"Seriously?"

"Yes. I learned something during the war. Well, I... I learned a few things, but one stands out at this moment. I had heard a person responds to fear by fight or flight, but I saw a third response, freeze. I saw men freeze where they stood from fear alone... perhaps because flight was not an option." Feeling like he was thinking aloud, he looked down to see Dewey looking up at him and continued. "Everyone came up with different ways to fight their fear. Some told themselves the other fellows would get it instead of them, and others resigned themselves to accepting the high likelihood of death and did their job as if it was like any other, hoping that if death came, it would be quick," Avriel said and paused when it struck him as strange that he was more comfortable than he would've expected to be talking about the war, and he wondered if it was because of the audience. Perhaps the boy, being a boy, was too innocent to judge, making him less self-conscious, or maybe thirty-plus years was a long enough time to pass. Then deciding not to overthink the reason and just to accept it, he said, "I expect you do not know that a soldier had a much greater chance of dying than surviving the war. Even civilians had poor chances of survival, some as low as perhaps twenty percent. And if certain groups lived in Germany or a country occupied by it, their odds of surviving were even less... much less. Did you know over twenty million Russians died in the war?"

"No."

"Well, they did, and that is almost the population of Canada," Avriel said, before pausing to collect his thoughts. "The whole concept of war, to me, is crazy, and it makes people crazy. I knew a fellow who truly believed the shells would not strike the same spot twice, making him believe the safest route forward would be from crater to crater. I would watch him run forward to the nearest hole, crouch down and wait, and then run ahead to the next one. I even started to believe he was right."

Then Avriel stopped painting and went silent.

"What happened to him?"

"Sorry?" Avriel asked, startled back to the present.

"What happened to the crater guy?"

"I... I saw him vanish. It turned out he was wrong."

"Was he your friend?"

"Yes, he was. He... he was my brother."

Catching himself as he was going silent again, Avriel excused himself to go into the house, and a minute later, Dewey heard a radio playing a rock song. And a minute after that and with the kitchen's garbage can keeping the back door open so they could hear the music better, Avriel returned with two glasses of lemonade.

Continuing with their painting, Avriel was going to ask Dewey if he liked the music, but when he looked down and saw him swaying and painting to its rhythm, he had his answer.

Before the women returned, Avriel and Dewey had finished painting the fence and had cleaned each other up. Avriel used a clean cloth dipped in turpentine to remove the bit of paint from Dewey's face and Dewey did the same for Avriel, making him sit on the floor for better reach.

Avriel was impressed with Dewey's ability to avoid getting paint on his coveralls. Most of the paint ended up on the top of his painter's cap, and that was mostly Avriel's fault. Dewey kept up with him so well that at times, he was painting directly beneath the old man who occasionally and accidentally dripped paint down on him.

When they had changed back into their regular clothes, Avriel offered Dewey another five-dollar bill for the completed work, but the boy refused to take it, telling him his wife had already paid him, and the old man only convinced him to take it by telling him that was regular painter's pay before they found out he was a professional and deserved professional painter's pay. Then, with the bill tightly in his fist, Dewey hugged Avriel's waist, causing him to tense up and pat the little boy on his shoulder, more to break the embrace than out of affection.

Then Dewey's day got even better. Before leaving for home with his mother, Ruth told him he could keep his work clothes and boots, saying, "They may come in handy at home too."

The next afternoon, after spending the morning watching the

street together, the two women brought Dewey with them while they got their hair and nails done, and afterward, they took him to have a haircut, which he hated since it required sitting still while pieces of hair fell around his face and neck, torturing him with tickles.

At the Dixon home, the women put on their makeup and changed into the new dresses that Dewey thought made them look like Cinderella and her fairy godmother, and he embarrassed his mother and took Mrs. Rosen's breath away when he walked to his bedroom to change, saying, "If you want to look perfect, Mrs. Rosen, you'll need a magic wand."

Several minutes later, Dewey shouted from behind his bedroom door, "Are you ready?"

"We're ready," his mother said as she and Ruth made their way down the hall to his room.

Then, with his bedroom door opening, he jumped out with his arms out to his sides, yelling, "TAH-DAH!"

Both women gasped as he stood proudly in front of them in his coveralls, work boots, and last Halloween's thin plastic ape mask, and with wide eyes, each tried to make sense of what they were seeing.

Breaking the silence, Mrs. Dixon exclaimed, "Dwight Dixon!"

Ruth said, "Oh, my,"

And Dewey asked, "What?"

His mother took a deep breath. "Dwight Dixon, why are you dressed up as a monkey in coveralls?"

"I'm not a monkey! I'm an ape, an ape from *The Planet of the Apes*! And Mrs. Rosen said I could dress up. Isn't that right, Mrs. Rosen? Remember, you said we had to dress up for the dinner."

Ruth couldn't help but break into a laugh, not her usual laugh but a full stomach laugh, and Mrs. Dixon couldn't help but join in, not so much because of Dewey's costume, but because of the old woman's laugh. And Dewey could only stand there confused and growing upset at their laughing — he was a scary ape, not a funny ape!

It took Ruth several seconds to get some control over her breathing, and when she did, she approached him and lifted his mask to reveal the face of the teary-eyed boy. Bending down, she hugged him and said, "Dear... when I said to dress up... I meant wear... wear nice clothes... not a costume." Releasing him, she felt pity when she saw a tear run down his cheek. "Why not show us how... how exceptionally handsome you look in... in your nice suit?"

"Ok," he said sadly, using his denim sleeve to wipe the next tear. "Ok."

As he turned to go back to his room, his mother asked, "Dewey, what did you do to your hands? They're brown!"

Turning back around, Dewey said proudly, "I colored them with my marker."

"Oh my," Ruth whispered.

"Dwight Paul Dixon, that will not come off easy! It'll take several hard washings!"

"Ok," he said, not understanding why she thought it was a problem.

Blushing, Mrs. Dixon took her older friend's hand and said, "I think we have to bother Avriel to watch Dewey again."

"It won't be a bother, dear."

And it wasn't a bother for Dewey either. If he couldn't go in his costume, he didn't want to go at all.

Half an hour later, the women were sitting in the back of the Cadillac, which was the first time it was ever used, and Dewey was sitting in front next to Avriel, whose discomfort diminished slightly when he saw the boy in his costume.

Dewey still wanted to wear his costume, dinner or not, and his mother only consented because she felt it would be easier for

Avriel to babysit a happy boy rather than a grumpy one, and despite the heat that had built up under the mask, Dewey kept it on during the drive to and the silent drive back from the Lord Nelson Hotel.

**

When Ruth and Mrs. Dixon entered the conservatively decorated ballroom, they found its fifty circular tables covered in white tablecloths with each of their six spots reserved with name cards, and after they found their table at the back of the room with the other late ticket purchasers, they claimed their designated seats and noticed on the other side of the room a display of paintings, photographs, and sculptures that were to be auctioned off later that night.

With Ruth pocketing her name card, the two women left their purses on their chairs to go view the art, and after several minutes of perusing it, Ruth asked Mrs. Dixon, "Is this parrot common here? It seems to be the focus of much of the art, and I think it's even on the provincial flag."

"Those are Puffins. They look like chubby parrots, but they don't make much noise. They live along the cliffs of the coastline."

"Well, that's interesting. Now this here picture, this is pretty, too," Ruth said as she looked at a painting of waves crashing against a shore of large, smooth-edged brownish-gray boulders, and to the right of the waves were small colorful shacks and several fishing boats moored to a wharf.

"That's Peggy's Cove. It's a big touristy place."

"You know, we've been here thirty years, and still we've seen very little. I'd love to see it. Is it far?"

"Maybe a thirty or forty-minute drive. We should go there sometime."

"Tomorrow? Would you be free tomorrow?"

"Tomorrow? Uh... we could. I have to get groceries, but other than that, I'm free."

"Great! Let's do it! And we can get groceries on the way back. I'll have Avriel take the day off tomorrow too, so he can drive us there."

"Ok, let's do it," Mrs. Dixon smiled.

After the women returned to their seats, the initial excitement of the event soon wore off as they listened to several slow presentations put on during the meal.

Bored, Ruth looked around the room and noticed there were mainly two types of people at the dinner: those looking to people-watch and those looking to be watched. Mrs. Dixon seemed content with the place, but to Ruth, it seemed pretentious. Without a large, colorful hat, as most women were wearing, she felt like an underdressed people-watcher — she considered herself a discreet people-listener — and with all the whispering going on at her table, it was difficult to eavesdrop, though even if she could, so as not to be rude to her friend, she wouldn't.

With their desserts finished and the presentations ended, Ruth whispered to her friend to follow along with her, and to her friend's initial apprehension and then delight, Ruth introduced herself to those at their table as Lady Ingrid, the second cousin to Queen Elizabeth the Second of England. Immediately, the table of guests started paying special attention to the two women and called over friends from other tables to introduce them to their royal friend, and when the few skeptics asked why they had never heard of her, Ruth responded that the royal family had cut off all contact with her several years before her second cousin became queen. Much like Edward the Eighth's abdication to marry a commoner who was a two-time divorcee, her marriage had broken two royal taboos: she married beneath her class and married outside her religion, though it was much less dramatic and much quieter, especially considering little was ever mentioned about royal second cousins. But if she had to do it all over again, she told them, she certainly would.

As word spread, the two were soon introduced to the charity's most prominent guests. They met the Mayor of Halifax, Edmund Morris, and had a brief conversation with the Lieutenant Governor, Clarence Gosse, whom they expected could destroy their charade but went along with it.

The only close call came when a merchant from Spring Garden Road recognized Ruth and tried to get her attention by calling out to her. Mrs. Dixon, thinking quickly, intercepted the older man and told him Ruth's real name was Lady Ingrid and Ruth was her alias, as she rarely disclosed she was the alienated second cousin to the Queen of England. Taking the man aside, Mrs. Dixon expanded on the scandal of Lady Ingrid eloping with a working-class Jew, and when she was done, she asked him to promise on his honor to keep the information to himself, and he did... for about a minute. When he returned to his table, he immediately told his wife, who soon told her friends, who told their friends, who told their friends, and before the night ended, Ruth's small purse was full of cards, and she had several invitations to private dinners.

**

Avriel and Dewey, who continued to wear his mask, sat in the Dixons' living room watching television, which Dewey suggested when Avriel asked him what they should do. They ate a chicken casserole that Mrs. Dixon had quickly prepared, and they ate on the sofa, which Avriel was uncomfortable doing until Dewey told him they always ate on it. The two watched Gilligan's Island, which interested Dewey, but not so much Avriel, who had a hard time believing Gilligan could be so stupid, and then they watched the CBC news, which interested Avriel but not at all Dewey, who had a hard time believing anyone could watch something so boring, and in the middle of it, he suggested they play Snakes and Ladders instead.

After explaining the rules to Avriel, the two sat at the kitchen table and quietly played the game, and feeling like he was playing against a robot, Dewey wished that Mrs. Rosen was playing too; she could've forced some life into the old man.

After losing the first game, Dewey decided the mask was the cause and as he removed it, Avriel showed some life by being melodramatically frightened and begging Dewey to put it back on. Laughing, Dewey put it on Avriel, and while the old man sweated behind the small mask that blinded him in one eye, Dewey won the next game. Then, during the next two games, Avriel, who became much more comfortable as he hid behind the mask, exchanged wisecracks with the boy, cracked several smiles and once even let loose a full stomach laugh.

It was dark when Avriel drove up to the hotel, where in the white light of its entrance, he was curious to see Ruth and Mrs. Dixon talking to a group of fellow guests who, when informed of Lady Ingrid's drive arriving, focused their attention on the Jewish man who had caused her fall from the royal family's graces. Seeing several strangers walking toward the car, Avriel quickly rolled up his window, locked his door, and tried not to disturb his sleeping little friend as he removed his mask.

Waking up, Dewey protested its removal, and then seeing his friend wearing it again, he laughed but stopped when he noticed a small group of people gathered on the other side of Avriel's door tapping on its window much like people do to get the attention of fish in an aquarium.

Behind the mask, Avriel asked Dewey to pretend they weren't there and Dewey obliged by trying to whistle while looking everywhere but at them. Then giving up on whistling, the boy hummed.

After two women waved farewell to their fans, they entered the back of the car, and as they settled into their seats, Ruth leaned over Avriel's backrest and was about to kiss his cheek when she noticed the mask and laughed.

Mrs. Dixon asked, "How was your evening, gentlemen?"

"It was great! I beat Avriel in snakes and ladders!" Dewey bragged. "So who were you talking to, Mommy?"

"Our new friends."

"That's strange because I didn't see anybody," Dewey laughed, confusing his mother and causing Avriel to smile behind the mask.

With his voice slightly muffled, Avriel said, "You two made a lot of friends."

"Lady Ingrid did," Mrs. Dixon said and laughed when she realized Avriel was wearing the ape mask.

"Sorry?"

"I'll tell you later, my working-class Jew," Ruth said, confusing her husband further.

**

The next day at Peggy's Cove, the four slowly strolled through the cool salty breeze as they made their way along the surface of flat rock about twenty feet from where the mild waves lightly slapped against the enormous boulders protruding from the ocean, and as the two women talked, Avriel and Dewey followed behind, neither very impressed with the sights.

Having enough of the boredom, Dewey asked Avriel if he wanted to play war, and Avriel agreed but only if they could be on the same side, which the boy thought was a strange condition until the old man pointed out the bunch of enemy soldiers trying to make their way onto the shore, and after they left to scout out the best position for their defense, the two women continued on their slow walk.

With Dewey directing Avriel to the left or right as required, the two sat where the flat boulders met the dirt and made gunfire sounds with their mouths as they fired their ground-mounted machine guns at the large force of enemy troops making their way onto the shore.

Shortly into their land defense, Avriel took his hands off his gun and mimed the pulling of a grenade's pin with his teeth, and then, after throwing it, made an explosion sound. Looking at Dewey each time he did it, the old man threw grenade after grenade until the boy was forced to stop firing and ask, "How many grenades you got?"

"Not one. They are throwing them at us with the pins still in them."

"Oh, we're fighting Newfoundlanders then."

What do you do when a Newfoundlander throws a grenade at you? Pull the pin and throw it back.

Beaten to the punch, except he was going to say they were fighting the Irish, Avriel laughed a low belly laugh and retook charge of his machine gun, shaking his arms and making shooting sounds as Dewey was doing.

**

A week later, on a Saturday morning and in the lobby of the Lord Nelson Hotel, the Rosens met Mr. Frank and his entourage of a tall, overweight lawyer and a short, fit operations manager, all three reeking of arrogance and condescension. When the group had finished their usual handshakes and small talk regarding their trip to Halifax the night before and the dramatic difference in weather between it and Toronto, to which Avriel simply nodded his head and murmured randomly, "Right," "Oh, you do not say?" and "Ok," Ruth took the reins of the conversation and steered it to the business at hand. Then, on the short ride to the Spring Garden Road location and noticeably uncomfortable talking business with Ruth, Mr. Frank tried to start a conversation with the old man but soon gave up and reluctantly accepted the old woman as the point man in the negotiations.

Throughout the day as they toured each drugstore, Ruth handed the lawyer a folder detailing the location's sales and profit history, deeds or lease agreements, and any other details relevant to the physical structure, and they ended the day at Morgan's Restaurant where Ruth gave a copy of her Policy and Procedure Guide to the operations manager before she and Mr. Frank discussed the total sales and profits for the last five years. When they finally discussed the selling price and the terms of the sale, the Rosens noticed Mr. Frank's not-so-subtle rolling of his eyes and the slight smirks of his entourage.

To the relief of Avriel, the dinner finally ended with the expectation that all would take that evening to reflect on what each had said and then meet the next day at Mr. Frank's hotel suite to continue negotiations.

"We'll have to meet in the afternoon, maybe twelve-thirty," Ruth told Mr. Frank. "I have an important phone call scheduled for tomorrow morning with Eric Bryson. Oh... maybe I shouldn't have said that."

Mr. Frank's eyebrows raised, and his entourage looked at each other. They all knew of Eric Bryson. He was the President of a much larger chain of pharmacies in the United States called Wilkins Drugs. If Wilkins Drugs moved into the Canadian market, Mr. Frank could count on tougher times ahead for all of his Canada-wide locations.

"And what would the call be regarding?" an agitated Mr. Frank asked.

"Oh, I'm afraid I'm not at liberty to say. Shall we say tomorrow at twelve-thirty then?"

"Fine. Twelve-thirty, it is. Until tomorrow then. We won't trouble you for a drive back to the hotel. The boys and I are going from here to explore the city's nightlife."

The next morning, as the Rosens shared the sofa while each read a book, Ruth asked Avriel to call Mr. Frank to move their meeting up to two-thirty with the excuse that her phone call with

Mr. Bryson was running longer than expected, and after doing as he was asked, when Mr. Frank pushed him for the reason for his wife's longer-than-expected discussion with Mr. Bryson, Avriel in his regular monotone voice told him he didn't know, and Mr. Frank believed him.

When the group met later that day, Mr. Frank had an offer drawn up, agreeing to all of Ruth's terms, including the purchase price she had asked for.

It was only three days later and with assurances from their lawyer when the Rosens signed the contract and couriered it back to Mr. Frank.

The speed of the sale astonished Avriel, and he continued to be amazed by how well his wife could read people.

CHAPTER 8
Something about the Dixons

Avriel, today is the beginning of our new life, and together, we shall start living it to the fullest.

Avriel folded the small piece of paper, placed it back in the paper bag with the wrapped roast beef sandwich, and returned his reading glasses to the glove compartment. Taking a deep breath, he placed the lunch bag on top of the uncovered cardboard box beside him that contained seven elastic band-wrapped bundles of envelopes.

Before the signing of the sales contract, the Rosens had decided to award their employees with a purchase bonus, giving each employee a check for their dedication to the store. The part-time employees would receive a straight amount while the full-time employees would receive two weeks' pay for each full year worked, and one employee, who had been with the Rosens since before the opening of their second location, would receive a check equal to three times that employee's yearly salary. To make sure the letters properly communicated their appreciation, Ruth had them printed up by a wedding invitation printer, and both she and her husband signed each one. There were ninety-eight letters and by the time they had finished signing them, Ruth's signature remained elegant while Avriel's was almost illegible.

That morning, Avriel would play deliveryman, delivering the

bundles to each of their six other locations with a request that they not be handed out until the following Monday, and the last bundle he would save for his final exit from their Spring Garden Road location.

**

The August sun gently woke Dewey out of his deep sleep. He sat up, rubbed the sleep from his eyes, and thought he heard someone crying. Getting out of bed, he struggled to pull up his Spiderman pajamas. Then realizing his heel was on the end of one leg, he lifted it and pulled them up with ease. Groggily, he made his way down the hall to his parent's bedroom, where the door was open and his mother, in her pink nightgown, was sitting up on her bed with her back against the oak headboard, her eyes red and a piece of tissue peeking out of her fist.

"What's wrong, Mommy?" he asked, expecting her to tell him to wash his face and brush his teeth.

"Nothing, Honey. I'm just tired. Coming up?"

Dewey climbed up on the side of the bed that had been undisturbed the night before, sat next to her, and leaned back against the headboard. "Where's daddy?" he asked before both recognized the sound of his father's car.

"Oh, uh...," she said, trying desperately to make the situation sound normal, "He couldn't come home last night."

"Why?"

"He... he was sick... and stayed at a friend's."

"Did he have to go to the hospital?"

"No, it wasn't that serious," she said, fighting not to cry again.

Both heard the front door open, the dropping of heavy work boots, the closing of the door, and then the kicking off of shoes.

"Dewey, go to your room, please. Daddy and I have to talk."

Doing as he was told, he was walking down the hall when his father spotted him. "Hey there, little man, where ya goin'?"

"To my room. Are you feeling better?"

"Better? Uh... yeah, sure. I'll be there ta see ya in a couple minutes."

Finding it strange that his father wore dress pants and a dress shirt, Dewey entered his room and closed the door. He knew that when asked or told to go to his room, he was to shut the door, too.

Avoiding eye contact, Mr. Dixon entered their bedroom and had begun unbuttoning his dress shirt when his wife whispered angrily, "Where were you? You never even called!"

"Where was I?" he asked, still avoiding eye contact while doing as he always did in the early hours of Friday morning, emptying a plastic grocery bag of Thursday's work clothes into the hamper. "Ended up stayin' at Tom's," he said as he undid his belt and the single button of his dress pants. "I was too drunk ta drive and forgots ta call. Remember Tom? He lives next'a King's. Moved there, so he'd be closer to it."

Mrs. Dixon raised her voice. "No! I don't remember! How would I know that? I don't know any of your friends!"

Raising his voice to match his wife's, he said, "Damn it ta hell! Look, it's never happened before and it won't happen again! I don't have time ta talk about it. It... it won't happen again, ok? Just drop it! I'm sorry, ok? I have ta shower and change for work and my freakin' head explodes every time I freakin' breathe! Now, fer Christ's sakes, just stop thinkin' whats yer freakin' thinkin'!"

Her husband left the bedroom, and as the shower started, Mrs. Dixon began to cry again. She had noticed a red mark resembling a hickey on the lower left side of his neck.

Forcing herself to stop crying, she got out of bed to put her husband's dress clothes in the laundry hamper and when she bent down to pick them up, noticed the familiar smell of cigarette smoke along with another smell, one that was becoming familiar. As she dropped the clothes into the hamper, a sickening feeling entered her stomach, and when she pulled the dress shirt back out and held it to her nose to confirm the smells, the pressure behind her eyes grew even stronger. Dropping the shirt back into the hamper, she returned to the bed, where a wave of intense anger washed over her, trying to make her scream. Then vanishing as quickly as it had come, leaving her again in grief, she tried to dry her eyes, but as soon as she had, they were wet again.

With a towel around his waist, Mr. Dixon returned to the bedroom, and while he put on clean work clothes, his wife tried to confirm the mark on his neck but had a hard time focusing her wet eyes. Finished buttoning his denim shirt, he walked over to his wife's side of the bed, bent down, and kissed her unresponsive lips. "Damn it ta hell! Lighten up! I'll be back at supper and we can discuss this then, fer Christ sakes! Just stop thinkin' whats yer thinkin'!" he said before he stormed out of the bedroom, and after putting on his work boots, the front door slammed and a minute later, the car left the driveway.

Dewey heard everything his father had said and knew well enough that when his father swore, he was angry. He had never heard of Tom and didn't understand how his father knew what his mother was thinking, and he wanted to know what she was thinking, too.

After Dewey had finished his lunch of a grilled cheese sandwich and potato chips and *The Flintstones* cartoon had ended, his mother, who had spoken very little that morning, told him that while she did her errands that afternoon, he would stay with Mrs. Rosen, and a few minutes later, they made their way to her house.

"Hello, you two! How are my two favorite people?" she asked with her usual smile.

"Good," they both answered, neither one cheerful.

Handing Dewey's left faded-brown hand to Ruth, who gladly took it, Mrs. Dixon said, "Ruth, thank you so much for the help. I wouldn't normally bother you with this, but it's an emergency."

"Dear, it's no bother at all. I'm just glad I can be of help, and I'm truly looking forward to spending some time with my little friend. Take all the time you need and don't think for one moment I'm being inconvenienced. It's all my pleasure."

Thanking Ruth again, Mrs. Dixon kissed the top of Dewey's head and reminded him to behave himself, and as a taxi pulled up, she left the two standing on the porch.

Looking up at Ruth, Dewey asked, "What's the emergency? Why couldn't she take me with her?"

"I was hoping you would tell me," she said. "Ok, come let's go find something to do to get my... our minds off of it."

**

Although they spent their preteens living six miles apart at opposite ends of the white Protestant community called Beaver Point, they were so many more miles apart in their upbringing and personalities that one could easily apply the cultural expression *opposites attract*, and like the attraction of two magnets placed at opposite poles, perhaps it's inevitable that over time, like the magnets, the couples' attraction would weaken until it no longer existed.

Tucked into the edge of the forest along Nova Scotia's Eastern Shore, a two-hour drive from Halifax, the small but spread out rural community of Beaver Point had an almost constant population of just fewer than five hundred residents and three social hubs: a gray-stone St. James United Church; a large wooden building along the main single-lane highway called Harvey's General Store/Garage, which sold everything from groceries and gasoline to hunting and fishing equipment; and a wooden eight-room single-story structure called Salmon River School, which taught grades primary to twelve.

It was at the school when they had started grade primary that a shy and chubby five-year-old named Paul Raymond Dixon first met a short, thin, and talkative five-year-old named Lisa Elizabeth Purcell. They met but didn't interact with one another for several more years as they kept to their group of same-sex peers, taking little interest in anyone outside of it except maybe to bother them.

Growing up in Beaver Point could mean a solitary life for a child, and by the age of seven, Paul had become a loner, not by choice but by geography. Great stretches of forest isolate the homes from one another and unless a child was driven or willing to walk a long distance along the highway and then along several dirt roads, they rarely saw their friends outside of school. However, even when at home among his family, Paul was a lonely loner and believed he couldn't feel anymore so if he were among strangers. His family was so cold and unaffectionate that the young boy often fantasized that the hospital had mistakenly given him to the wrong parents, and someday his actual birth parents, who were rich in his fantasy, would arrive at the door with smiling faces and tear-filled eyes to claim him back, but it would never happen.

Paul's twin brothers Rob and Rod, rarely seen apart and often cynical and rebellious, were close with each other but not so much with their much younger brother, whom they included in their activities only when it was convenient or necessary, like when they performed electrofishing at a nearby lake.

When the twins had gotten a hold of a discarded hand-cranked telephone, they took their brother along to help with the collection of fish, and while one twin rowed the wooden boat in circles and the other cranked the lever on the magnetic generator of the phone, sending seventy volts at one amp down its improvised wires and into the water, Paul scooped up the stunned speckled trout with a metal dip net and quickly learned to scoop only when his brother had stopped cranking the machine; otherwise, his screams from the electrical shock sent his brothers roaring with laughter.

After an hour of stunning and collecting the fish, the three brothers each used a fishhook to put tiny holes in the mouths of the fish, so it appeared to their mother that they were caught with a fishing rod.

Paul's mother, a thin, light-haired teetotaler reaching just over five feet and who rarely spoke more than a few words at a time, was the matriarch of Paul's very conservative, strict, and emotionally handicapped family, and like most who considered it poaching, she didn't approve of electrofishing, and if she had discovered what they had been doing, their father would never have hesitated to wield his leather belt with its large metal buckle. The buckle deterred any potential public shame brought on the family by his children's actions. That shame could lead to labeling, and the labels didn't drop off quickly and could follow a person for the rest of their life, even spilling over to their immediate family and on to the next generation.

His father, a self-employed lobster fisherman, was the yin to his mother's yang. He was a large man whose thick coating of fat covered his once well-toned muscles, whose large beer belly seemed to defy gravity, who confused being loud with being outspoken, and who relished being the disciplinarian of the household, and for as far back as Paul could remember, the first words his father would utter when he arrived home from a day at sea were, "Which one today?" meaning which boys required his discipline.

From the age of eight, Paul's favorite pastime was fishing off the nearest wharf, where he would sit for hours at its edge, enjoying the pacifying tranquility of the harbor as he waited for the fish to bite. He even enjoyed the trip there, walking along the dirt shoulder of the highway for twenty minutes while daydreaming about the many fish he would surprise his mother with and maybe even receive a smile, but he only enjoyed the trip back if he had caught an impressive number.

Next to fishing, Paul enjoyed snaring rabbits. In the forest around his home, he would patiently make snares by tying thin metal wires into noose-like hoops and attaching them from low-hanging branches so the nooses hung six inches from the ground, and after anxiously waiting the night, Paul would return to the forest to check his snares, hoping to find several strangled rabbits that his mother would cook and furs that his father would sell to Harvey's and split the proceeds with him.

Paul had wanted to hunt with his father and brothers, but they refused to take him along until he was in his teens, expecting his youthful excitement to both annoy them and alert the animals to their presence. So one summer, with his money from his fur trade, he purchased a spring-piston pellet rifle. His game was the many squirrels in the woods surrounding his house, and he would often return home with more than a dozen and a sore shoulder from repeatedly breaking the barrel to pump the rifle and load the pellet.

Paul had heard of people eating squirrels and would've liked to experience it himself, but unlike rabbits, his mother refused to cook the squirrel meat, saying, "I might as well cook rats!" And just as with the rabbits, he thought he could sell the squirrel furs too, but when he brought his six-inch pile of tiny furs to his father to take to the general store, his father laughed, asked, "What're ya, nuts?" and slapped his small son on the back of the head. Not to be defeated, he reversed his disappointment when he found a cash market for the skins at the school. A few boys wanted them, but mostly the girls purchased the dried and stiff skins to use as bearskin rugs for their dollhouses. Every young girl seemed to have a handmade dollhouse.

Not having to split the revenues with his father, he made more money from the squirrel skins than he did from the rabbits, but the squirrel skin market was short-lived. Since there were a limited number of girls at school and few needed more than one bearskin rug, the demand quickly dried up and left him with several dozen that he couldn't even give away. He still hunted the rodents, but he left the small corpses where they fell.

Paul saw nothing wrong with hunting. Most men in the village and even some women did it, and he never considered animals as anything more than objects for his trade, until one day as he was returning home through the woods casually swinging two strangled rabbits by their hind legs, he spotted a third in a snare that had been empty just minutes earlier. He released the metal noose from around the lifeless animal's neck, picked up the warm body, and made his way to a short, wide tree stump behind his house, where he dropped the two colder rabbits to the ground and laid the freshly killed one on the stump. Holding one of its front legs, he swung his father's machete and was surprised by the usual amount of blood coming from the dead animal. Then a high-pitched shrill stunned him; a pain in his finger caused him to release his grip on the animal, and he froze as he watched the screeching rabbit hop into the woods on three legs. Looking down again at the blood-covered paw on the stump, he vomited violently until nothing more could come out of him, and once he recovered, he vowed never to hunt or trap another animal, and he wouldn't.

By the age of twelve, he was even more alone at home. His brothers, having each got their driver's license, quit school and after working with their father for a short period, pooled their money, purchased a used pickup truck, and moved out to British Columbia. Except for the move to the other end of the country, the twins' actions were normal and expected.

Beaver Point's rite of passage to male adulthood was a driver's license. The license gave the young adults an opportunity for independence. With their independence came the need for a car. With the car came the need for a job, and with the job came the need to quit school. Most of the male residents of Beaver Point never finished high school.

Gone, the twins never phoned but jointly wrote short monthly letters containing just enough information to let their parents know they were alive, and after the first few letters, which never once addressed or referenced him, Paul learned not to look forward to them.

In sharp contrast to Paul's parents, Lisa's parents smothered their only daughter with attention and affection. Her parents were slim, light-haired, and very good-looking, and the folks in the village would often comment that God maintained His Purcell Standard when He gave them Lisa. They were such an attractive family that their family photos could easily have been mistaken for the photos that came with the frames.

Besides being attractive, the Purcells were popular. Several times a week, almost as a routine, they would visit their friends, or their friends would visit them, and however it worked out, Lisa always played with their friends' children. She preferred playing with the girls, but where her parents' friends had none, she would tolerate playing with the boys.

Lisa did what most young girls did growing up in Beaver Point: played with her dolls, helped her mother around the house, and read. She read whatever books her father, a traveling bookkeeper, would bring home to her, but she especially enjoyed the Harlequin Romance novels. She also enjoyed knitting, but could never master it. Often one mitten, slipper, or arm of a sweater wouldn't exactly match its mate, but despite that, nothing deterred her from the hobby, even when her father couldn't help himself and teased her about not having to bother considering bookkeeping as a career, since she was legally blind to detail. But her father never teased her about her cooking. After reaching the age of eleven, Lisa proved to have a gift for it. She could follow a recipe and know instinctively how to enhance its flavor, and before she reached her teens, Lisa's offer to make the family's weekend dinners was accepted with enthusiasm.

By the age of thirteen, most of Paul's fat had seemingly transformed into muscle, and the girls at school had taken an interest in him. He enjoyed the attention, but by then had developed an interest in Lisa, causing him to become shy around the pretty girl.

The change in his behavior caught her attention, and one spring day during lunch at school, she surprised him by aggressively pulling him aside and placing a small wrapped package in his hand.

"What's this?"

"A birthday gift," she said with a huge smile. "Go ahead and open it."

Paul nervously unwrapped and opened the small box to discover a three-inch pocketknife. "What's this fer?" he asked. "I ain't huntin' no more."

"I know. It's for whittling, so maybe this will help with a new hobby."

Handing the empty box to Lisa, he pulled the blade out from its shiny metal handle. "This is nifty! I might start doin' that!"

"Ok, now kiss me," she demanded.

"What?"

"Kiss me! I gave you a gift, so now you have to kiss me!"

Shocked, Paul stared at her for a second, and then after looking around to make sure no one was paying attention to them, he closed his eyes, puckered his lips, and let Lisa place hers on his, making it their first kiss.

He soon relaxed around her, and after their second kiss, they were officially *going together*. The young couple spent their time together a few minutes before and after school, and during their lunch breaks, but so as not to distract them from their learning, Lisa made it a rule that they wouldn't interact in class.

Paul wasn't a particularly motivated student and after finishing grade ten and receiving his driver's license, he lost what little motivation he may have had and quit. With Paul no longer with her at school, Lisa, who had maintained consistently high grades, lost interest too, and to the quiet disappointment of her parents, she soon dropped out.

Both Lisa and Paul were eager to start living the family life. Lisa wanted three children, Paul wanted two — he had once suggested they meet in the middle — and both wanted to live in the city. But to make their plans happen, the couple needed to save money that they would first need to earn, so Paul began helping his father with the lobster fishing, and when the village's first grocery store opened, which was the talk of the village for several months, Lisa found work there as a cashier.

Paul enjoyed lobster fishing, but while he quietly hauled in the traps, emptied them of the live lobster, baited them again with pieces of fish, and dropped them back into the salty water, his father did little else besides repeatedly belittle him and complain about his current situation and bleak future.

After a few months of what should've been tranquil work, but wasn't, Paul bought a clunker of a car and quit working for his father. He had found a job in the local forestry industry, where he used a chainsaw to remove the branches from downed trees. The job paid much more than his father did and was far more harmonious.

From the first day he started his new job, Paul enjoyed it. He enjoyed working in the open air, liked the physical, fast-paced work, and enjoyed working with people close to his age. Though initially shy around his coworkers, he made friends much easier than he had expected, especially since his coworkers made it a group challenge to get him to loosen up by including him in their conversations, jokes, and pranks.

Paul was happy, and Lisa was happy for him, and just four

months into working with the logging company, three of Paul's older coworkers invited him to share a house, and since the tension at home had become thick due to him offending his father by refusing to work for him, Paul jumped at the opportunity and was flattered when his new roommates threw him a party that following Friday. He soon learned they threw a party every Friday and Saturday night, which included much drinking and drugs, and ended after the sun came up.

    Lisa joined Paul at the party. He enjoyed it, but she didn't. She felt out of place. She had nothing in common with the older girls who showed up drunk, stoned, or both, and she felt the men were vulgar, obnoxious, and opinionated, and at the second party she attended, she spent most of the time by herself, bored and nursing a beer while waiting for Paul to drive her home. After that, she never went to another party, but she was happy that Paul had found a group he fit in well with.

    Soon the couple agreed that the weekday evenings would be their time together, which pleased Paul since he enjoyed the weekend's parties with his roommates whom he looked up to. They were free spirits who were making the most out of life and had before then performed various other jobs around the province and country, making them seem worldly to him. He quickly got over the initial shock with his roommates' constant drinking, and on weeknights, when he arrived back from Lisa's, expected and usually found them sitting around the sparsely furnished living room, drunk and talking or arguing. Their drunken conversations usually involved exchanging stories about women, fights with bosses, and general hate for blacks, Native Indians, and Jews. Besides Native Indians, Paul had never met anyone of a different religion or race and actively listened to the opinions of his roommates with what he would call an open mind.

    With all the drinking opportunities, Paul's new taste for alcohol grew into weekend binges, and he drank so much that twice when he was elected to drive some of their party guests home, the Royal Canadian Mounted Police arrested him. The first time, while fighting to keep his eyes focused as he struggled to keep his car from staggering along the dark highway with only his high beams showing the way, Paul tried to outrun them, and after almost five minutes with the flashing lights in his rear-view mirror and frustrated by the passengers' protests, he pulled over to perform the expected sobriety tests. First, he was told to recite the alphabet backward, but he refused, saying, "I can't even say 'em forward when I'm sober!" The second test required him to close his eyes, extend his arms out to his sides and by only bending the left elbow, touch his nose with the tip of his left hand's index finger, and he did it easily, but it was at the last test when he was to walk a straight line one foot in front of the other, that he decided it would be easier to throw a punch at the officer. The second time the flashing lights were in his rear-view mirror, he pulled over immediately and went passively with the officer. Both times, he was locked in a single-bed cell to sober up, and in the morning, with the sheets, blanket, and pillow thrown around, they released him with a fine. Neither time was Paul charged with drinking and driving.

Losing a driver's license in Beaver Point would have dire results on the individual's livelihood, and the RCMP officers were well aware of that, and, to keep the level of animosity toward them low, they were careful about laying charges. They didn't need the surprise of a rifle's bullet *accidentally* exiting the woods as they drove along the quiet highway or rural roads.

When Paul was sober, he was ashamed of his arrests, but when drunk, he was proud of them. He never told Lisa about them, but after the first year of his living with his coworkers, the arrests wouldn't have surprised her. His drinking and his new habit of smoking had become almost constant. He swore much more often, was more aggressive and self-centered, and had adopted his roommates' bigotry and racism.

With the extreme change in her boyfriend's previously shy and gentle character, Lisa decided to break up with him, but a few days before she would have the chance and the courage to do it, she discovered she was pregnant.

Lisa wasn't happy about the pregnancy. It was too soon, and she didn't want a child with the *new* Paul if his change was permanent. And to make matters worse, they had both heard of girls becoming pregnant to trap their boyfriends into marriage, and she feared Paul would assume she was doing the same. Those pregnancy traps forced the father-to-be into a wedding, a shotgun wedding, and she expected her wedding would feel as if it involved a double-barreled shotgun.

Teenage pregnancy was common within Beaver Point. It was such a common occurrence that the community easily accepted it as long as a wedding soon followed. Most residents of Beaver Point even considered pregnancy a catalyst to marriage, almost a prerequisite, making a wedding without a pregnant bride a pleasant surprise to all, with the parents of the bride and groom bragging about it before the wedding and for years after.

Fighting against her nerves, Lisa met Paul as he parked his car in her parents' driveway, and he knew something was up when she got in and asked him to stay seated. Then with him staring dumbly at her, she decided she wouldn't work the conversation toward the news by asking him when he wanted children, did he still want two, and would now be a good time to start. Instead, she took a deep breath and said, "I don't know how to say this, so I'm just going—"

"What? What is it?" Paul asked, nervously expecting her to announce they were breaking up.

"I'm... I'm pregnant."

"What! With a baby?" Paul asked, both surprised and relieved.

"No, a puppy. Of course, a baby, our baby!"

"What the Hell? How'd this happen? How could this happen?" Paul asked so loud that Lisa thought his words could reach her parents sitting in their living room.

"Lower your voice. I know this is a shock and you know how this happened, could've happened. Something went wrong with the condom or something. Now, if you're going to blame this on me, don't! I don't want this as much as you, maybe even more! This is not a trap!"

Lisa's assertiveness put Paul out of place, and he said, "Ok, ok, calm down. Whats we do now?"

"I guess we tell our folks."

"Ok, ok, let's tell yers first. It'll be like a dry run for mine."

"All right, but let's wait a week to get over our shock before we shock them too, ok?"

"Yeah, that's a... that's a good idea."

"And maybe we should try to think of this as starting our life together a little sooner than planned?"

"Ok, ok. Looks, I feels like I gotta be alone now. How abouts we calls it a night and I'll come back tomorrow night."

"All right, I'll see you tomorrow then," Lisa said before leaning over and quickly kissing him.

Lisa watched him drive away. She knew he would go back to his shared house to drink and talk with his roommates, and she would have to wait and see if his attitude would change overnight. She was glad he didn't get too upset, and she was relieved he didn't mention abortion.

Just over a week later, in the living room of her parents, the two nervously told the Purcells about their pregnancy. The news didn't surprise them much and both tried to regard it positively. Though they felt the pregnancy was too soon, they hugged their daughter and told her they were certain she would be an excellent mother and loved the idea of having a baby around their home again. They said nothing regarding Paul as a father, and Paul noticed. Over the previous year, they couldn't help but witness the change in his personality and they dreaded the idea of him marrying their daughter, though neither mentioned it to Lisa.

Mr. Purcell offered to go along with Paul to inform his parents, but Paul insisted on going alone, even without Lisa. Three days later, and as Paul had expected, his parents didn't accept the pregnancy well. His father exploded in a rage and called him some harsh names, and his furious mother called Lisa even harsher ones. Hearing their words, Paul's temper ignited and for the first and last time, he punched his father straight in the face, knocking him on his back, and if not for his mother distracting him with slaps across the back of his head, he might've given into his desire to kick the man as he lay bleeding from the nose. Then the *new* Paul showed unusual self-control when he only lightly pushed his mother aside as he left the house.

On the way home, he pulled over onto the dirt shoulder of the road, and with tears blurring his vision, he angrily beat his fists against the steering wheel. Then, after calming down, he decided to disconnect himself permanently from his family and marry Lisa.

It was a combination of his lack of romance and the stress of the situation that caused him to propose to Lisa in such a stoic manner that he appeared to be offering her a beer, and it was the stress of the situation that caused her to appear as if she was stoically accepting one.

With the proposal, Lisa had a bit of hope that it was a sign of Paul's old self since she expected his new self to leave her and their baby, and later that week, Paul reinforced that hope by suggesting they use some of their savings for an engagement ring. But Lisa disagreed and suggested they buy only the much cheaper wedding bands. With a baby coming, they couldn't afford a flashy ring.

As the news of Paul's attack on his father spread through the village, soon to be followed by the news of his and Lisa's marriage, the Purcells had a family sit-down with the young couple. To save them money, they offered to have their future son-in-law move into their home until they were prepared to purchase a home of their own, and they also offered to look after their coming grandchild until the young couple had settled down into their new home and were prepared to look after the child on their own. Fearing the loss of his new friends and, therefore, losing his social life, Paul refused the offer to move in with the Purcells but agreed they could look after their child until he and Lisa had settled into their new place. Disappointed with both of his decisions, Lisa went along so as not to create more tension than necessary.

With much less excitement than she had envisioned as a young girl, Lisa began arranging the marriage, and with Paul and her parents in agreement, she set the date, booked the church, arranged the invitation list, picked out invitations, and together she and her mother searched through wedding dress designs.

All seemed on track with their plans until Paul let his temper get the better of him and had a fistfight with one of several Mi'kmaq Indians who worked with the company during the busier summer months. As their fists flew, Paul found an opening and connected with the man's jaw, knocking him unconscious and getting himself fired, and with the loss of his income and the strong possibility of having to move in with the Purcells, he returned devastated to his shared home. His roommates were sympathetic, and that night after quite a few drinks, they convinced him he had a case for getting his job back, so the next morning, hung over, he went to speak to the manager, but when the nervous man refused to allow him into his trailer-office for a private talk, his temper ignited again and the situation quickly became heated, ending in Paul's second fistfight of the week, and his coworkers, including one roommate, having to subdue him until the RCMP arrived to arrest him. The manager charged him with trespassing and assault but later dropped the charges. The company didn't need any bad blood in the small community.

Six weeks earlier, one of Paul's roommates had moved to Halifax and had taken partial employment on the docks as a stevedore, and desperate to get his life back on track, Paul packed up his car and moved to Halifax to join him.

The young couple's plans had changed. Paul was to find an apartment and have it furnished by the time they were married in Beaver Point, and after the marriage, Lisa would join him in Halifax.

Sleeping on his friend's sofa, each morning Paul went with him to the dockyard where they waited in the bullpen, the name given to the waiting room for casual workers hoping to find daily jobs, and after only a month of getting jobs almost every other day, a manager noticed Paul, his roommate, and another man's hard work and offered them full-time employment. Paul was more than happy with the full-time job and welcomed the fluctuating hours and occasional weekend work, and soon after, he found an apartment and began slowly furnishing it with used items.

With the only friend he had in the city spending more time with his girlfriend (who moved in when he moved out), Paul quickly found himself bored. He considered passing the time by drinking in a bar, but since he had yet to find any drinking buddies, it would mean he would have to drink alone, and since only pathetic losers did that, he spent his evenings sober and in front of his small black and white television. Then growing lonelier by the day, he expected the next several months to be painfully boring, so much so that he viewed his little apartment as not much more than a prison's solitary confinement... but with a television, and he was soon spending his nights drinking more than several beers in front of the television while fantasizing about a future life in a house within the city where he was the successful breadwinner while his wife looked after their two children.

For almost two months, all seemed positive again until one Sunday, three hours after the Purcells were expected home from their regular Bridge Night, a worried Lisa answered the door to find an RCMP officer standing there. While driving home, the Purcells had lost control of their car, hit and flipped over a side barrier, and tumbled down an embankment, coming to rest upside-down in five feet of cold salty water.

With his pregnant fiancée in distress, Paul took time off work to help with the funeral arrangements, and soon after the burial, the couple headed to Halifax.

Lisa was thankful she had Paul and was even more thankful after seeing the damage to the right side of his car and hearing about the accident he also had earlier that week in Halifax, and two weeks later, with Paul's old roommate and his roommate's girlfriend as witnesses, Lisa and Paul were married in the Halifax Court House. The wedding didn't come close to Lisa's childhood dream: it wasn't in a church; there was no wedding service with a crowd of smiling onlookers; neither the bride nor the groom's parents were present, and neither dressed up. It seemed only a little more than four people ordering at the counter of a McDonald's restaurant.

With Lisa inheriting her parents' home, its contents, and what remained of their savings after paying the funeral expenses, Paul arranged for the sale of the Purcells' home to one of his old roommates and the couple used the money for a down payment on a much more expensive bungalow on Gilmore Street.

Paul liked the all-white neighborhood. It was a new subdivision and a new house, the perfect beginning for a new family. Lisa, with all the sudden changes in her life, was indifferent to the location and the house and would've been content with only a simple apartment, but she stoically followed behind her husband as he proudly led her into their new life.

Furnishing their new bungalow with pieces from Lisa's parents' home, they used their oval, chrome-legged melamine kitchen table with its four matching chairs, their beige sofa and matching loveseat, and their heavy wooden coffee and end tables. Their thick oak bedroom set went into the newlyweds' bedroom and Lisa's cast iron bed went into the child's room for future use. They purchased a crib, fridge, stove, and a washer and dryer, and exhausted their cash and credit by ending their purchases with a new two-door Oldsmobile Tornado, a sporty sedan with its trademark of a curved down trunk. And to prepare for their child, Paul painted the baby's room blue and pink. "In case it's a boy or girl," he told Lisa.

When their baby was born at the IWK Hospital, they named the six-and-a-half-pound baby boy Dwight Paul Purcell and for the next two years, the child would sleep in his parent's bedroom before moving into his own.

For the first five years on Gilmore Street, the Dixons lived what they considered the perfect family life, with Paul working while Lisa did the traditional tasks of taking care of Dewey while doing the chores around the house, and a year after moving to Gilmore, the couple found a babysitter through one of Paul's coworkers, and they began going out shopping together, to the cinema and occasionally to restaurants. Paul drank very little during those first few years of their marriage, only occasionally going out after work with his coworkers.

With Dewey in elementary school, Lisa volunteered at his school's library and enjoyed it so much that it motivated her to finish her high school education through the General Education Diploma program, or GED, so she could then go on to Teacher's College to become an elementary school teacher.

Expecting his wife's plans to be just a passing fancy, Paul was still supportive and soon found himself alone with Dewey three nights a week while she attended her evening classes, and at other times, he had to keep himself and Dewey quiet while she studied in their bedroom. And after a couple of months into the program, he began to resent Lisa. He worked all day, came home, ate, and then had to watch Dewey until eight o'clock, and after four months into the program, he began going out more often after work and sometimes arrived home too late for her to make her evening classes. Lisa wanted to be angry with him but she could only be angry with herself for starting the program prematurely, and she dropped out a month short of her diploma.

Over the next year, Paul returning home late became Paul returning home drunk, and it was becoming much more frequent. At Lisa's insistence, he refrained from showing his bigotry and racism at home, but the more he drank, the more he brought it home, and she soon found herself resenting him as they gradually grew apart.

Then, one Saturday morning, Lisa mustered the courage to tell Paul that she and their son had had enough of his drinking, and she put on a strong front as she warned him she would leave him unless he started controlling his drinking and then proposed a compromise: if they were going to continue with the marriage, he could only go out once a week. With the reality shock of a potential divorce, Paul agreed to go out only on Thursday nights.

Lisa was content with seeing Paul's aggressive side only once a week, and Paul was content with having a regular schedule for releasing his tension, which he did with the patrons of King's bar who generally shared his views on most things racist.

Paul was comfortable at King's bar. He felt popular, and the other patrons seemed to enjoy listening to him rant on, and he ranted on often. Like his father, he also confused being loud for being outspoken and could easily put on a twenty-minute diatribe concerning the problems of a particular race, usually the same problems but with the race changed, and during his performance, most of the patrons would cheer him on, but occasionally, a situation occurred where someone disagreed with him, and Paul had two responses for it. His first involved simply calling his opponent a lover of the particular race and declaring that the opponent had been brainwashed by them, and his second, his favorite, was to ask his opponent if he would approve of his daughter marrying a man of that race. If the response was negative, he would claim victory. If positive, he would call the opponent a sick bastard and tell him he wanted nothing to do with him.

Maybe it was the alcohol, but Paul never seemed to realize that most of the spectators were anxiously waiting for the fight that could conclude an argument, or if he did realize it, maybe he just liked the attention. It was always a good bet that an argument would turn into a fistfight with him losing or winning, depending on how drunk he was. When not too drunk, he was a good fist fighter, and he knew it and liked to prove it, coming home at least once a month with dried blood on his face and bruises on his body.

The residents of Gilmore Street normally kept to themselves, though when passing one another, they didn't hesitate to exchange a few pleasant words ranging from the weather to minor gossip, and it was always minor since nothing of great significance occurred on or around there.

Over the years, Lisa came to know the first names of almost every woman on the first three blocks of the street and some of those of the men. Paul, on the other hand, knew only a few names but would claim to know everyone. His loud personality tended to force his neighbors to distance themselves from him, causing him to only know the names of a couple of men living directly across the street and those on each side of his house, or he used to know those on each side of his house.

At the end of the previous summer, Paul's neighbor on his left informed him he was moving and had sold his home to an old Jewish couple, and since he was never on good terms with his neighbor, he was certain the sale to the Jews was a personal dig at him and believed the neighbor had even discounted the house to ensure an easy sale, and more so since Jews never paid the asking price for anything.

Being the first Jews he had come across, the Rosens moved into the two-story house next to his smaller bungalow and shared a driveway where their large black Cadillac overshadowed his smaller car. They had their driveway plowed while he shoveled his, and they used a gas mower while he used a push. They were screaming out that they were better than him, and he would've liked to confront them and let them know they weren't welcome on the street, but he restrained himself for the sake of his wife, though he was somewhat pacified with them having no children or grandchildren to further *contaminate* the street and was pacified more when they kept to themselves, not attempting a conversation with him or his family. As long as they were not in his life or his family's, he felt he could tolerate them, but he would still drop the occasional complaint to his wife regarding their sloppy shoveling of the snow from their section of the sidewalk and in the late spring, not cutting the small strip of grass separating the two driveways. Then there were those multi-armed electric candles they displayed in their two lower-level windows during their first Christmas on the street. He couldn't understand, "If they really are Jews, why does they celebrate Christmas?"

CHAPTER 9
Chaos

Lisa bought a double-pack of exterior doorknobs at The Met department store and then walked almost three hundred feet to the other end of the mall to enter the Canadian Imperial Bank of Commerce. After reviewing the balance of their joint savings account, she withdrew eleven hundred dollars, leaving a balance of two hundred and forty-seven dollars and eighteen cents. Then looking at the time, she figured she could save three dollars and take the bus home, and like a machine going through its motions absent of all emotion, she cut through the parking lot to Herring Cove Road, crossed to the other side, and waited for the #20 Herring Cove Road heading toward Gilmore Street. When the blue and gray bus stopped and with a loud hiss, opened its door, she entered, dropped the change in the metal box separating her from the driver, and walked to its almost empty back.

That morning was the fifth time Paul had come home with the same perfume on his shirt, and like the other times before, Lisa had never asked about it, knowing nothing would come out of it except, perhaps, anger aimed at her for noticing. Over the last couple of years, Paul's anger had become intense, and although he had never been violent with her, violence now seemed a possibility.

Around eleven that morning, Lisa had called King's under the pretense of looking for Tom. She had told the man answering the phone that she was afraid Tom, a regular customer there, could be in trouble since he didn't come home the night before and yet he lived so close to it, and the man confirmed her suspicions when he told her he had worked the bar the night before but didn't know of any Tom being there and didn't know of any regular by that name either. He ended the call by politely suggesting she was calling the wrong bar. Disappointed with herself since she should have said Tom was with Paul Dixon, Lisa was going to call back, but then decided against it when she considered he might catch her lying and lie to cover for Paul. After all, she couldn't be the first wife to call the bar concerning her husband.

**

Ruth was more than happy to extend Dewey's stay until eight. The two had spent the early afternoon playing Go Fish, which the boy had taught the old woman, and after that, they read *Alice in Wonderland*, each taking turns reading aloud alternate pages, with Ruth helping her little friend as needed.

When they ended their shared reading, Dewey asked about one of the few non-books on the bookshelves that interested him, a bronze statue of a funny-dressed woman with four arms.

"That's a statue of Aditi, the Hindu Goddess of Fertility, and other things that escape me. Avriel purchased it after our wedding. He thought we should cover our bases," she laughed. "Everything here has a story, just like everything in your bedroom has one."

"Neat. What's the story of the plate there, the plate with the lady on it?"

"That's Queen Elizabeth the Second. We got that after her coronation. Weren't able to be there, so we purchased the plate with her picture on it. We have a plate of her father too, but that's somewhere in the basement."

"What's the story with this plate for the cookies?"

"We got that with a set of dishes over thirty years ago. Not much of a story there. Some things have better stories than others."

"Over thirty years ago! That's a long time! It's time for a new set, no?"

Ruth smiled. "You sound just like Avriel, and I can only tell you what I tell him: we still have each piece and they're still as good as new."

"But thirty years is old. That's really, really old!"

Ruth laughed again. "Yes, but I follow the adage, *if it isn't broken, don't fix it*, or more to the dishes, *if they aren't broke, don't buy new ones*."

Before Ruth prepared the burger patties and sliced the vegetables, she made her final phone call to the office. She would've called her husband several times that afternoon to give him support and to see if he had seen Mr. Frank and shown him around the office, but she kept losing track of the time.

**

His wife's call moved him. He needed to hear her voice. He needed to be reminded that he wasn't alone.

After waiting for the click of her putting down the receiver, Avriel hung up the phone and checked his watch. It was almost four-thirty. He placed his glasses in his shirt pocket, stood up, and stiffly shook hands with Mr. Frank and his people who had been familiarizing themselves with the files. Grabbing the last bundle of envelopes and almost forgetting his briefcase containing only a monogrammed envelope opener and a paper lunch bag full of hundreds of Ruth's notes that he had saved since she began writing them, he picked it up and did a final walk of the store, awkwardly shaking hands with the employees as they traded goodbyes.

He was both relieved and disappointed that no one had used what he considered empty phrases: drop by and see us sometime; let's stay in touch; let's get together over coffee one of these mornings, or drop me a line and let me know how life is treating you. He had heard them used in the past, felt it was just empty talk and it bothered him to hear them, but that afternoon, he felt like a hypocrite as he almost wished someone would've used one on him.

When he reached the manager, Avriel handed him the bundle of envelopes, except for one, and asked him to give them out on Monday, as the other locations were doing.

Finished with his repeated goodbyes, he took a deep breath, wiped the sweat from his brow, and headed down to the receiving area where he paused when he saw Thomas who paused when he saw him, and after they silently shook hands and Thomas jokingly pushed him toward the door, Avriel forced an envelope into his hand.

Through the hot wind, he made his way to his car, and as he was reaching into his back pocket for his keys, a strong hand on his shoulder spun him around, and with one hand stuck in his back pocket and the other holding his briefcase, he found himself tightly embraced by Thomas. A second later, his friend broke the embrace, nodded his head nervously, and returned to the store.

After watching Thomas return to the building with his unopened envelope in his hand, Avriel took a deep breath, unlocked his car door, and tried to clear his mind by reminding himself to pick up the hamburger buns and another board game. Strangely, he looked forward to both the hamburgers and his time with Dewey, and for a moment, he even considered how to sneak some cheese on their burgers, but realized the risks outweighed the short-term pleasure.

When Avriel walked through the door, Ruth wasn't standing there to greet him as he had expected. Instead, she was sitting back on the sofa watching Dewey standing where the coffee table should've been as he tried to show off his skills with the Yo-Yo by performing Walk-the-Dog. Focusing so much attention on it, the boy didn't hear the front door open and close.

With a smile, Ruth welcomed her husband, who placed his briefcase down at the door, removed his shoes, and watched Dewey wind the string on the Yo-Yo, try the trick again, and huff when, after spinning at the end of its string, it refused to return to the palm of his hand.

After the third failed attempt, Ruth joked, "He's not a very obedient dog, is he?"

And Avriel couldn't stop himself from saying. "Dewey, perhaps the Yo-Yo is a dodo."

Turning around to find Avriel watching him, Dewey said shyly, "Hi, Avriel."

"Hello, Dewey. Perhaps you are having a hard time with the trick because you are using your left hand. You are right-handed, correct? It is more awkward with your left hand, is it not?"

"Yup, I think you're right," Dewey said, appreciating Avriel's legitimate excuse for his repeated failures.

As Dewey rewound the string of the Yo-Yo, Ruth struggled slightly to stand up from the sofa. "I'm going to leave you two alone while I grab the hamburgers warming in the oven," she said before slowly walking up to Avriel, pulling his head down to hers, and kissing him. Then, taking the bag of buns, she headed toward the kitchen.

Instinctively taking a deep breath, Avriel walked into the living room and held up the plastic bag containing the board game. "Dewey, I picked up another game. This one is called Monopoly. Have you heard of it?"

"Sure, we have that one at home. Maybe next time I can bring a game over. Hey, I can go get ours now."

"That is a good idea, but seeing how I hate returning things and how I enjoy watching you open them, perhaps you could break open this box?"

"Sure, ok," Dewey said, taking the bag and sitting on the sofa as Avriel slid the coffee table back to its spot. "This game takes a while to play, so we might have to decide the winner by who has the most stuff. That's what we do at home. But you'll have to do the adding like Mommy does because it's too much for my little head."

"Sounds good," he said, not understanding what Dewey meant and surprised there was math involved and because of it, expecting his wife to win most of the games. Sitting back in the leather chair, he watched the boy tear off the plastic wrapping, open the box, fold out the game's board onto the coffee table, and then use his teeth to open a little plastic sack containing several small metal pieces. "Careful, you do not choke on anything," Avriel warned him as he bit into the plastic wrapping of a pack of cards.

"Nope, I'm a professional," he said and lightly spat out a tiny piece of plastic.

Curious, Avriel leaned forward to examine the metal playing pieces, trying to understand what the random little things, like a top hat, a shoe, and a thimble, had to do with the real estate-themed game, which looked rather boring and made him wish he had instead purchased the Mouse Trap game with its many plastic pieces to build a contraption to catch the plastic mice. He had spotted the curious game on the store shelf that afternoon but thought it would be too exciting for his wife.

**

Having to pick up his watch from the night before, Paul arrived home later than usual, around six-thirty. He parked his car next to the Cadillac and walked up to his front door, noting he'll have to remind Lisa that the grass needed cutting. When he went to turn the doorknob, it wouldn't budge. He tried shaking it — nothing. Putting his key in the lock. It wouldn't turn. He tried shaking the key — nothing. Puzzled, he removed the key and knocked on the door — no answer. He rang the doorbell — still no answer. Confused, he looked through their large living room window on his left. Their television was off and there was no light on in the back hall. With the closed floral curtains blocking the view into their bedroom window on his right, he walked to the back of the house and tried the door there. It too was locked, and his key wouldn't work. Through Dewey's closed window, he couldn't see the boy, and when he tried to see through the bathroom window, the fog effect on the glass made it impossible. Lastly, he checked the small kitchen window on the right — nothing.

Sitting on the back steps, he considered either waiting at the front of the house or waiting at Rob Smith's, but both would make him look pathetic. The best option would be to wait in the air-conditioned Spryfield Mall and from there telephone his wife every few minutes.

Back in his car, he drove up Gilmore Street, turned left onto Herring Cove Road, and tried to remember when he had last used his house keys but couldn't remember the last time he had come home to an empty house. *If there's somethin' wrong, she should've left a note on the door!* With anger replacing his frustration, he followed Herring Cove Road through two intersections while trying to control his speed, made a right turn just past King's bar, and then a squealing left turn into the mall's parking lot. He tried finding a parking space close to the entrance, but it was Friday evening, the day after payday, so he had to park almost at the end of the parking lot, feeding his anger more.

The cool air hitting him at the mall's entrance did nothing to calm him as he impatiently went in search of a payphone, and finding a group of four next to the entrance of The Met department store, he picked up a receiver, searched his pockets for a dime, slid it in the slot, and dialed his number. After three rings, Lisa answered and he tried to control his anger as he asked, "Ya just gettin' home?"

Trying to control her fear, Lisa said, "No, I've been home all day."

"Where were ya then? I knocked! I rang the bell!"

Then, feeling safer on the other end of the line, she said, "I know. I was home. You don't live here anymore."

"What the hell? That's my house!" he said with his voice growing louder and the shoppers entering and leaving The Met taking notice. "Ya don't locks me outta me own house!"

"Rob Smith is holding the boxes of your things until you're ready to pick them up. I have his number if you want it."

"What? WHAT THE HELL!? HOW LONG WERE YA PLANNIN' THIS BULLSHIT!?" he shouted, drawing the attention of shoppers further down the mall.

"Since this morning. I know what you've been up to."

"UP TO? SCREW YA, YA BITCH! YA DON'T KNOW NOTHIN'! I'M COMIN' BACK NOW!" he said, slamming the phone onto its receiver so hard that it jumped out and swung from its cord.

With his shouting having brought customers and salespeople out from the stores to check on the commotion, a husky mall security guard four stores away began walking toward him but stopped when Paul exited the mall.

Driving the short distance to King's bar, he intended to calm down with several drinks.

**

Full of hamburgers, the three sat on the floor around the coffee table. With Dewey using the small metal car as his playing piece, Ruth, the shoe, and Avriel, with his tie off and sleeves rolled up, using the top hat, almost half of the Monopoly properties had been purchased, but no one had a complete set to buy houses and hotels, which Avriel and Dewey were eager to do.

As Dewey was shaking the two dice in his cupped hands while hoping he wouldn't land on one of Avriel's properties, he heard his father yelling outside. Dropping the dice, he jumped up and ran out of the house in his socks.

With his knees stiff from having them folded for a while, Avriel stood up, asked Ruth to wait inside while he tried to persuade the boy to return, and left in his socks too.

Paul was beating on the door with the bottom of his fists when Dewey ran up to him, saying, "Daddy! Daddy! What's going on?"

Surprised for only a second to see his son, Paul grabbed him roughly by the back of his T-shirt and yelled, "BITCH, OPEN THIS DAMN DOOR BEFORE I HURTS YER PRECIOUS BOY!"

Dewey couldn't speak or move. His father's words, actions, and the anger filling his face froze him, and he had to be pulled back to the cement walkway so his father could have a better view of the bungalow's two front windows.

"DO YA HEAR ME, YA DAMN BITCH!"

"You should release the boy."

Paul turned around, swinging Dewey along with him

"Jew, mind yer own business! Don't try actin' like no hero. It's not in ya."

With tears running down his cheeks, Dewey said, "His last name's not Jew. It's Rosen. He's my friend, Avriel, Avriel Rosen."

Paul glared down at Dewey. "What the hell?! Can this day get any more screwed up?!" he said as his anger jumped up yet another level and he pushed Dewey down onto the front lawn, giving Avriel the uncommon feeling of anger. "MY DAMNED SON'S FRIEND'S THE OLD JEW!" he yelled before lunging forward and throwing a punch at Avriel.

As Avriel stepped to the side to avoid it, it struck the nose of Mr. Smith, who had just come up behind him, and falling flat on his back, the man was knocked unconscious by his head's impact with the cement walkway.

On her porch and horrified to see the commotion beyond the

parked cars, Ruth yelled, "Avriel!" and with her breathing becoming rapid, she made her way down the steps and tried yelling out to him a second time, but no sound came out.

When Paul threw a left hook, Avriel ducked it and slid behind him to try and lock his arms, but an elbow to his chest sent him stumbling backward toward Dewy who was crying as he was getting up. Falling into him, sending the boy rolling several feet, Avriel rolled over onto his stomach, and as he tried to get to his feet, Paul was on top of him, flattening him and pushing the side of his face into the grass.

Ruth's racing heart reached its peak, her vision blurred, and she failed again to yell her husband's name, and as she was passing the back bumper of their Cadillac, she stopped, dropped to her knees, and fell onto her back.

While Lisa rushed from her house to grab her crying son and pull him over to Ruth, Avriel roll Paul off him, and when Paul rolled back and grabbed at him, the two men rolled over the grass until Paul was on his chest with both hands around his neck. "LIGHTS OUT, JEW!"

Fighting for air, Avriel spotted from the corner of an eye Dewey's Yo-Yo. Grabbing the string, he pulled it toward him, but the Yo-Yo just spun where it was. Grabbing more string, he was able to pull it closer, and using what seemed like the last of his strength, he slammed it against the side of Paul's head, stunning him, and as Paul fell forward, Avriel head-butted his face.

Dropping the two pieces of the Yo-Yo, Avriel pushed the unconscious Paul off of him and struggled to stand. Then leaning over with his hands on his knees, he was coughing up dirt when he heard multiple sirens screaming in the distance. Straightening up, he looked around to see on his right, Mr. Smith unconscious on the Dixon's walkway, and to his left, Lisa and Dewey kneeling, crying, and holding his wife's hands as she lay on her behind his car.

Feeling an enormous fear, one stronger than he had ever experienced in his life, Avriel ran to his wife.

Feeling a strange peaceful sensation wash over her, Ruth looked down at Avriel kneeling beside her as he blew into her mouth before placing his hands on her chest and pushing down several times. She watched Dewey crying helplessly on the other side of Lisa who took over blowing into her mouth so Avriel could focus on the chest compressions, and she watched two ambulance technicians run over to her, force her husband out of the way, put a mask attached to a transparent plastic bubble over her face, and direct Avriel to squeeze the bubble as they placed her on a gurney. After Avriel followed her into the ambulance, two more technicians and two police officers arrived and went to Mr. Smith, who would've appeared to be resting peacefully on his back if not for the blood around his nose and mouth. As her ambulance pulled out, she watched Dewey shrinking in size as he stood staring at the vehicle while crying and hugging his crying mother. She would've felt pity for the child, worry for the mother, and concern for her husband, if not for the continuing peaceful sensation.

CHAPTER 10
The Aftermath

Dirt and grass stains covered his face, clothes, knees, and arms, and the edges of his cast had been cracked or crushed, exposing its cloth. In Lisa's rush to get to the hospital, she hadn't thought to clean her son until they were seated in the back of the taxi. She tried cleaning him with a tissue from her oversized fake leather purse, but the stains were too ground in. Even the bit of saliva she used did little to help.

Still stunned by the evening's drama, Dewey asked if his father would come home later that night, and to his relief, she answered, "No." Then trying to make sense of that evening, he was silent through the rest of the drive.

It was close to nine-thirty when a red-eyed Lisa, with Dewey in hand, entered the Queen Elizabeth II Hospital's Emergency Department, where almost every woke face in the waiting room turned to them.

When Dewey spotted Avriel standing out like a defeated Titan among the mortals, he yelled his name, pulled his hand from his mother's, and ran to him.

The broken man, his tall body bent forward in a chair, elbows on his knees and face in his hands, straightened up in his chair to reveal the dirt, grass stains, and blood on his white shirt and the vertical streaks on his cheeks where his tears had forced paths through the dirt. Before that evening, it had been a very long time since he had last cried, and it was in the ambulance when he first noticed the unfamiliar pressure growing in his face. After taking a moment to recognize it, he tried to control it but failed.

"Avriel, are you ok?"

Avriel slowly came out of his trance-like state. "Hello, Dewey. Yes, I'm fine, thank you. Hello, Lisa," he whispered before moving over a seat so each could take one next to him.

"Have you... have you heard anything?" Lisa asked, starting to cry again.

"No... nothing... nothing at all," Avriel replied, tears building up in his bloodshot eyes in reaction to hers.

With tears running down his cheeks, Dewey didn't know why they were crying, but it was impossible for him not to when those he loved did.

When Lisa leaned over and hugged Avriel, Dewey stood up and stretched out his arms to hug them both, and Avriel reciprocated the hugs since sorrow always trumps shyness. After several seconds, they broke their embrace, wiped their eyes, and settled back in their seats to stare down at the floor.

Then after some minutes of silence, Avriel said, "You just missed Mr. Smith. He came to in his ambulance, and after a doctor came out and set his nose, he left. He has to work early tomorrow and needs at least six hours of sleep. He also told me he had wanted to wait with you while you waited for your husband, but he didn't want to risk making the situation worse. He waited by his window and called the police when your husband started yelling. He seems like a good man. I did not explain Ruthy's situation... since he rudely slept through the whole thing," With his attempt at humor failing, he added, "I believe he assumed I was here to be examined as well."

Dewey, then aware that something was seriously wrong with Mrs. Rosen, placed his small hand on Avriel's arm and caused him to fight off another attack of tears.

While looking in her purse for some tissue, Lisa said, "Avriel, I almost forgot!" Pulling out his dress shoes, she kneeled in front of him, placed them over his dirty socks, and tied their laces. "I... I hope you don't mind, but I went over to your place for your guys' shoes."

"No, not at all. But that reminds me... Dewey, I owe you a Yo-Yo."

"It's ok. I have another one. Mommy always buys me more than one of the little things. I always break them too fast."

Finished tying his shoelaces, Lisa returned to her chair, and the three sat silent again.

Dewey thought about the events of the evening. He had never seen his father so angry. Even after he woke up and the police took him away, he was yelling, swearing, and threatening to come back and finish what he started. He never knew his father was strong enough to knock out Mr. Smith, and Carl was wrong when last winter he told him, "My daddy can beat up your daddy!" Then there was Avriel who fought his dad like a professional wrestler and won, making him the strongest of the three. And what about Mrs. Rosen? She fainted just as he had seen women do in movies, and then the men with the ambulance carried her away instead of tapping her cheek as they do in the movies. She was somewhere in the hospital, but why? It had to be something serious, something scary.

Lisa sat thinking about how terrible the night had been. Was this Paul's fault, hers, or both? She had expected him to freak out, but not to turn on Dewey. The delay between his phone call and his showing up should've set off an alarm, but it had never even crossed her mind, and once the commotion started, she found herself frozen watching it... until Ruth's collapse snapped her out of it. *I should've known he would've gone drinking! I should've called the police as soon as he arrived! Did I truly believe he'd have just left? Do I even know him anymore?*

For the first time since arriving at the hospital, Avriel looked around the room. He found it curious how, with their chrome chairs, their sounds and smells, and the color of their walls, the two different Emergency Departments looked and felt identical. If not for the size of the patients, it would be almost impossible to tell which he was in. *Perhaps Ruthy was right. Perhaps there was a sale on beige paint.* A tear escaped his eye.

As a set of swinging doors opened inward, a man in his late forties dressed in green hospital scrubs appeared and called out, "Mr. Rosen? Mr. Avriel Rosen?"

One after the other, Lisa, Dewey, and Avriel stood up.

"Hello, I'm Doctor Rogers. I'm sorry... but we... we couldn't revive your wife."

Avriel's knees weakened, but he caught himself and remained standing with his arms hanging loosely at his sides, and as tears streamed down their cheeks, Lisa and Dewey each took one of his hands.

"Her heart was much too weak. Its deterioration was too far gone."

Avriel tried to say something, but couldn't. He was doing all he could just to keep standing.

The doctor waited for the old man to take in what he had said, and after a few seconds, he gave up on him, looked at Lisa, and said, "We have some papers to be signed... but they can wait until tomorrow if you... he'd like."

With Lisa unable to say anything, the doctor looked again for a response from Avriel, who seemed to look through him. "I'll... I'll have the secretary hold—"

Then when she gently squeezed his hand, Avriel blurted out louder than he meant to, "I'll sign them now."

"Ok... uh... please sign at the bottom."

The doctor handed his clipboard and pen to Avriel, who, with shaking hands, quickly signed it and handed it back.

"Uh... sorry... please sign the third and fourth papers too, at their bottoms."

Avriel awkwardly flipped through the pages, signed twice more, and handed the clipboard back again.

"We'll keep your wife here until she's picked up by the funeral home. They'll get the death certificate too, and until then, Mr. Rosen, your wife will be treated with the utmost respect."

"Right... right," nodded Avriel, appreciating the doctor's words but not able to show it.

As the doctor stiffly turned and walked back through the swinging doors, Lisa and Dewey wrapped their arms around the broken old man, and all three stood hugging and crying before he forced out, "We... we should leave."

Taking their hands, he led them out of the emergency room and headed toward the parking lot. Then remembering how he had gotten there, he stopped, released their hands, and turned around, and after his friends did the same, he took their hands again and followed the walkway toward the waiting taxis at the main entrance.

He had expected that when the time came years from then, Ruth would be resting in a hospital bed, making Death wait impatiently while she consoled him in her selfless and habitual way of putting him before herself. He had expected many more kisses and hugs, and he expected to be able to tell her goodbye many times over before the annoyed and impatient Death took her from him. He had never expected that they would part without any goodbyes.

CHAPTER 11
Alone

With each staring into the other's eyes, the two slowly waltzed to the fast rhythm of their song, *Puttin' on the Ritz*. Wearing her wedding dress, she looked just as she did on their wedding night, and he only realized he was wearing a tuxedo by the unusual tightness of what must have been a bow tie around his neck.

With everything behind her washed out, Ruth mouthed the words, "I love you."

Avriel replied, "I love you too."

And she mouthed, "I know," before pulling his head down to whisper in his ear, "Look around you."

Not wanting to break eye contact with her, he reluctantly did, and as a ballroom came into focus, followed by a small standing crowd, he saw his father, and it took him a second to recognize his mother beside him. She was older than he remembered, about his father's age, and she had aged well. He noticed his uncles and an aunt, and it took two tries before he recognized his father-in-law, whose out-of-character smile dramatically changed his appearance. Standing between several older people whom he hadn't yet recognized was an old schoolmate Tommy Crombie, or a young schoolmate since he was still about ten years old, and Avriel was happy to see him since the last time he did was in elementary school, the day before he drowned under what turned out to be only thin ice covering Cameron's Pond. Then Avriel saw three of his brothers standing together and wondered where the fourth was.

"He's not here yet," Ruth said as if reading his mind.

One by one, all the faces became familiar. There were fellow students from Cambridge and several people he was close to during his military service, including Timothy Jenkins, who was giving a slight wave. There were even acquaintances he had made before the war and a few ex-employees from their first couple of drugstores.

Startling Avriel, Ruth released him, stepped back, and said, "Av, I have to go. It's going to be a time of many changes, and you'll need to accept and embrace them. Lisa and Dewey are good for you, and you're good for them." Then she smirked and added, "And remember, I'm never wrong."

Avriel attempted to grab and pull her in for a kiss and a squeeze, but his hands grabbed nothing as she faded away with the guests.

With the song fading out as it ended, Avriel reflexively yelled, "I'M A NINCOMPOOP!" And with the words echoing off the walls, he stood alone, looking about as the empty ballroom faded away with the echo.

He woke in an armchair and had difficulty opening his eyes — the tears from the night before had formed a weak glue along the edges of his eyelids — and as he lifted his forearms from the leather armrests, they made a soft sound like that of slow tearing paper. Standing up, he stretched his stiff back, and then suddenly feeling lost, he sat back down, straightened out his long legs, set his forearms back on the armrests, and stared straight ahead at nothing. Noticing the subtle scent of his wife's favorite perfume, he expected she had last worn it the night of the charity dinner, but couldn't be certain. He was certain he had smelled it, but when he took a deep breath in through his nose to get a stronger dose, there was nothing.

He needed to get himself together and deal with the situation. His mind was on Ruth and he could've easily stayed in the chair the entire day thinking of her, but he needed to function and the only way he could do that was to think about something else, something besides his wife.

Using what had become his coping tool over the last year and a half, he thought about the past. He thought about the long voyage to Halifax when his wife would force him out of their room and onto the ship's deck for an evening stroll. He thought about their small apartment in The North End and, soon after moving into it, how they had enjoyed painting over its smoke-stained walls. He thought about when they had purchased their first drugstore, how a delighted Ruth had come up with the name Rose Son's and acted as the buffer between him and the customers, and just when he was going to give up on his coping mechanism, his mind jumped to their last place together. The bloody house! The house, or rather its location, was Ruth's only mistake, and an enormous one at that. *Location, Location, Location!* If it weren't for the location of the house, they would never have met the Dixons. If they had never met, he wouldn't have been involved in the situation the night before, and if he weren't involved, Ruth wouldn't have been so excited. The location had caused her premature death, or maybe, he reconsidered, it was her need for friends.

He forced himself to his feet, picked up his reading glasses from off the edge of a bookshelf, put them on, and looked at his watch. It was almost seven-thirty; he would have to call the rabbi.

After retrieving the pink folder from Ruth's sewing room's filing cabinet, he went into the kitchen to call the large numbers written on the inside of the folder's cover, and it took several tries before his shaking hand correctly dialed the first number.

Hello, this is Rabbi Lavigne.

"Ruthy is dead."

Hello? What's that?

"My wife... my Ruthy... has died."

There was a moment of silence.

Mr. Rosen?

"Yes."

Mr. Rosen, it saddens me to hear this. Is she at the QE Hospital?

"Yes."

Ok, I'll make the arrangements today and call you back in the afternoon. I understand the service will be held at the plot. Mr. Rosen, if you need to talk, please call or come over any hour. If you'd like, I could come over after the service today.

"Plot where?"

Right, it's at the Baron De Hirsch Cemetery along Windsor Street. The entrance is on the east side, but don't worry about that. I expect Parker's funeral home will send a car for you and your group.

Avriel thought he had heard himself say, "Thank you. I appreciate your help. Goodbye," but what he actually said was incoherent.

Taking several deep breaths, he dialed the second number, and after stating his condolences, a tired Mr. Parker told him he would pick up Ruth from the hospital and Rabbi Lavigne would work with him regarding her preparation. He would dig and prepare the gravesite that day; the pine casket was ready in storage, and before Avriel hung up, the man told him he would call back later that day to confirm the details.

Pine casket remained in Avriel's head. It wasn't even a coffin. He would've preferred to build a mausoleum and place his wife in an elaborate coffin, but Ruth wanted to follow Jewish custom, and that meant placing her in a simple pine box without even an interior lining.

Trying to ignore those two words, Avriel went through the folder's papers. There were several paid invoices, including one dated over a year earlier for a gravestone that he made a mental note to talk to Mr. Parker about. His wife had placed modest words on it, but there he could have his say and would ensure it said all he thought it should in its limited space.

Then he pulled out from the back of the folder an eight by eleven sheet of paper with a handwritten list detailing the monthly household expenses, including the telephone, electricity, water charges, the synagogue's monthly fees, and the suggested amounts to donate annually to several charities. He set the list on the kitchen counter so as not to forget about it, and as he closed the folder, something green caught his eye. He opened it again, pulled out the small piece of paper, and read, *Avriel, my love, you're stronger than you believe, and now's the time to show it.*

Assuming the note was the one replaced by the half-piece of toast weeks before, he placed it in his shirt pocket, laid the folder and his glasses down on the counter, and went to the front door where he locked the doorknob and set the deadbolt. After closing the living room and dining room curtains, he returned to the armchair, and hoping to see Ruth again, he took a deep breath, closed his eyes, and was soon snoring softly.

Waking to the scent of her perfume, he tried confirming it, but like before, there was nothing.

Forcing himself out of the chair, he slowly made his way up the stairs to go through the filing cabinet twice before reflexively calling down, "Ruthy, have you seen the pink folder?" And with the pressure growing in his face again, he wiped his eyes with his dirty sleeves and slowly made his way down to the phonebook in the kitchen, where he was surprised to see the pink folder reminding him of what he had already done. Sitting on his chair, he placed his elbows on the small table, placed his head in his hands, and silently cried. He wanted to die a quick death rather than the painfully slow one he was experiencing.

A light knock on the front door startled him and being in no condition to answer it but curious who it was, he stood up from the kitchen chair, stretched his back, and wiped his eyes with his fingers before creeping over to the far side of the dining-room window and peeking out to see Lisa holding what looked like a casserole dish.

He crept back to the kitchen.

Minutes later, the phone rang.

Looking up at the clock on the wall, he was sure it was too soon for Mr. Parker or the rabbi, so he let it ring.

Then, with his growling stomach reminding him he was hungry, he found crackers in the first cupboard he checked, poured a glass of water, and sat down to eat while staring at the wall.

Ten minutes later, several whiffs of his body odor reminded him to shower, and like a man on his last leg of life, he walked up the stairs to the bathroom where in its mirror he saw a broken old man with dirt, grass stains and dried blood on his shirt and face and some bruising around his neck, and after removing his shirt, saw the bruises on his thin chest and arms and only realized they hurt when he touched them.

Changed and showered, but forgetting to shave, Avriel answered the phone. It was Mr. Parker. The funeral was to be the day after next — the Monday. Half an hour later, the rabbi called to tell him the same thing.

He needed a drink, needed to drink something mind-altering, and he knew better than to look for it in the house, and since his car could make enough noise to bring Lisa out to check on him, he would have to walk down Herring Cove Road to the liquor store about a mile away. So, after peeking out the window to make sure Dewey wasn't playing in the front, he left the house, walked up Gilmore Street, and turned left at Herring Cove Road.

Starting in the afternoon and continuing through the evening, he drank. The first time he did it alone, ever. After pulling out the book *Paradise Lost,* which he enjoyed for its words rather than any religious significance, he sat down to lose himself in it and the alcohol.

Having finished two trays of ice and half the bottle of whiskey, Avriel fell asleep again in the living room chair, but this time with the book on his lap and just to the right of the chair, a shattered glass lying in a pool of whisky.

With his reading glasses still on and his head hurting, Avriel awoke around five the next morning and cleaned up the broken glass and its spilled contents. He placed Ruth's many tiny notes scattered over the Monopoly board still lying on the coffee table back into their paper bag — he didn't remember taking them out — and put away the game, leaving out the metal shoe that he placed on a bookshelf. He emptied the remaining half of the forty-ounce bottle in the kitchen sink, hid the evidence in the garbage, and with the last of the milk, made a bowl of cereal and sat down at the kitchen table.

Having forgotten the spoon, Avriel stood up, pulled out the top drawer, and was surprised to find the cooking utensils. Pulling out the second drawer, he found the cutlery, and as he picked up a spoon, spotted a small pink piece of paper at the side. He picked it up too, went to get his reading glasses, and then, realizing they were resting on his nose, sat back down at the table.

Avriel, you are so very easy to love, but you must let people in to see it.

He had never read that note and wondered how it had gotten into the drawer, and then it hit him: there was only one reason for him to open that drawer. The pressure growing again in his face was becoming the norm.

While going through the motion of eating, he figured out what he would do. He would read. He would escape into books until he was ready to face the world, which at that moment felt like never.

Later, he would pull out books and make a small stack of them, which would take much longer than expected. As he pulled out a book, he would stare at the title for a time, experiencing a flashback to the moment in their lives when he or Ruth had first purchased and shared it with the other by reading it aloud to them.

**

A limousine pulled up to the house and a husky young chauffeur wearing a tight-fitting suit, which made him look more like a bodyguard, opened the door to the back and had to wait only a second before Avriel rushed into the vehicle, and while the man continued to wait at its opened door, Avriel closed it to let him know there was no one else coming.

Dressed in a black suit and a matching yarmulke and with enough room around him for five more people, he was reminded of how alone he was. There was the physical loneliness and there was the much more difficult mental loneliness.

Avriel wanted to ask Mr. Parker to view Ruth resting in her pine box, but the limousine never stopped. When it reached the funeral home, it turned into the driveway, positioned itself behind the hearse, and then followed it out onto Herring Cove Road. Seeing the hearse, Avriel tried not to shut down. Ruth was almost twenty feet away, so close but at the same time so far away. Forcing his mind from the vehicle, he thought about his last couple of days and what she would've thought about his behavior. She wouldn't have been impressed. Then he remembered the gravestone, and it being the one thing in which he could have a say, and again, he made a mental note to talk to Mr. Parker about it.

The two vehicles passed through the opened iron gates of the cemetery to drive along a paved road cutting through the fields of gravestones. Coming to a row of parked cars, Avriel's heart sped up as both vehicles slowed to make their way to the front of the row, and as the limousine stopped, he took a deep breath, exited without waiting for the driver to open the door, and walked slowly toward the grave. Conscious of each step, he made his way up a recently mowed hill and passed several rows of gravestones to stop at a deep rectangular hole, which would be Ruth's resting place. Most of the thirty folding chairs to the left of the grave were claimed by people around his age, and though he had never spoken to them, he recognized some from the few times he and Ruth were at the synagogue.

As several women sitting in the front row beckoned him to join them in an empty seat, he ignored them and chose to stand alone on the opposite side of the grave next to a pile of dirt poorly hidden by a green sheet held down from the breeze by a shovel.

When the rabbi made his way to him, said a small prayer, and then offered him a piece of black ribbon with a safety pin, Avriel shook his head and pointed to his suit pocket, which the rabbi then struggled to tear, all the time saying a prayer in Hebrew.

Minutes later, several younger male members of the synagogue quietly removed the casket from the hearse and carried it toward the gravesite, stopping several times as the Rabbi repeated a holy verse followed by a prayer. When the pallbearers reached the grave, they gently placed the pine box on two cords tightly strung across the hole.

It was no longer than twenty minutes before the rabbi was saying a prayer while the pine box was being lowered into the hole by four men, two on each side, turning metal levers to lower the cords evenly, and after another man closed the ceremony with a final prayer, Avriel picked up the shovel, moved the cloth aside to reveal the pile of dirt, and pushed the shovel into it. Dropping the dirt down onto Ruth's casket, he laid the shovel next to the pile, and after each mourner bent down, picked up a handful, and dropped it into the hole, they silently made a line in front of the widower, who had never been physically touched by so many people in such a short time. As some shook his limp hand, others grabbed his arm, and some aggressively hugged his stiff torso, Avriel could only reply with nods.

As the last person passed, he watched them line up to dip their hands in a water basin sitting on a tripod. Taking a deep breath, he turned around to look once again at Ruth's final resting place and noticed a lone mourner still standing to the left of the chairs. It took him several seconds to recognize Thomas Robinson. He had never seen him in a suit or with his salt-and-pepper hair oiled back or with his face so closely shaved, and as he was wondering how he had heard about Ruth's death and funeral so soon, he noticed the yarmulke, not the sort the synagogue would lend to visiting non-Jews but a well-fitted black one with thick white edging that was noticeable from a distance. All these years working together and he never knew Thomas was Jewish. *Robinson? Perhaps his mother was a Jew.*

The two men stared at each other for a moment before Thomas reached for the morning newspaper under his arm and gestured with it. Walking over to Avriel, he picked up a handful of dirt, scattered it in the hole, and wiped his hand on the leg of his suit pants before shaking Avriel's hand. Saying nothing, both waited until only the limousine and one other car remained before crossing the road and sitting on a bench at the edge of another field of gravestones, where Thomas handed him a section of the paper.

After a while, they exchanged sections.

Fifteen minutes later, Avriel stood up and handed his section back to Thomas, who folded the paper and stood to join him, and with neither saying a word, they shook hands a second time before Thomas reached into his breast pocket, pulled out a square envelope, and handed it to Avriel, who took it and watched

Thomas walk to his car.

While they had read, Avriel failed to notice the workers filling in Ruth's grave. The grave previously marked by a hole was then marked by a well-shaped rectangular mound of dirt covered with the green sheet.

Entering his home, he locked the door, removed his shoes, and remembering the envelope, he pulled it out of his inside breast pocket and walked into the kitchen to sit down at the table.

He expected a condolence card. The type of card that put into words what the sender couldn't and what Avriel considered just a lot of blah, blah, blah. Was he supposed to put it on a counter with whatever others may follow? Was he supposed to keep it as a souvenir, as a memory of good times? Was it supposed to be the official recording of their concern for him and his wife?

Without bothering with his reading glasses, he opened the envelope to find a simple birthday card with Thomas' signature and a phone number inside it.

The day before, his sixty-fifth birthday had quietly marked his entry into lonely seniorhood.

CHAPTER 12
A Bad Day and a Good Day, All on the Same Day

What's the difference between a Jew hit by a car and a dog hit by a car? There are skid marks leading up to the dog. What's the difference between a Jew and an onion? You cry when you cut up an onion. What do you throw a drowning Jew? His family.

With three days of dark facial growth, he sat on the sofa in his brown bathrobe, reflecting on the rhyme,

Sticks and stones,
Will break my bones,
But words will never hurt me.

He agreed with its logic but disagreed with its simplicity. If the words fall short of their desired effect, then the sticks and stones were sure to follow.

Several times as a youth, he had the words hurled at him, but that morning, he received his first stone, or granite gift as he downplayed it, covered with a piece of paper held on by an elastic band. Some minutes earlier, after forcing himself out of bed and down the stairs, the light reflecting from the shattered glass on the floor caught his eye and he followed its sporadic trail from the broken living room window to the stone near the opposite wall.

In an armchair holding the fist-sized package in both hands, he leaned forward, placed his elbows on his knees, and examined it with a morbid curiosity. It was strange how he felt nothing, not anger or fear, neither sadness nor frustration. He needed to feel something and anger seemed the only emotion close enough to grab, but still, he couldn't reach it. Then gently, as if fearing he would damage the stone, he pulled off the elastic band to remove the piece of paper, and on it was printing so large he could easily read it without the aid of his glasses. *ONE JEW DOWN ONE TO GO.*

After laying the piece of paper on the coffee table and using the stone as a paperweight, he walked into the kitchen, where he grabbed the broom and dustpan, and ten minutes later, he found an almost untouched roll of duct tape and used it to tape up the jagged hole in the bottom of the window. Deciding to tape up the window from the outside too, he pulled the front door open and found the same message spray painted on it.

ONE
JEW
DOWN
ONE
TO
GO

Leaving the door open, Avriel went upstairs to Ruth's sewing room where the pride of finding a red marker in the first place he had looked, the top drawer of her desk, was pushed aside by someone calling out to him from downstairs.

"Hello? Hello, Mr. Rosen?"

The doorbell rang.

"Hello? Mr. Rosen?"

The wave of anxiety covering him was quickly replaced by

frustration. It had been six days since he had isolated himself in the house while refusing to answer the door, and he would've appreciated another six.

"I will be down in a moment," he blurted out loud enough to be heard downstairs.

Gripping the red marker in his fist, he reluctantly descended the stairs to find Mr. Smith nervously standing just outside the entrance with a bandage over his nose and red and blue marks beneath his eyes. Dressed in pressed jeans, a yellow tennis shirt, and sneakers, he had the distinction of being the first neighbor to come to the door besides Lisa, who had come carrying food at least twice a day only to have her knocks ignored. But instead of food, Mr. Smith carried a long object rolled up in a bedsheet.

"Hi, Mr. Rosen. Sorry to bother you, but I've been waiting for you to come home. I saw the writing on your door this morning and brought something I think you should have."

"Just one moment, please," Avriel said as he took the top off the marker and turned his attention to the door where he placed a large comma behind the word *DOWN* and, after the word *GO*, added an underscore with a question mark beneath it as if to ask what should be there, a period, an exclamation point, or a question mark. "That is about correct. Yes, just about correct," he said to no one as he placed the top back on the marker, dropped it into his robe's waist pocket, and then bent down to scoop up the few newspapers that he had let accumulate over the last few days.

Normally, Avriel would've stood inhospitably at the door while his visitor said his piece before being sent on his way, but instead, he surprised himself by saying, "Come in, please. Come into the living room." Leaving the door open, he dropped the papers by his shoes, tightened his robe, and added, "Please leave your shoes on. There could still be glass."

Leading his unexpected guest into the room, he sat on the nearest armchair and motioned for him to sit on the sofa, which he did after quickly scanning the library-like living room.

"Sorry if I caught you at a bad time, sir. I saw the graffiti this morning and figured by your opened door you only just got in."

"Please call me Avriel. I would rather you call me Avriel," he said if only to avoid explaining his behavior over the last few days.

"Ok, and you can call me Rob. It's legally Robert, but no one calls me that, and I don't like the name Bob. It seems like a silly name, being a palindrome," he said before gesturing toward the rock on the coffee table. "I didn't realize he broke your window, too. When I say he, I'm assuming we both know who did this, right?"

"Ok," Avriel said, neither agreeing nor disagreeing.

"Avriel, we know who did this, right?" Mr. Smith asked again. "He even picked up his car sometime last night, so we know he was on the street. It must have been in the early hours of the morning for no one to hear anything."

"I have my suspicions, Rob, but we may never know for sure," Avriel said, unknowingly relaxing by their use of first names.

"Is there anyone else you suspect?"

"No."

"Ok... well, let me say this. Paul Dixon's head isn't screwed on well, and we don't know what he's capable of. I heard from a neighbor he was even screaming for revenge when he was being arrested... so I think you should have this," Mr. Smith said, handing the bedsheet-covered item to Avriel, who took it and immediately recognized its feel. "I've never used it. It was my uncle's and I expect it could use a good cleaning and oiling, but as it is, I'm sure it works fine."

"Mr... uh... Rob, I appreciate the thought, but if a rifle were to help, I would require several around the house. It is not something I could carry around with me. Also, I am not good at aiming."

Avriel wasn't exaggerating. He had only once fired a rifle under duress. It was a long time ago, but the memory was still there.

Amid the blasts of heavy artillery and cracks of gunfire, Avriel had been crouching down in a foxhole's growing pool of water when between the almost deafening sounds, a cry came from a wounded soldier. Reacting to the call as he was conditioned, the medic fought with the muddy sides as he struggled to climb his way out and make his way in the distress's direction. Reaching the soldier, Avriel was quickly snipping away at the man's clothes to locate the wound in his stomach when out of the corner of his eye, he saw mud splash up. After it happened a second and third time, getting nearer each time, a bullet hit the soldier's side, causing him to scream again, and a second piercing the side of his helmet silenced him. With the man beyond help, Avriel threw himself into the closest crater, where a corpse cushioned his fall. Trying to roll off the dead soldier, a pain in his right calf stopped him, and assuming he'd been shot, he was surprised he didn't feel the initial bite of the bullet. Then trying again to roll off the corpse, his calf's scream drew his attention to the bayonet blade sticking out from the bottom of his pant leg, and without the concern he should've had for the wound, he slid his calf from it. As he crouched down in the hole, he ignored the pain as he popped his head up several times to locate the shooter, whose smoking barrel gave away his position as he took shots at the medic's head. The lone German soldier, who had somehow gotten behind the British and was shielding himself behind a large boulder only a grenade throw away, was making it his mission to kill the medic.

With his pistol in hand, Avriel wiped the rain from his eyes and anxiously returned fire until it was empty. Throwing it aside, he grabbed the corpse's rifle, and after checking it for ammunition, returned more fire until it too was empty. Again crouching down in the hole, he was considering how long he might be forced to stay there when his frustration sparked an idea, and purposely avoiding looking at the face of the dead soldier, he unclipped a grenade from its uniform and, in his excitement, prematurely pulled its pin and released its lever. "Bloody hell!" Popping up, he threw the time bomb, but maybe too far, and when he popped up to confirm his failed attempt, expecting the grenade to explode harmlessly behind the soldier, it exploded above him, killing him.

A sudden joy overcame him, a pure joy that made him yell, "Yes!" He wanted to shout to his mates, to brag, to dance, and then the reality hit him and he lay defeated in the muddy water with his back against the wall of the crater. He had just killed a man who was certainly a son. Two parents would mourn for him. And if he had brothers, sisters, nieces, and nephews, and his grandparents were still living, there would be many more mourners. What if he was close to his aunts, uncles, and cousins? That would be even more. And what if, to Avriel's horror, the soldier had a wife and children? There would be several more broken-hearted mourners. Avriel might've just shattered the lives of dozens of people, and with him having maybe a dozen mourners, being the lighter of the two on the mourner scale, it should've been him to die.

Unable to differentiate the rain from the tears in his eyes, Avriel looked at the wet face of the corpse beside him and recognized it as it stared back... and blinked. It was his mate, Ronald. He was alive but seemingly unable to move.

Avriel handed the rifle back to Mr. Smith. "But I could use a grenade."

"Yeah... I can't help you there," said Mr. Smith, who took it and bent down to place it gently on the floor beside him. "If you change your mind, just let me know." Then, after both men sat awkwardly silent for a moment, he said, "I... I have to say I'm sorry to hear about your wife. Lisa told me what happened when we were moving Paul's boxes of stuff to his car. Last Friday... at the hospital, I had no idea it was so serious. I feel pretty bad for leaving you there alone. If I had known, I certainly would've stayed."

"Would you like anything to drink?" Avriel asked, trying to change the subject.

"No, thanks," the man said, shaking his head. "I don't know if you know this, but I lost my wife three years ago."

With the disclosure moving Avriel, Curiosity took over and he said, "No... I am sorry... I–I never knew that... and if you... you do not mind me asking, how long did it take for you to accept it and move on?"

"I still haven't accepted it... not fully anyway, but I had to move on. I had no choice. I found... and find things to distract me... and it's easy to distract yourself when you have a three-month-old and a three-year-old. Of course, they're three and six now, but I'm reminded of Becky every time our little girl smiles," Mr. Smith said before clearing his throat and asking, "Avriel, do you have a hobby?"

"No... no, but I shall have to find one. I always wanted to learn how to build a ship in a bottle, but those bottles are so small that I may have to start slow and find one maybe six feet high for my first try," Avriel joked in his deadpan manner, trying to lighten the conversation.

Mr. Smith chuckled, and then abruptly stopped as if suddenly realizing the old man was serious.

"And placing a bottle that size on a shelf could be a problem, too."

Mr. Smith chuckled again. "Yes, it could be."

Then an idea came to Avriel, and he went with it. "I am considering finding a guard dog. If anything, I would not be alone in the house."

"A guard dog? They can be pretty vicious. I guess they're meant to be, but I'm not sure that would be a good thing for the street... a residential street like Gilmore, I mean."

"Right... right, I am sure you are correct. Perhaps a dog that only barks when it hears strange noises at night."

Avriel's neighbor smiled. "That's a better idea, but no offense. I've heard your snoring from the street, and it could just make a dog like that bark all night." With Avriel slightly blushing, Mr. Smith dropped his smile. "Maybe you should give it some more thought. I know when Becky passed, I had some pretty impulsive thoughts that seemed normal at the time, but looking back, were quite out of character, to say the least. I considered going somewhere... someplace like the Australian Outback, just to be alone. Imagine, a father of two considering going somewhere alone, considering only himself. It was crazy, and, thankfully, those thoughts are gone now," Mr. Smith said, and then bringing the conversation back to the reason for his being there, asked, "Avriel, would you agree that you... we should at least call the police and report this?"

"No, I believe I should let it go. I am sure Mr. Dixon, if that is who has done this, will cool down sometime."

"Avriel, it's been several days since his blow-up, and according to the rock and the spray painting, there's been little, if any, change in his temper. If we report it and if he did this, it could end this whole thing now."

"I suppose it could."

"Great. Where's your phone? I'll call and wait with you."

"Right... thank you. It's in the kitchen at the end of the longer section of counter," Avriel said, feeling pushed into action but comfortable with his visitor taking charge.

Mr. Smith made the phone call, and afterward, both sat down at the kitchen table where he took Avriel up on his earlier offer of a drink by asking for a cup of coffee, which Avriel made for the first time and it showed. Not sure how many grinds to use, he used nearly twice what was required, causing some to enter the pot of very strong coffee.

Without asking how he took his coffee, Avriel gave his guest and himself black and sat back down at the table.

Taking a sip, Mr. Smith's eyes enlarged slightly before he set the cup down to never pick it up again, and after using his tongue to wipe the grinds from his teeth, he said, "So, you're... you're Jewish?"

"Yes... yes, that is correct."

"That's interesting. You're the first Jew I've met, that I know of. I only guessed by the candles in your windows last winter. Those are for hun... hun—"

"Hanukkah. Yes, we light a candle or, in our case, screw in a bulb for each day."

"Right. You folks have gone through a lot of bad times... and overcome them."

"I suppose they... we have."

Then, with both staring down at the table for a moment, Mr. Smith asked. "So, what is it you do for a living?"

"I am retired." It felt strange to say it, so he added, "I am a pharmacist and owned a chain of pharmacies called Rose Sons."

Surprised, Mr. Smith smiled and said, "Really? I often went to the one at the Simpson's Shopping Center. It's too bad for me, I didn't know you sooner. I would've liked the friend's discount." Then he told Avriel about his job as an air traffic controller. He worked three twelve-hour days in a row and was off for four, which made it easier to be a single parent since it only required his or his late wife's parents to watch his children for the few hours outside of daycare those three days a week, and after sharing some humorous anecdotes about his job that made Avriel glad to have never taken a plane, he asked Avriel how he had started his chain of drugstores.

Preferring to be a listener rather than a talker, Avriel only said, "It is a long story, too long... and... much too boring," and then asked about Mr. Smith's children.

Mr. Smith talked for close to thirty minutes before the police arrived and disappointed both: Mr. Smith was enjoying talking about his two children, and Avriel was appreciating the distraction.

With the graffiti on the opened door hinting at the situation, Avriel and Mr. Smith greeted the two police officers, who were the same two who had arrested Paul, though neither Avriel nor Mr. Smith knew it, and after Avriel brought them into the living room and nervously went through the details of what he had found that morning, with Mr. Smith suggesting Mr. Dixon was the guilty party, one officer frowned and said, "Let me be upfront with you. With no substantial evidence like a witness, there's little we can do. We can always question Mr. Dixon about it, and we'll do that, but unless he admits to it, little will come out of it, except, hopefully, for him to take it as a warning and back off." And when the second officer reminded them they could still place assault charges against Mr. Dixon, Avriel declined, explaining it could hurt Mrs. Dixon financially if Mr. Dixon was to lose his job over the matter, and hearing Avriel's reasoning, Mr. Smith also declined.

As the officers' car pulled away, Mr. Smith went to pick up the bedsheet-wrapped rifle, and when he returned, said, "Well, I best be leaving you to shower and change."

"Right... and thank you again for the thought," Avriel said as he shook his neighbor's hand.

"It's no problem. Like I said, if you change your mind, just let me know. Hey, I'm off for the next couple of days and the kids are on a weeklong road trip with Becky's parents. So, Avriel, don't hesitate to come to me for anything, even just to talk," he said, and just as he was about to leave, he stopped and turned around. "You know, sometimes people say that sort of thing just to say it, but I mean it. Come over whenever you want."

Avriel nodded and said only, "Right."

"Well, hang in there."

After nodding again, he watched Mr. Smith jog across the street to his house, and just as Avriel was about to enter his, someone called his name, almost sang it. Looking in the voice's direction, he saw Lisa and Dewey walking down the sidewalk toward his house from the direction of Herring Cove Road and he had to fight the urge to run and hide. Besides not wanting them to see him in his bathrobe, he didn't want to explain his perceived absence over the last several days or that morning's discoveries.

Lisa, in a knee-length pink skirt, white blouse, and white running shoes with her large purse over one shoulder, was carrying two plastic grocery bags in one hand and holding Dewey's hand in the other, and as they got closer, Dewey's black shorts revealed what had previously been scabbed knees as then being only pale blotches, and the darker tan on his face accentuated the pale blotches on his forehead and cheek, making them look like reversed birthmarks.

Hoping to block the graffiti, Avriel positioned himself in front of the opened door as they made their way onto his porch. "Hello, Dewey, Lisa."

"Hi, Avriel!" Dewey said, waving his liberated and conspicuously white right forearm as he invited himself into Avriel's home.

"Hi, Avriel," Lisa said before whispering, "I'm so sorry about your door," and then looking past him at it, asked, "Did you really correct the punctuation?"

"All is good. The... the squirrels and I are getting along poorly, almost as poorly as their grammar," Avriel whispered back as he closed the door behind his second and third visitors of the morning.

While Avriel cleared the full cups of cold coffee from the table and grabbed two clean ones from the cupboard, Lisa placed her bags of groceries on the kitchen counter and took what was Ruth's seat, and when Dewey sat down across from her, he immediately stood up to find the source of the discomfort. Sitting back down, he moved his bottom to the left side of the seat.

As Avriel poured the coffee, Dewey waved his right arm a second time and asked with a large grin, "Avriel, do you notice anything different? Huh, do ya?"

Turning around, the old man took a second before saying, "Yes. You got a haircut."

Lisa smiled.

"No! Uh... yes, but that's not what I'm talking about!"

"You lost twenty pounds?"

Dewey huffed. "No! Seriously? Well, I guess I lost a couple of pounds because I GOT MY CAST OFF!" he yelled, waving his arm again.

"My, so you did, so you did," he said with a genuine smile.

Then Lisa startled the old man when she gave in to the urge and stood up to put her arms around him, giving him a strong hug. Releasing him, she whispered, "How are you holding up?"

Uncomfortable with the touching and concern, but strangely appreciating it, he downplayed the situation by whispering, "Fine. It will take some adjustment... much adjustment."

Confused by their whispering, it suddenly occurred to Dewey that Mrs. Rosen wasn't there and why, and he was ashamed of himself for forgetting.

After setting the two cups of black coffee down on the table, Avriel poured Dewey a glass of lemonade and joined them at the table, taking for the first time a seat other than his scratched-up one. "When did you have it removed?"

"This morning. We could've kept the cast, but Mommy said it stunk too much. It did. It stunk bad," Dewey said, with none of the excitement he had shown a minute earlier.

"Oh, I see. It is probably a good thing you left it there. You wouldn't want the neighbors complaining about it stinking up the street."

Dewey grinned and said, "Then you should shower before they

complain about you, too."

As Lisa tried to hide her grin by dropping her head toward the table, Avriel cracked a slight smile and said to her. "From the mouth of babes, no?"

Still grinning, she looked up and nodded.

Placing the cup to his lips, Avriel caught some grinds in his teeth before noticing the coffee's much stronger taste, and he was about to warn Lisa not to drink hers when Dewey said, "We saw Mrs. Rosen's grave yesterday."

Lisa lost her grin. "Uh... yes, I got a hold of the synagogue, and Rabbi Lavigne, if I remember his name correctly, let us know where she was buried. It's a beautiful place. I think she'd be very happy with your choice."

"Thank you, but it was her choice," Avriel said, both surprised and impressed by the disclosure.

Taking a sip of her coffee, a surprised Lisa forced herself to swallow what was in her mouth and teeth and set the cup back down on the table. "Avriel, have... have you eaten breakfast yet?"

"Uh... no. No, not yet."

"Then you go shower and dress and I'll make breakfast," she said in a way that wasn't too pushy but left little room for argument.

After Avriel bashfully nodded, he left the two at the table and discreetly picked up the *package* in the living room to bring upstairs it with him.

The first thing Lisa did was make a fresh pot of coffee. After going through several cupboards, she found the coffee grinds, and while scooping them out into the paper coffee filter, it struck her as strange that there was little in the cupboards other than cereal, oatmeal, spices, sugar and a few cans of soup. Out of concern, she looked in the fridge and found only an almost empty glass jug of lemonade, some butter, a couple of bottles of partially used jams and condiments, and something that resembled soup. In the freezer, there was some hamburger, about a pound of fish, a brick of vanilla ice cream, and two empty ice cube trays. She assumed Avriel had been eating takeout, but when she checked the garbage bin to confirm it, it was half-full and had an empty liquor bottle and several shards of glass resting on top of empty boxes of crackers, cookies, and oatmeal. There was nothing resembling takeout containers.

Taking out the groceries she had purchased that morning, she placed them in Avriel's fridge and cupboard, and to Dewey's delight, she gave him ten dollars and for the first time in his short life, sent him to pick up eggs, milk, bread, and bacon from the store at the corner of Gilmore and Herring Cove Road.

When the fresh pot of coffee had finished brewing and so as not to bring attention to it and possibly embarrass Avriel, she poured some into the sink so the remaining amount reflected the previous quantity of much stronger coffee.

Showered, shaved, and in his black dress pants and a white dress shirt, Avriel struggled to control the anxiety he had been conditioned to connect with the smell of bacon and had to stop halfway down the stairs to take a few seconds to collect himself.

In the kitchen, the bacon was warming in one frying pan and from another Lisa was sliding fried eggs onto three plates. Adding the bacon and toast, she placed the plates on the table with fresh cups of coffee for her and Avriel, and a glass of milk for Dewey.

As Avriel stared at his plate while nervously picking at his first proper breakfast in a week and the Dixons ate their second breakfast of the day, Dewey broke the silence by proclaiming his triumph in going to the store for the first time.

Genuinely impressed, Avriel recognized it as being quite the accomplishment, and after taking a sip of his coffee and noticing it tasted better, he figured Lisa must have known how to fix his poor attempt. Then strangely more relaxed, he began eating at his usual speed while wondering why he was much more comfortable than he would've expected to be. He had only known the Dixons for a few weeks and yet they seemed very familiar, a comfortable familiar. Perhaps it was because of the time they had spent together until that moment. Perhaps it was because they were together during the recent drama in their lives, or perhaps it was both, but whatever the reason, he decided not to overthink it.

Finished eating and not sure what to say, the adults were quietly having a second cup of coffee when Dewey asked, "So, Avriel, what're you doing today?"

With his shell half down, Avriel surprised himself by saying, "I am considering getting a dog."

Jumping to his feet, Dewey asked, "Can I go with him, Mommy? Can I?"

"You'll have to ask Avriel."

"Ok. Can I go with you? Can I?"

Avriel broke a slight smile before admitting, "Well... I would appreciate the company of the two of you. I know nothing about dogs and you could both help me in my decision if you are up for it."

At Lisa's suggestion, and with Dewey sitting between the two, they were soon on their way to the SPCA.

"So what kind of dog do you want? A big one, a small one, or a medium one?"

"Dewey, I have no idea."

"There are those large furry ones. The coli ones like Lassie."

"Perhaps."

"And there are those small ones, the tiny ones. They aren't furry or anything, but they bark a lot and attack your toes. No, you don't want those," he said, shaking his head. "They look like long-legged rats."

Smiling at the description that sounded like something his wife would say, Avriel said, "I expect you are right. We will avoid those."

"Then there are the Krout Shepherds. But those can be scary mean."

"By Krout, do you mean—"

Dewey laughed. "Yes, German Shepherds. I just said that to see what you'd say! Oh, yeah—"

"Oh, yes," his mother corrected him.

"Oh, yes, there's the Benji kind too! I don't know what they're called, but they're small, shaggy, and very, very smart. The kind Benji is from the movie *Benji*. Yeah! Yes! You should get that kind! Did I say they were really, really smart?"

"Yes, you did, and I like smart dogs. Maybe it could help me with my crosswords."

After Dewey and Lisa laughed, Dewey said, "I don't think they're that smart, but he can fetch your slippers and newspapers and tell you things with gestures."

"Great, we will get the small, shaggy, and really, really smart kind of dog that gestures."

"Seriously?"

"Seriously."

"That's so great! Then we'll have to name him Benji, too!"

"Then it is decided. We will get the Benji kind and name it Benji."

Satisfied, Dewey was quiet the rest of the drive as he imagined what he and the little dog would do together.

At the animal shelter, the three met a slim young man in his early twenties slouching behind the counter looking like he would rather be somewhere else.

"What can I do for you?" he asked with disinterest.

"Hello. We are looking for a dog," Avriel said.

"The Benji kind!" Dewey added. "The kind from the movie Benji!"

Failing to conceal his frustration, the young man said, "Nope, don't have that one, and it's a mutt, not a breed."

Placing his large hand on the small shoulder of his disappointed friend, Avriel said, "Then we will have to see what you have."

"Ok, come this way," the man said, leading them through a door and down a hall. "The dogs are down the end of this hall, to the right. We keep the cats to the left for obvious reasons."

They were about to turn right when Avriel thought he heard Ruth's voice in his head. *Av, a dog?* Then suddenly stopping, the others stopped with him, and the SPCA worker looked as if he expected the old man to ask where he was and who they were. "I am thinking that perhaps I should start small... with a cat," he said, feeling stupid for being so indecisive and expecting the young man to tell him there is a world of difference between a dog and a cat, much like there is between a car and a truck, and that people were set on one or the other before arriving there.

With an expression that asked if the old man should be taken seriously or just patronized, the young man looked for a sign from Lisa, and not seeing one, he asked impatiently, "A cat or a kitten?"

"A kitten," Avriel replied, though he wasn't certain of that either, but hoped he would be once he saw the selection.

Dewey was further disappointed; he didn't know what a person could do with a cat. He only saw them on the street and they were never as interested in him as most of the dogs he came across were.

The worker led the three to the left, where along two opposing walls were three levels of shelves holding large metal cages containing a single cat or several kittens, water, and a litter tray, and then, after telling them to take their time selecting a kitten and that he would return shortly, he left.

With Dewey ahead of them, bouncing between the cats and

kittens on both sides, Lisa walked with Avriel as he looked at several kittens hoping one would jump out at him, but not literally, and when an orange tabby alone in a cage halfway down the room caught his eye, he stuck his index finger through the metal wire and watched the kitten cautiously approach, smell the finger, and then bite it. Quickly pulling his stinging finger back, the kitten skirted backward to slam against the back of the cage, and then feeling bad for causing its fright, Avriel again put his finger through the wire, and when the kitten cautiously approached again, instead of biting it, it licked it and purred.

"I think he's apologizing to you," Lisa smiled while putting her hand on his shoulder.

"You know, I believe he is," he nodded, and then feeling certain of his choice and with a rare excitement, he yelled out, "Sir, we found one! Sir?" Embarrassed, he looked at Lisa with a smile covering her face, raised his dark, bushy eyebrows, and said, "He already believes I am crazy."

"Who?" Dewey asked, drawn back by Avriel's yell.

"Nobody," answered Lisa.

"And everybody," added Avriel, who surprised Dewey by picking him up under his armpits for a better view of the kitten.

The man soon returned, apparently offended that he was shouted to, and after Avriel pointed out the kitten, he impatiently fiddled with the cage's latch and roughly scooped it out with one hand so its four legs hung down in a pathetically submissive posture. With a warning that he would have to keep a good hold on it, he handed the small animal to an excited Dewey, who held it securely to his chest as it began purring so loud everyone could easily hear it, making Avriel more confident with his choice.

After a late lunch with Lisa and Dewey at A&W, his first time there and his first time being served in a car, Avriel arrived back to his empty home with a content Sam (the name Dewey and he had agreed upon) in his arm and three plastic bags in his hand. Setting Sam on the floor, he carried the bags into the kitchen and pulled out from them a litter box, fresh litter, a cat toy, and several simple groceries.

The day had started badly but ended well. His first day out of the house without Ruth had gone better than he would've expected, but that was only because of the company he had with him. He liked Lisa and Dewey, not because his wife did, but because he did. He had enjoyed their company and appreciated that Lisa never brought up Ruth's funeral, never questioned where he was over the last few days, and didn't go on about the graffiti, and he appreciated that she and Dewey had visited Ruth. Then with newfound motivation, he decided that the next morning he would use the green fence paint to cover over the door's graffiti and he would call the glass replacement people, whoever they were.

Later that evening, Sam's jumping onto his lap woke him to the smell of Ruth's perfume mixed with the smell of a burning Swanson TV Dinner. Sniffing the air to confirm the perfume's presence, he failed to notice it again, and as the kitten curled up on his lap, he worried he could be going crazy and then a moment later decided not to worry about it. If he were crazy, he may never know it and to boot, he had read or heard somewhere that most crazy people were happy beyond normal levels.

Then, as the kitten's purring relaxed him, he realized the burning smell wasn't in his head and jumped to his feet, launching the startled kitten across the living room.

CHAPTER 13
Friends Helping Friends

Lisa was in a bad situation. She couldn't count on Paul for financial support and the savings she had pulled out from their joint account the week before wouldn't last more than two months. She had to find a job quickly, and on the Monday after Paul's arrest, she had gone through the employment section of the paper, but there were few opportunities. Most of the jobs required a high school diploma, experience, or both, but refusing to give in to the initial discouragement, that Tuesday and Wednesday and with Dewey in tow, she visited several businesses to fill out job applications. It was hardly a positive experience. At least a few people, recognizing she had a child with her, gave her an application just to humor her. Some even tossed her sympathetic smiles, silently telling her they were guilty of wasting her time.

**

Being both a laundry room and a storage room for extra furniture and other items, there was never a reason for him to be down there, but now that he was, the hanging light bulb inadequately illuminating the unfinished basement and the morning's rays coming through its two small windows failing to help brighten the space made him wish he wasn't

As the light bulb swung from its recent contact with his head, animating his shadow across the washer and dryer, Avriel stood holding a full laundry basket while staring stupidly at the washing machine's overbearing dial that was almost screaming at him. He felt helpless, and more so when he noticed Sam standing by his feet, purring and looking up at him as if to ask, "Do you know what you're doing?" He didn't know what he was doing. He didn't know which settings to use on the wash cycle: gentle, regular, or extended, and he didn't know which water to choose: hot, warm, cold, or the several combinations of them. He considered using the settings Ruth had last used: hot and cold, and regular cycle. *Hot and cold? Would that not be warm?* Hot water would certainly clean everything, but it could harm clothes of certain materials; otherwise, why offer the other combinations? And was the regular cycle good for everything or just most things? There must be a reason for those other settings, too. And what's the difference between regular and delicate clothing?

He didn't care so much about damaging his clothing as he did about his wife's. What would it matter if he destroyed some of his many almost identical clothes?

But he wasn't a complete idiot. Without knowing why they were or even what it was, he knew to dry-clean his suits, dress pants, and Ruth's dresses, which she had always kept separate from the laundry, but washing clothes was a different beast, and he was surprised that from a distance, the machines looked simple enough, but up close, their complexities were revealed.

Then, as he was considering taking the fellow widower across the street up on his offer from the day before, he appreciated the doorbell's ring.

Setting the basket on the washer, he went upstairs and opened the front door to find a teary-eyed Lisa holding what looked like a thick extra-large pizza box with another much smaller box on top, both covered in wrapping paper.

"Avriel... I'm... I'm so sorry! I-I forgot your birthday! Ruth asked me to hold your gift at my place... and with... with everything going on, I completely forgot about it."

"Lisa, there is no reason to be upset over such a truly trivial thing," Avriel said as he took the packages out of her hands and moved to the side so she could enter. "All is fine. I had even forgotten myself. At my age, a birthday is rather a negative thing. They should probably have the age count backward after forty... or somewhere after thirty."

As Lisa smiled through her sad face and wiped an eye with her fingertips, he set the boxes down on top of the small pile of newspapers beside the door and found himself engulfed in her arms. As he automatically tensed up, she said, "Well... happy belated birthday, Avriel."

"Right... thank you."

Releasing him, she added, "You have to get used to my hugs. They're free and I got lots of them."

"Right... and since... since you are here, I could use your help. I have to admit I know nothing regarding the washing of clothes and am rather embarrassed that I never considered all that Ruthy did."

Lisa was happy to help and seeing it as a chance to redeem herself, she followed him down into the basement, where she gave her older friend a quick lesson on using the washer and dryer, telling him, depending on what sort of clothes he was washing and drying, which settings to use, but after explaining what the symbols on the tags of the clothing meant and seeing the confusion on his face when he realized doing the laundry required reading glasses, she suggested they do theirs together that afternoon at her place, and he accepted. He would learn better by being shown rather than by being told.

"Ok, so we'll say around three?"

"That would be fine. And afterward, I would like to take you two out to dinner as a thank you."

"You don't have to thank me... and I already have a... a casserole prepared. Why not join us for dinner at my place? We can have it while the clothes go through the washer and dryer."

"Right, let's do that."

"But maybe we should make it four," Lisa said, giving herself enough time to prepare the casserole.

"Then four it is."

Later, while searching for something to do, Avriel would muster the courage to open the two gifts to find another black suit from his wife and a silver tie clip from Lisa and Dewey.

Almost at exactly four, Avriel, with his reading glasses in his shirt pocket, showed up at the Dixons' house with the full laundry basket in his arms.

After Dewey answered the door and the two greeted each other, the boy reached into the basket, grabbed the purring furry bundle, and ran off with it.

"Oi, come back here with that. It has to go in the wash, too."

Laughing, Lisa met him at the door. "First lesson, anything with fur should be dry-cleaned. Tsk, tsk, there's so much to teach you. Ok, let's take that downstairs now and we'll get started," she said, taking the basket from him and leading him into the house and to the hall where she demonstrated her motherly skill of opening the door to the basement with her hands full.

As he followed her down the bare wooden stairs to the unfinished basement that was as large as his but with more available space, he noticed it was brighter than his and didn't have its musty smell, and after watching her empty the hamper onto a long homemade wooden table standing next to the laundry machines, she explained why she was separating his clothes into several piles before mixing her small amount of laundry in with his.

Avriel had blushed when Lisa handled his unmentionables, and he blushed again when he saw hers added to the piles, and he blushed yet again when he realized by her small amount of laundry that she was only doing hers for his benefit. But lucky for him, she was too busy to notice his dark-red complexion because if she did, he would've blushed more... and then blushed even more because of his blushing. Avriel hated how blushing had that strange domino effect.

While the two did their laundry, Dewey and Sam played together, taking a break only when Lisa called up to her son to tell him to go next door to get Sam's food dish and litter box, and Avriel gave him incentive when he told him where he could find the cat toys.

As the casserole cooked in the oven and the piles of laundry took their turns with the washer and dryer, Avriel and Lisa sat in the living room talking over coffee, or more accurately, she talked and he listened. She talked about her recent job search and what she would like to do rather than what she was qualified to do, whispered about her concerns regarding Dewey's future relationship with his father, and talked about Dewey soon starting school and his excitement with being around children his age again. She had mentioned Ruth but changed the subject when Avriel suddenly looked uncomfortable, and she changed the subject again after asking about his retirement plans.

All the while Lisa talked, Dewey and Sam played. Initially, they played behind the sofa with a cat toy, and after becoming bored with that, they chased each other around the house, with Sam sometimes jumping onto Avriel or Lisa's lap to use them as platforms to jump at Dewey.

About an hour into her talking, she received a phone call, and Avriel tried not to eavesdrop, but sitting in the living room with her while she was on the phone made it difficult not to, and with only hearing her side of the conversation, he could still guess the reason for the call.

When she hung up the phone, a huge smile covered her face and through excitedly fast talking that would've put the old man off if he had just met her, she explained the reason for the phone call, confirming he had guessed correctly. She had received a call for a job interview.

Then, telling him she had to call Rob Smith, it took her three times through her excitement before she could dial his number correctly. "Darn, he's not home," she said aloud to herself. "Uh... Avriel, if you're free tomorrow afternoon, would... would you be up for babysitting Dewey for a couple of hours?"

"Babysit! I'm not a baby!" Dewey protested.

Avriel cracked a smile at the boy's protest. "I would like that. I enjoy spending time with the munchkin."

"Munchkin!?" Dewey protested again.

Avriel broke a full smile. "Right. Little person then," he said, causing Dewey to huff.

"Are you sure you don't mind?"

"Yes. I tend to enjoy his company, especially now with too much time on my hands. What do you think, Munch... little person?"

Dewey grinned. "Sure, giant... uh... tall person."

"And the next time you need to do your laundry, I'll do it for you."

"That sounds fine, but I believe I am coming out ahead in the trade."

The following day, Saturday, Lisa left Dewey with Avriel to take the bus to her job interview.

Earlier, Avriel had offered to drive her, but she declined since the bus ride would allow her time to prepare herself mentally for the interview. Also, the drive would've been only for her benefit, going against her new independence that she was unwilling to compromise.

Twenty minutes after she left and with Sam protesting from behind the Dixons' closed door, Avriel took his little friend to the toy store on Spring Garden Road. There were closer stores, but since he had already been to that one twice, he was more comfortable there.

Standing in the aisle of board games, Avriel asked Dewey, "Have you ever played Mouse Trap?"

"Nope, but I'd like to. I've seen the commercials on TV and it looks like lots of fun."

After Avriel picked up the game, Dewey dragged him to another section of the store. "There's the G.I. Joes I told you about!" he said, pointing to the boxes of action figures just beyond his reach. "And look way up there at all the stuff for them! See the helicopter! And there's the space capsule! Those giant boxes over there are the headquarters!"

"That is much stuff," Avriel nodded.

"Can you tell me how much the men are? I got to figure out what I can get with my savings."

"Right. They all seem to be six dollars and ninety-nine cents."

"What about the clothes over there?"

"One dollar and ninety-nine cents," Avriel said as he shuffled through the thin boxes. "They look to be all the same price, too."

"And the helicopter up there? How much is that?"

"That is... that is twenty-nine dollars and ninety-nine cents," the old man replied, who then looked at the tank's box, the box of the space capsule, and the one containing the headquarters. "I believe that is the least expensive of them."

"Wow! That's a lot!"

Then Avriel surprised Dewey when he asked which 'fella' he should buy for himself, and he surprised him again at the checkout counter by adding to the board game and his redheaded G.I. Joe action figure, a scuba diving outfit for Dewey's G.I. Joe at home.

Later, Dewey would figure out that he had saved enough money for three more action figures or ten sets of clothes, or some combination of both. He didn't yet understand the concept of sales tax and would be disappointed when he did.

As the two sat at the kitchen table engaged in their second game of Mouse Trap while a bored Sam slept on the floor, Lisa arrived home carrying a plastic bag and a large paper one. Setting the paper bag on the kitchen counter, she greeted the two with a smile that seemed to take up her entire face, before saying, "Tah-dah!" and pulling out from the plastic bag a one-piece outfit that looked like something between a straight dress and a smock. After holding the uniform up for them to see, she threw it aside, gave each a hug, and announced they were celebrating her new job with Chinese food.

Avriel and Dewey quickly cleared the game from the kitchen table and while Lisa and Dewey got the plates, cutlery, and drinks, Avriel apprehensively removed the assortment of containers from the paper bag, and during the meal, which Avriel was surprised to find he enjoyed, she talked about what her new job involved as a cashier at Gary's Groceries, a mile further down Herring Cove Road. She was excited about the job and, at the same time, nervous. She would have full-time hours spread out over weekdays, evenings, and some Saturday shifts, and for the first two weeks, she would train with the head cashier whom she had met and felt wasn't very friendly.

Seeing it as an opportunity to help, Avriel didn't ask to be the regular babysitter but surprised Lisa, Dewey, and even himself by implying he would be. As bits of food escaped his mouth, he forced out that the hours were great since he would have a little friend to do things with more often, and when he asked Dewey what he thought, the boy purposely put more food in his mouth before energetically agreeing and with bits of food escaping with his words, listing off things they could do together. And Lisa made sure she also had a mouth full of food when she interrupted her son to say, almost incoherently, that it would be a big help but she would have to pay him. Getting the hint, Avriel made sure to swallow what was in his mouth before saying, "I will only accept payment in the form of meals. I will be working for food."

CHAPTER 14
Out with the New and in with the Old

It wasn't long after Avriel and Dewey began hanging out (the term they settled on to replace *babysitting*) when the pranks began, and they started with Dewey's fondness for wearing the same socks for several days.

"They feel better than a fresh pair, and if they don't smell, why not?"

"I believe smell is rather subjective and if you are not careful, the neighbors may start complaining," Avriel replied, and when he asked the boy, he was relieved to hear he didn't hold the same fondness for his underwear.

Then the next morning, after his mother had left for her day shift, Dewey was getting dressed for school when he put on the previous day's socks and was surprised by a cold, creamy sensation on his toes. Earlier that morning, while the boy slept, Avriel had snuck into his room, grabbed the pair of socks on the floor, rolled them back, and released shaving cream into each. Dewey wasn't impressed but thought it would've been funny if it happened to someone else.

That following Saturday, as the two watched television, Dewey offered to make them each a baloney and mustard sandwich for lunch, and after Dewey had finished his sandwich and Avriel was halfway through his, the boy asked him to look inside it. Fearful, the old man pulled a piece of bread away and found the only baloney in the sandwich was hanging out around the edges. With most of the slice of boloney's center cut out, it was pretty much just a mustard sandwich. Saying nothing, Avriel gave a thumbs-up and continued eating as if there was nothing wrong, making Dewey believe he had mixed up the sandwiches.

The next morning, as Dewey slept in while his mother left for work, Avriel made bacon and eggs, and as the smell of burning bacon filled the house, Dewey woke and rushed out to sit at the kitchen table in his pajamas.

"Have you brushed your teeth and washed your face?" Avriel asked as he used a fork to scoop the bacon from the grease-spitting frying pan.

"Yup! I'm ready to eat!"

Avriel looked over at the boy and smiled. "No, you have not. Now to the bathroom, you go."

Wondering how his old friend would've known, Dewey huffed and made his way to the bathroom, where he pulled out his small wooden platform from beside the sink, stood on it, adjusted the taps for warm water, and lathered up his hands. Then looking into the mirror, he roared with laughter.

Earlier that morning, Avriel had discovered Lisa's eyeliner pencil lying out, and while Dewey slept soundly, he gently drew a mustache on him.

That evening, as Avriel was leaving the Dixons' home, he discovered his shoelaces had been reversed and tied at the bottom. Impressed by the boy's effort, he struggled to loosen them and put them on.

"Avriel, do you notice anything wrong with your shoes?" Dewey asked, grinning.

"No," he replied, and with Sam in his arms and Dewey

confused, he left the house.

He kept the laces as they were for several days, until one evening, when he was leaving the Dixons' house, Lisa noticed his laces and laughed. "Avriel, I think I'll have to have Dewey teach you how to lace your shoes."

"Why? What is wrong with them?" he asked with raised eyebrows, confusing Lisa and causing Dewey to laugh so hard he almost peed himself.

Fearing a worse prank to come, Dewey made it difficult for Avriel to pull one on him. For the next week, he slept with his door closed and his half-full piggybank on the floor a few inches away from it, and throughout the days, he was careful to check everything, sometimes twice, before wearing it or putting it in his mouth.

Then one morning, after Lisa had gone to work, the noise from the bedroom door hitting the piggy bank woke him, and sitting up in his bed, he yelled, "Ah-ha! Caught you!"

Standing at the door with worry on his face, Avriel said, "Sorry, no prank here. I need you to get up and get ready for school quickly. I lost track of time and we are going to be late."

Dewey sleepily washed up, brushed his teeth, and dressed, and after Avriel grabbed his schoolbag, he ate his buttered toast on the walk to Herring Cove Road. Crossing the unusually quiet street, they walked about three-quarters the way up the Cowie Hill subdivision to stop where Lisa felt he could walk the last five minutes safely without the embarrassment of being seen with an adult escort.

After Dewey took his school bag from Avriel and left him to walk the rest of the hill by himself, the aged babysitter normally would have left for home, but that morning after seeing the little boy disappear over the hill, he stayed where he was, and about fifteen minutes later, saw Dewey slowly walking back and when he was within hearing distance, asked, "Was there a problem?"

"I guess! Today's Saturday!" the frustrated boy exclaimed.

"Really? You do not say?"

"Yes, I say! The janitor told me so when I was waiting outside!"

"I guess he cleans on Saturdays. Lucky for you, or you may have been waiting there all day. What can I say? You know I am rather old, correct?"

"That was funny! Ha, ha, ha. See, I'm laughing!" Dewey said as he passed him. "Ok, I surrender!"

"Surrendering makes it sound as if there is a winner. Maybe we should just call it a ceasefire?" Avriel said as he joined the boy

"Then I ceasefire!"

Reaching Herring Cove Road, Avriel broke their silence by saying, "You know when I was your age, we had school eight days a week. That is probably where I was confused. And we had to walk uphill both ways in two feet of snow every day during the winter. We also had to do it barefoot since boots had not been invented then. Now in the summer, we had to swim uphill both ways. I remember that well. We only had two seasons back then, with no gradual change between them. You munch... kids have it pretty good these days. The world did not even have color back then. It was only invented in the last ten years or so. That is why all the old pictures are in black and white."

Dewey only huffed.

Then, five minutes later, and just before reaching the house, Avriel broke their silence again. "Do you suppose we should work together and make your mother our target?"

Stopping, Dewey looked up at him, huffed, and said, "Seriously? She'd ground us both! I guess groundings weren't invented too when you were a kid!"

The next day, Dewey woke earlier than usual and reminded himself it was Sunday, in case Avriel tried a repeat performance of the previous day, and forced his tired mind out of bed to feed J.C.

Rushing into his room in jeans and a blouse, his mother ignored the door hitting the piggy bank, and said, "Have fun with Avriel today, Honey," and kissed him on the forehead.

"You're going to work? But it's Sunday."

"It's our day for counting inventory. We do it every three months, so have fun and I'll see you tonight."

"Ok, have fun at work, Mommy."

After his mother rushed down the hall, Dewey picked up the small container of fish food and was about to shake some into the fishbowl when he noticed an unusual amount still floating on the surface from the day before, and when he tapped the glass with the can, J.C. continued to float upside down. Tapping it several more times, the capsized goldfish didn't move. He had to be certain, so he placed his hand in the aquarium's cold water and nudged the tiny fish. Still not getting a response, tears built up in his blue eyes, not so much because his fish had died — he knew J.C. was going to at some point — but because he neglected to notice his death.

Drying his hand on his Spiderman pajamas, he sat down on the side of his bed, and with his feet hanging six inches from the floor, dwelt on his little goldfish being ignored while crying out for help as he drowned.

Seconds later, Avriel showed up at his door. "Good Morning, Mr. Dixon. What would you like from the breakfast menu this fine morning? This morning's specials are cereal, porridge, eggs, lasagna, and corned beef and cabbage."

Dewey would've laughed at the last two specials, but at that moment of his morning mourning, he just looked at Avriel and waved a weak salutation.

"What is wrong?"

Looking down at his feet, Dewey replied, "J.C. died. I don't know when he died, but he died."

Relieved that it wasn't his joke that wasn't funny, Avriel walked into the room, tapped on the aquarium, and bent down for a better look. "Yes, you are correct," he said before joining the boy on the edge of the bed. "Should we perform a burial at sea?"

Dewey looked sternly at him. "Do you mean down the toilette!?"

That was exactly what Avriel meant, but instead of admitting it, he said, "That is one way, but it would... it would be a crude way to the sea. He would have to travel through the sewers system and go into the harbor with the city's waste." Avriel wasn't exaggerating. The city's waste went directly into the harbor, and only two years earlier, the pollution had forced the closing of Black Rock Beach next to the dockyard. "I think a better way would be for us to carry him to the harbor. It would be respectful."

Then, relaxing, Dewey nodded in agreement.

"Ok, get dressed, wash your face, brush your teeth and we shall get breakfast on the way back from the funeral... but do not expect any breakfast specials as interesting as the ones here."

Neither said a word during the twenty-minute drive. Dewey was still too upset to talk, and Avriel wasn't sure what to say about the death of a thirty-two-cent pet.

Soon they were standing on a wharf in Halifax's old waterfront just across from the Bluenose II schooner, both looking into the morning fog of the harbor with its foamy water eight feet below them. With Dewey taking J.C. out of his pocket and holding the tissue-wrapped fish in his hand, Avriel considered the environment to be appropriate for the occasion: an overcast sky blocked the sun; the saltwater made a soft, slow rhythmic sound as it rubbed up and down against the wharf's pillars; the seagulls' frequent calls seemed to cry for the moment, and the foghorn of the Dartmouth Ferry mourned along with them.

Clearing his throat, Avriel asked, "Should we say a few

words?"

"Yes. Can you do it, please?" Dewey asked softly.

"Certainly," Avriel said before clearing his throat again and searching for the words. Hebrew was the first thing to enter his mind, but that would be incomprehensible to his little buddy, so he searched for something English and Christian-like, and finding it, he said, "Dearly beloved, we are gathered here today to join..." Pausing when he realized his mistake in choosing a quote, he glanced down at Dewey for a reaction, and when there wasn't one, he told himself he could make it work. "We are gathered here today to join this goldfish, Jacque Cr... Crouton—"

"Cousteau!"

"Right. Jacques Cousteau... once again to the ocean whence he came. We thank You, Lord, for bringing him into our lives. He was a great fish—"

"A loyal fish," Dewey interjected.

"A loyal fish—"

"A faithful and obedient fish."

"A faithful and obedient fish," added Avriel, who paused a moment for another interjection. "Who brought comfort and joy into our lives."

"And the lives of others."

"And the lives of others. Take this fish, deliver him from evil, and forgive his trespasses as he forgave those who trespassed against him. For Yours is the kingdom, the power, and the glory, forever and ever, amen."

"Amen," Dewey repeated before extending his hands out past the wharf and dropping the tiny fish into the cold, salty water.

Then wanting one more look at his pet, Dewey stepped out to the edge of the wharf and peered down to locate the fish, but because of the height, the fog, and the debris in the water, it was impossible to see where it floated.

After waiting in silence for almost a minute while watching

protectively over Dewey standing in front of him, Avriel said, "It is time for J.C.'s memorial breakfast," and placing his hand on Dewey's shoulder, the two slowly walked back toward the Cadillac.

After they silently ate breakfast at a downtown diner, they stopped at a pet store where Avriel picked up some cat food and, to Dewey's delight, had him pick out a new goldfish.
The old man smiled his first full smile of the day when the boy told him he was going to call his new goldfish J.C. the Second.

**

Avriel was becoming accustomed to sleeping alone or, more accurately, sleeping with Sam, and to minimize the fur on the bed, he had placed a white towel on the other side of it for the kitten to sleep on, which Sam had become so accustomed to that if it weren't on the bed for whatever reason, he would protest with loud meows while refusing to join Avriel.
Retired, Avriel would've expected to sleep in on the morning of the days he wasn't watching Dewey, but he was getting up even earlier than he was used to, around five-thirty every morning, including Sundays. It wasn't by choice. Sam woke him every morning around that time by pushing his furry face against Avriel's stubbly cheek, and if that didn't wake him, his second tactic, running his sandpaper-like tongue over the full length of Avriel's nose, did.

One afternoon, while Lisa was home with Dewey, Avriel needed something to do. He would never have considered rearranging his closet and removing his wife's clothes, so he decided to rearrange her sewing room. He couldn't remember when he had last seen or heard Ruth using the sewing machine, but she would never have discarded it. She believed every woman should have one, just as every man should have a set of tools, and except for his hammer and a couple of screwdrivers, Avriel had hardly ever used his tools.

After calling and offering the machine to Lisa and learning she had a smaller one, he unbolted it from its desk and lugged it and the desk into the basement, where among the other stored furniture, he found the three pieces of his banker's desk. Sweating, he struggled to carry each part up the two flights of stairs and into the almost empty room, and when he had finished putting the desk together, the room appeared as a well-organized office. Avriel wasn't sure what he would use it for, but he could use an office more than a sewing room.

Then the following Saturday and to Sam's apparent amazement, in the living room's windowless wall of bookshelves about a third of the way from the front window, Avriel removed three bookcases to make room for a new floor model color television being delivered early next week and to create a small reading area, on the same wall about another third of the way from the back window, he removed another bookcase and created a semi-wall by placing the four bookcases, two-wide and back-to-back, perpendicular to the wall. He placed the two leather armchairs in the space between the new semi-wall of bookcases and the back window and moved the sofa and coffee table into the basement to make room for the delivery of four reclining chairs, which he was amazed to discover in the first furniture store he and Dewey had visited on their search for a television. Each recliner would have its owner. Avriel's was purple, Dewey's blue, Lisa's orange — the store didn't have pink — and the fourth, for Sam, was green. He would also have cable television installed, increasing the number of English channels from two to twelve.

A week later, on a Saturday evening, Avriel prepared lasagna from a recipe book he had recently purchased and the next morning, eager to show off his work, surprised Lisa by phoning her to invite the two to a lasagna supper. When Lisa asked him what she should bring, he answered, "Well... lasagna, of course," but after a brief silence on her end, he had to say, "It is a joke. I am joking. Just bring Dewey. I prepared the lasagna last night." He was a bit disappointed that Lisa thought he might've been serious.

When mother and son arrived, Avriel proudly showed off his new living room arrangement and, as he expected, Dewey was the more excited of the two, and more so when he discovered Avriel had installed cable.

In the dining room, Avriel, who couldn't help but feel he was playing grown-up, had covered the table with a tablecloth and used Ruth's fine dishes to set three places at one end, and while eating their lasagna dinner, Lisa and he sipped their glasses of red wine while Dewey sipped his grape juice from a wineglass.

When they had finished dinner, Dewey claimed the channel knob and sat on the floor in front of the television, going through the channels until they found a show they all wanted to watch, and after two hours of watching television, when Lisa decided it was time to head home, she quietly found a blanket in an upstairs closet and placed it over their inherited friend, who had fallen asleep during the second hour of television and was snoring heavily.

After watching the Dixons leave the house, Sam made himself comfortable on the blanketed lap of the old man, whose snores he had become immune to.

As they were walking back to their house, Lisa asked, "So, Honey, did you have fun at Avriel's?"

"Yes, but he snores loud. It was funny at first, but later, it was annoying. It was hard to hear the TV."

"I think his loud snoring is a good thing. It means he's comfortable around us."

"Ok, but next time we watch TV at his place, can we make it so he's not so comfortable?"

CHAPTER 15
And Then the Strangest Thing Happened

That Sunday, just over seven weeks after Ruth's death, the paper had called for clear skies and an unusual high of seventy-three degrees, and with the sun promising to fulfill the forecast, Avriel phoned Lisa to propose they all take advantage of the weather.

Lisa refused to relay Dewey's first suggestion of going to a movie, but she relayed his second of playing catch, and after the two had changed into their shorts, T-shirts, and sneakers, both were amused when Avriel arrived at their house wearing a short sleeve dress shirt, dress pants, dress socks, and his regular dress shoes. Ignoring her urge to ask him why he wasn't wearing a tie, Lisa made a mental note to take him shopping for casual clothes.

Half an hour later, and with a tall chain-linked fence behind him and two weathered wooden benches fifteen feet away on each side of him, Avriel, with a bat over one shoulder and a baseball in his hand, looked out toward the green field. To his right, almost halfway between him and the forest surrounding a smooth hill of rock peeking out from over the trees, Dewey patiently waited for the ball, and to his left, Lisa punched the cup of Paul's glove just as she had seen others do and shouted, "Come on, batter, batter, batter!" just as she had heard others shout.

Seeing and hearing his mother, Dewey was thankful there were no other kids around. Though, the kids in the small houses to his right lining the other side of the street that separated them from the field might see and hear her.

It had been over four decades since Avriel had used a bat, and it showed. In his day, he was rather good at batting, *was* being the keyword. Several times that early afternoon, as he tossed the ball into the air and attempted to swing at it, he missed, and when he did finally begin hitting it, it sped along the ground, causing the mother and son to chase after it, and soon both were exhausted from running after the rolling ball and switched to walking after it, making it less fun and more of a chore.

It took almost twenty minutes, but Avriel finally found his old swing and was hitting the balls into the air, proving Dewey to be the better catcher than his mother, who would line herself up so the ball was coming down on her right side, turn her head away, close her eyes and stick her glove straight out to her side, and to everyone's surprise, including hers, she caught a few that way.

With renewed confidence and a slight sweat accumulating on his forehead, Avriel called out to Dewey to go further back, and doing as he was asked, the boy went further out than the old man had wanted, stopping almost twenty feet from the tree line. Then accepting the challenge, Avriel tossed the ball in the air and as it dropped, swung the bat with a fury, causing a loud crack as the ball took off high into the air, and as it fell back to earth, it passed over an amazed Dewey and landed in the thick of the trees. Though impressed with his swing, Avriel was also worried that they might have lost the ball, ending the fun that was only just beginning.

To Avriel, it looked like it had landed near the base of the rocky hill, but to Dewey and Lisa, who had seen the ball from different angles, it landed just inside the tree line, and each made their way to the spots.

Passing through the densely populated trees while avoiding their many attempts to snag his clothes with their branches, Avriel reached the base of the rocky hill that blocked any potential breeze, making the air seem stagnant, and as he began searching for the ball along the rock base, he noticed a scent, froze for a moment, and then sniffed lightly to confirm it was there. It was. With his initial reaction being to walk away, he forced himself to search for the source. Walking along the almost vertical rock wall until the odor became almost nonexistent, he reversed direction and was soon walking through the growing pungent odor toward a three-foot-high pile of rocks stacked against the rock base. Trying to calm down, he instinctively took a deep breath and breathed in so much of the noxious gas that he bent over and vomited, and when he recovered, he forced himself to toss away the smaller stones from the top of the stack, exposing a thin crack in the rock base. As more stones were removed, the crack widened, and the smell became so thick it was almost visible. Trying to ignore both the foul air entering his lungs and the sweat stinging his eyes, the anxious old man rolled away the large stones at the bottom, and then dripping with sweat, he stepped back several feet to stare into the bottom of the wide crevice where the white rubber soles of a small pair of sneakers peered out at him.

"I found it! Avriel! Mommy! I found it!"

Snapping out of his shock, Avriel heard the small footsteps closing in on him, and trying to sound calm, he yelled back, "Great! Take it to the field. I will meet you there." With the small footsteps coming closer, he panicked. "Dewey! The baseball field, go there now!" When the footsteps stopped, Avriel waited for a second before making his way through the trees toward the spot where he had last heard them, and there, he met a stunned Dewey holding up in his small hand the ball that seconds before he was so proud to find, and as the two stared at each other, their eyes watered. A moment later, a curious Lisa joined them, and with Dewey watching and trying to listen in, Avriel whispered into her ear. Then with her face revealing her shock and her eyes beginning to water, she gripped Dewey's hand and without a word, led him out of the woods.

As they traversed the baseball field to cross the street to the nearest house, Dewey tried to figure out what he did that was so wrong. Reaching the steps of a bungalow, Lisa said in a desperately controlled voice, "Dewey, I need you to stay here for a minute," and Dewey could only nod before watching her walk up the steps and knock on the wooden border of the screen door. Then, when a cautious old woman answered, she continued fighting to control her voice. "There's been an accident. Would it be possible to use your phone?" Spotting the young boy waiting for his mother, the woman opened the screen door and allowed her in.

Two minutes later, she returned and not thinking to take his hand, he had to almost run to keep up with her as she headed back to Avriel who was sitting on one of the wooden benches. "They're on their way," she told her friend.

Having had a few minutes to think about how he would handle Dewey, Avriel tried to sound upbeat as he said, "Great! Dewey, you may soon get to ride in a police car, seriously."

Dewey said nothing as he and his mother sat with Avriel, and with them also not saying anything, fear, sadness, and even anger bombarded the boy, who felt no joy with the possibility of riding in a police car. He had by then figured out that he had done nothing wrong and that Avriel had discovered something bad in the woods. He wanted to know what it was and would've asked if not for the lingering shock from his friend's unusually loud, stern voice.

A few minutes later and with their sirens screaming, two police cars followed a dark-gray car onto the baseball field to stop near the baseball diamond. When Dewey stood up with Avriel, Lisa pulled him back down onto the bench and both watched Avriel walk over to the dark-gray car whose driver, a slim man almost six feet tall in a gray suit and sporting a thin mustache, exited the vehicle to meet him and seconds later, three uniformed police officers join them.

Lisa and Dewey watched as the officers and the man in the suit formed a semi-circle in front of their friend, which worried the boy since they looked like they were standing off against him, and he worried more when all five disappeared into the woods.

As a curious crowd slowly formed around the police cars, Avriel returned with one of the police officers, and trying desperately to sound upbeat again, said, "Dewey, you are going to get that drive. Officer Richards here has offered to give you and Mommy a ride home in his police car."

Taking his cue from the old man, the officer also tried to sound upbeat. "That's right, and you get the choice of riding as a policeman or a bad guy. Which'll it be, sir?"

"Policeman, I guess," Dewey said apprehensively.

"And I'll be the bad guy!" Lisa said, also trying to sound upbeat while putting on a fake smile that Dewey easily saw through, making him even more apprehensive.

With Dewey in the front seat and his mother in the back with the two gloves, bat, and ball on her lap, both waved goodbye to Avriel, who waved back while trying to hold a poorly constructed smile — he didn't seem to realize a genuine smile also showed in the eyes — and as they drove away, a local news van passed them.

Heading up to Herring Cove Road, Dewey looked back through the metal screen dividing the front from the back to see his mother quietly sobbing, and as tears filled his eyes, he wanted to be in the back with her. Even though she was just on the other side of the screen, she was still too far away.

CHAPTER 16
The Darker Days of Fall

As the season progressed, and the days became colder and darker, so too did the atmosphere on Gilmore Street.

The news of the discovery of the dead child hit the neighborhood like a nearby explosion, stunning all those around, and the aftershock, which almost knocked the residents over, came when it was revealed that one of their own had made the gruesome discovery. The murder of a child was such a shock to the usually quiet neighborhood that speculation soon spread. Some residents believed the killing was the work of a man of wealth taking out his frustrations on the lower class, or at the opposite end of the social class spectrum, the work of a drifter passing through and acting out his sick desires. Others, including Mrs. O'Brien, believed that since the small victim was white, it was racially motivated and a black man or men had performed the killing in revenge for the city's destruction of Africville, an unofficial name given to a small black community in the city's North End whose residents were forced from their houses and into public housing so it could create a dump on their land. Rumor was the city had even moved the residents' belongings out by garbage trucks.

There was another speculation too, one involving the street's most recent resident, the same resident who had found the child. Some felt he could be the killer. They knew almost nothing about him and by keeping to himself, befriending only Mrs. Dixon, he appeared to be hiding something. And to reinforce their suspicions, there had been little to no drama before he had moved to the street and yet he was involved in the two recent dramatic events occurring directly on it, making more than a few residents believe that a cloud of evil surrounded him. To top off their suspicions, there was the question as to why he was living there when the rumor was that he had more than enough money to live in the upper-class area, causing the many who didn't suspect him of being the killer to feel it best to avoid him.

Days later, when the news came out about the police arresting the child's uncle for the crime, the residents' negative feelings toward their neighbor didn't subside. If anything, they worsened. With the many whispers circulating about him, another rumor had spread about him and Mrs. Dixon having an affair. Many felt certain of it while others felt the relationship was at least suspect since a recent widower spending so much time with a woman soon to be a divorcee and young enough to be his daughter was more than frowned upon. Even Mr. Smith believed an affair was a strong possibility.

Lisa and Avriel knew nothing regarding their neighbors' suspicions. They noticed the tense atmosphere on the street and believed the discovery of the young body was its cause.

The discovery of the body continued to shock Lisa and it had pushed her close to her breaking point. Several times during the first couple of weeks, she had broken down in tears, including once at work when she overheard two women at her checkout line talking about the grisly find.

The discovery continued to shock Avriel too, though it was much less of a shock than what he had experienced during the war, which had conditioned him to such atrocities much like a warhorse is conditioned to loud, sudden noises. The shock had created an anxiety that would've forced him back into his introverted shell if not for his concern for the Dixons. He was able to be there for Lisa through the crises simply by listening to her talk about her concerns while he said little, which he was rather good at. With the child being around Dewey's age, it struck deep for Lisa, who couldn't imagine losing her son and expected that if she did, she would want to die too. How could a person take a child's life? What if the murderer wasn't the uncle? Could a killer be walking free in Spryfield? And to pacify her concerns, they agreed they wouldn't let Dewey out of their sight when he was playing outside.

Even through the shock, Lisa had a lot of sympathy for Avriel. He had found the body on their first outing together and he found it by recognizing the odor of a rotting corpse, and she wanted to know how he knew the smell but couldn't bring herself to ask since it might add more guilt to what she was already feeling for having brought him out to the baseball field that day.

From the way Avriel had handled the discovery, had been there to listen to her concerns, and had more than once offered a shoulder to cry on, Lisa had come to believe he was, at least emotionally, the strongest man she had ever known, and unbeknownst to him, he had started a humble knight-in-shining-armor image when he directed her to his lawyer. Before giving her the contact information, he had arranged for his lawyer to inform her that the divorce would be pro bono because of a regulation within Nova Scotia's Legal Act requiring so many free hours of legal service by each of its barristers and solicitors. Avriel would pay for the service and felt the deception was justified since Lisa would've certainly refused any offer of financial help. He had come to understand that even though it placed an enormous strain on her, her new independence was something for which she was proud, and though it was difficult seeing her in that situation, he had come to respect her more for it.

**

Normally by the last week of October, Dewey would be excitedly planning his costume while counting down the days until the thirty-first, or The Night of Candy as he had preferred to call it, but that year he gave little attention to it. He had so little care for the occasion, that two days before Halloween, his mother was forced to buy him a costume off a shelf at The Met, where she impatiently chose a pirate costume while Dewey stood in the aisle indifferent to the many surrounding them. Then on Halloween night, he wore it over his fall jacket and jeans as he and his mother went door-to-door, where he said his trick-or-treats only when he had to and said them as if it was a bother. His lack of excitement embarrassed his mother, who thought the cold responses from most of their neighbors were because of his lack of gratitude.

Two weeks later, for Dewey's birthday, Lisa gave her stoic son a rectangular 110-film camera and several rolls of film, and with a "Tah-dah," Avriel presented him with a new ten-speed bike, which Lisa thought was too much, but to his disappointment, the little boy was unexcited by the gift, making Avriel believe his lack of interest was due to it being the wrong season for riding it, causing it to tease the child until the spring.

Then, a month later, rather than take part, he preferred to sit and watch Avriel and his mother set up and decorate the artificial Christmas tree. Surprising himself, Avriel became engrossed with the occasion and had a new understanding of why some Jews would set up a Hanukkah bush for their children, which Ruth felt was wrong. However, he didn't bring his excitement home with him and did nothing special there, except to place the electronic menorahs in his first-floor windows as a tribute to Ruth, though it gave him a chance to explain their religious significance to a disinterested Dewey.

Dewey's response to Christmas was even worse than that of

Halloween. His mother had to force him out of bed, and then he just sat on the sofa as they passed around the gifts. From Avriel and Dewey, an excited Lisa received several romance novels and a large bulky microwave, which she thought was too much. From Lisa and Dewey, a smiling Avriel received a few pairs of jeans and two turtleneck shirts, one dark blue and the other light gray. From his mother, Dewey received a second G.I. Joe action figure, a black one, and his standard *boring* gifts of clothing, and from Avriel, he received another action figure, a white one with a short and fuzzy black beard, which could've passed for a young rabbi. "An army rabbi," Avriel told him. And when Avriel surprised his little friend with a G.I. Joe helicopter, he just nodded his head as the old man showed off the oversized toy's retractable hook at its bottom while repeatedly pressing the spring-loaded button to make its blades rotate. It wasn't until Avriel placed a G.I. Joe snuggly into the cockpit, saying, "See? Look at that! Is this not great?" that Dewey cracked a smile... if only to pacify him.

By January, Dewey had stopped smiling altogether, not even cracking one. Whenever anyone attempted to have a conversation with him, he regularly responded with one-word answers. When it came to venting his feelings, bitter sarcasm had become his main tool, and if something didn't go his way, he began saying, "Damn it to hell!" causing his mother to threaten to ground him if he continued saying it. On the weekends, Dewey's pastime became sleeping in late and watching television. He had no interest in going outside to play or even playing with Sam, who would only annoy the boy with his attempts. He had no interest in playing G.I. Joe with Avriel and no interest in going to the movies with his mother. At school, during recess and lunch, Dewey refused to take part in any group activities, preferring to sit silently in the background. And when his school marks dropped, his mother grounded him from television, theirs and Avriel's, until he brought them up again on his next tests, which he reluctantly did.

Lisa and Avriel had attempted several times to get Dewey to tell them what was wrong, and in each of those times, Dewey denied anything was wrong, besides them asking him what was wrong.

Dewey's change worried his mother and Avriel, who worried so much that he suggested a psychiatrist for his little friend. Lisa thought it was a good idea, but also thought they should wait longer to make sure he wasn't going through a temporary phase, like growth pains or puberty, keeping it to herself that she feared if her son saw a psychiatrist, he would negatively label himself.

Dewey also worried about what was happening to him. He knew he was in a bad mood, a terrible mood, and didn't understand why he couldn't just shake it off. Bad moods weren't new to him, but before then, they would only last for several hours, never several months. When the mood first came on, he had put on a happy act but couldn't keep it going for very long and soon replaced it with just being quiet, which was easier to maintain, but recently he began verbalizing his mood through sarcasm, and he couldn't seem to control it.

He considered maybe he was turning into one of those introverts he had once heard Mrs. Rosen talking about with his mother. She had said they would rather read a book than socialize, and that sounded like him. They would rather be alone thinking, reflecting, and even daydreaming, and that sounded like him, too. They also seemed rude because they didn't appreciate small talk or social pleasantries, and that pretty much matched how he felt, and she had told his mother they chose their friends carefully and then were very loyal to them, and that sounded like him, or he hoped it did. But she had also said they were highly intelligent, and he didn't feel highly intelligent, and she had mentioned that many introverts were scientists, musicians, doctors, artists, and authors, and he had no interest in being any of those. Dewey worried that if he wasn't becoming an introvert, what was he becoming? Crazy?

**

Normally, Avriel made his monthly visit to Ruth's grave on Sunday mornings, but that January he changed it to Saturday, and on the second Saturday morning of January, instead of asking his little friend if he wanted to go with him, he startled him by telling him he was.

Parked on the street near the opened iron gates of the cemetery and in their heavy winter coats and boots, they walked along the plowed sidewalk, and as they passed through the gates, Avriel broke their last twenty minutes of silence by asking Dewey if he knew why they put fences around cemeteries. When the boy shook his head, he told him it was because people were dying to get in and received a sarcastic laugh.

After following the plowed road past several snow-covered fields of gravestones, an anxious Avriel turned to walk through the foot-high snow covering another field of them, and after passing its first few rows of gravestones, he stopped in front of one almost completely covered in snow. Brushing the snow from its top with his leather-gloved hand and using his booted foot to sweep away the snowdrift covering its front, he stepped back to look at the stone. "You are welcome," he said before walking past a short space to the next gravestone and removing the snow from it too. Finished and satisfied that the snow trapped in the engraving made it easier to read, he stepped back to stand next to Dewey.

RUTH ABIGAIL ROSEN
FEBRUARY 24, 1910 –
AUGUST 20, 1976

WIFE, FRIEND & CONFIDANT

YOUR NINCOMPOOP MISSES YOU

As the two stood staring at the gravestone, Avriel reflected on Ruth while Dewey reflected on his grandparents, his mother's parents. He knew they had died together in a car accident and probably shared a gravestone, but why had he never seen their grave? He knew it was in a small village called Beaver Tail, or something like that, but why hadn't his mother ever taken him for a visit? Was she on bad terms with her parents like she had once described his father's relationship with his? Maybe bad terms ran in his family — that would explain a lot. Then reading the words on the gravestone a second time, he surprised Avriel by asking, "What's a confidant?"

"It... it is a person you tell secrets to, knowing they will tell no one else and will not judge," Avriel answered, still looking ahead.

"Ok, what's a nincompoop?"

"A jerk."

"Why didn't you just write jerk?"

"I did not know how to spell it."

"Ok," Dewy nodded, accepting the reason. "Why's there a space between her gravestone and that one?"

"She dislikes that person. They get along poorly."

"Seriously?"

"No, that space is reserved for me. People are dying to get in, remember?"

Dewey nodded his head and then, after a few seconds, whispered, "Are you still sad about her... her dying?"

"Yes, but not because she died, because I miss her. The same sadness I would have if you and your mother were to leave and go somewhere far away from me."

"You aren't sad she died?"

"That sadness has passed. The sadness of missing her still lingers. We shall all die someday, so no matter how hard it is to accept, we have to. I think her death would have been easier to accept if I would have been able to admit it to myself. I expected she was going to die, but I refused to accept she would, but I have to say I am thankful her death was not a surprise. If she had died with no warning, it would have been much harder to handle. It would have come as much more of a shock." Then hoping to turn the conversation toward Dewey, he said, "Like the poor little boy we found. The suddenness of his death must have shocked his parents greatly, and I expect they are still having a difficult time coming to terms with it. They probably blame themselves, believing they could have avoided it when there might have been nothing they could have done.

"You know the way he died was rare, correct? I mean to say there are few if any crazy people out there going around killing people, and as for us finding the body... well, that was even rarer. Most people never experience such a thing. You understand that, correct?" With Dewey nodding his head while staring at the gravestone, Avriel continued, "It was a shock to find the boy and because we found him, we might think that sort of thing happens all the time and the world is an evil place, but it is not. That sort of thing almost never occurs, and it is because it almost never occurs that we hear much about it when it does, making us think it occurs all the time. We have a better chance of being hit by lightning twice than finding a dead body, correct?"

Continuing to look ahead, Dewey said, "Yeah, I guess. Did they ever find the person who did it, the person who killed him?"

"Yes... well, they think they have him, but they will only know after the trial," Avriel said, turning his head to look at Dewey. "Does it still bother you about the boy?"

Dewey returned his look. "No. It never really bothered me. It bothered me to see you and Mommy upset, but that's over now. I think finding the body was sort of cool. I never saw it, but would've liked to."

Avriel was perplexed. He had felt certain the discovery of the boy's body had pushed his little friend into a depression, but it seemed only to have affected him in a detached way, like a dead dog on the side of the road. Then not sure what to say, he pointed his gloved finger toward Ruth's gravestone and asked, "Do you miss her?"

"Yup, I miss her. She was nice to me."

"To me as well."

"But I miss my daddy more."

"You miss your father?" Avriel asked with surprise in his voice, before realizing how idiotic his question sounded.

"Seriously!? Of course!" Dewey blurted out as tears built up in his eyes. "He's my father! He never called since he left, never even sent a card for Christmas or my birthday! Never nothing! And he's not even dead! I don't think he even misses me, and if he doesn't miss me, he can't love me! If he did, he'd've done something by now!"

Avriel dropped to one knee, placed his hand on his little shoulder, and said to the boy who was looking down at the ground, embarrassed by his tears. "I am sure your father loves you and misses you, and that may be why you have not heard from him."

"Huh!?"

"Ok, that does not sound correct. Let me try again," Avriel said, before clearing his throat. "I should have said your father went through a very stressful situation and those situations can affect people in different ways. I am certain your father never wanted to leave you and your mother, but they could not stay together. I do not know the reasons. It is only between the two of them. Nevertheless, when something dramatic happens to a person, they can react in several ways. Now I am not a psychiatrist, mind you, but I believe some can brush it off by placing it in the back of their mind and go on living as if nothing had happened. For others, it can change their personality negatively, and for some..." Avriel took off a glove and used his warm fingers to wipe away Dewey's tears. "There, caught those before they turned to icicles... and for some who may include your father, they may need to take some time to accept it. Perhaps your father has to accept all that happened before he can come back to you. I am sure he will come back, and I am sure he loves you." Avriel said, wiping away two more of Dewey's tears. "Especially when you consider that if you can make an old grouch like me love you, then your father certainly does."

For the first time in what seemed like a long time to both, Dewey broke a smile. "You... you love me?"

"What? Of course, I love you. You are the biggest littlest thing in my life! Perhaps, you think differently because I dragged you into the cold and through the snow, only to stare at a piece of rock. Well, young man, I did it because I love you... and you have to walk home, too."

With his smile growing bigger, Dewey laughed.

Content that he had found the reason or one reason for the boy's depression and with his knee hurting from the cold ground, Avriel twisted around, reached back to wrap his long arms around Dewey's legs, and stood up to piggyback him through the snow toward the plowed road.

"You know, you helped me adjust to Ruthy being gone. Without you, I would have been lost."

"Seriously?"

"Seriously. Without you, I would not have known what to do with myself. Perhaps, I would have become a shut-in, those old folks who never go outside, or... or perhaps, I would have moved to the country, or perhaps, I may have even died from a broken heart. It happens, you know."

"Sure, Mommy told me Mrs. Rosen died of a broken heart."

"Right. That is a different, a more literal broken heart. I was speaking figuratively."

Dewey was going to ask what he meant by *literal* and

figuratively but figured it would require several explanations, so he asked the other question on his mind, "Who do you love more, me or Mommy?"

"Well, you, of course... but keep that to yourself. We do not want your mother jealous. She could ground us both, you know," Avriel said as he set Dewey down on the road, took his mittened hand in his leathered one, and headed toward the gate. "You know, perhaps your father also thinks you do not miss him. Perhaps he is thinking the same thing you are, right at this very moment. Perhaps he thinks you are mad at him because of his actions that night. Do you suppose we should have your mother try to talk to him and tell him you forgive and miss him?"

"Yeah, and maybe Mommy can tell him I love him too."

"I am confident she will," Avriel nodded, and then said with an unusual excitement, "Dewey, look! I am smoking!" Holding two fingers up to his mouth, he puckered his lips, inhaled as if he was sucking on an invisible cigarette, and then exhaled the smoke like vapor.

Dewey groaned before he too held two fingers up to his mouth, puckered his lips, inhaled as if he was sucking on an invisible cigarette, and then exhaled the smoke like vapor. After pretending to cough, he smirked and said, "Me too."

Smiling, Av asked, "What did the big chimney say to the little chimney?"

"What?"

"You are too young to smoke."

Dewey groaned again. "What did you do, buy a joke book?"

"Yes, but obviously not a good one."

"Hey, remember when you said I might think the world was an evil place?"

"Yes."

"I don't."

"That is good to hear."

"Ya wanna know why?"

"Certainly."

"Because you're in it."

Avriel stopped walking for a moment and then, as he continued, said, "That... that is nice to know, thank you."

"You want to know something else?"

"Sure," Avriel nodded, uncertain if he could handle another warm remark.

"You talk funny. I don't mean your accent, but the way you talk."

Avriel stopped walking. "I talk funny? Seriously?"

"Yup. You don't connect your words. You say *do not* instead of *don't*."

"I do? I do not use contraction?"

"See, you did it again! Sometimes you sound like Spock from *Star Trek*."

Avriel huffed as Dewey would. "I do not! Seriously?"

"See, you even did it again!"

"I did not! I did... *don't*. Interesting, I guess I do... *don't*. I had never thought about it or even noticed. Should I start?"

"Yup. It'll make you sound more real and friendly, like you are. More like who you are inside."

"I will... *I'll* do that. You have to help me, though. Let me know when I do... *don't* do it, but should."

"I can do that," Dewey nodded.

"That will be great."

"You just did it again!"

"*That'll* be great."

"Perfect!"

That evening, as the three watched television and snacked on potato chips and pop, Dewey seemed more like his old young self, and to Lisa's initial surprise and then amusement, he corrected

Avriel's lack of contraction several times.

Later, after Dewey had gone to bed and Avriel and Lisa had talked about his recent enlightenment, Lisa was covered by a blanket of guilt: Paul had called on both Dewey's birthday and Christmas, but because he was drunk each time, she wouldn't let him talk to his son.

The next morning, Lisa spent several minutes mentally preparing to call Paul and when she finally found the courage, she did, and it wasn't as she had expected. The call confused a hungover Paul, who immediately became excited. He assumed something tragic had happened, but once Lisa had corrected him, he was relieved, calm, and friendly, and by the end of their brief conversation, he agreed to visit Dewey each Sunday morning.

Instead of hanging up the phone, she handed it to Dewey who had been eavesdropping, and the longer father and son talked, the higher Dewey's voice got and the more animated he became, making Lisa smile and wonder when she had last seen him so excited.

**

Paul followed their schedule and picked Dewey up in front of their house at the agreed time, and the first thing he did was surprise him with two late Christmas and birthday presents. Unwrapping them in the car, Dewey discovered two Lego sets, and he made his father promise to build them with him, and he would.

Over the next month and armed with his camera, Dewey spent each Sunday with his father. Paul took him to the movies. They walked through the chilly forest of Point Pleasant Park searching for the nineteenth-century military structures scattered throughout *click... click*. They toured Fort George, the large fortification built on top of Citadel Hill, looking out past downtown toward the harbor *click, click... click* and they tobogganed down the hill's longer and less steep side opposite the harbor *click, click*.

At Fort George, Dewey had a million questions and his father tried to answer them all, answering those he could and lying for those he couldn't, like when Dewey asked how many people had died defending the city. Paul didn't want to disappoint his son by telling him it had never seen battle, so he made up a grand story. He described a battle involving a large fleet of enemy ships in Halifax's harbor and a major enemy ground assault up the banks of the hill, and in the end, and to Dewey's delight, Halifax won the battle with over three thousand of the enemy dead or captured and only six Haligonians wounded.

With each of Paul's visits, both focused on enjoying their time together, and neither brought up the *event* of the past summer.

Paul was proud of himself. He was able to control his emotions when he was surprised to hear about the Jew finding the body of the murdered child, and he was even able to control them when he was shocked to learn his son had been there with him. He had controlled his anger when he had learned the old Jew had become a large part of his son's life and controlled it again when learning his son was still playing with dolls and had even gotten two more: a black one from Lisa, and a Jewish one from the Jew. He was only able to control his anger by telling himself the situation was only temporary. It was just a picture in time but a negative of the picture he expected. As things developed, the next picture would be better and he would make certain of it.

**

Dewey returned to his old self, but a more mature self. He started helping with the cleaning of the house, helping with the dishes, and helping Avriel with the laundry. He had even begun assisting his friend as he attempted to cook dinners, including spaghetti with meat sauce when under the advice of the old man, he threw several noodles at the wall to determine if they were ready by whether they stuck to it. And when Lisa arrived home later that afternoon, she was confused by the several strands of dried spaghetti noodles stuck to the kitchen wall and several more on the floor near it. She was amused to hear the reason for it, and she was thankful they didn't use the same method for testing the sauce.

As a hobby they could do together, Avriel began purchasing plastic model airplanes and twice or three times a week, he and Dewey spent a few hours at the kitchen table carefully assembling them, and while it took between one to two weeks to finish a model, a stack of unopened model airplane boxes began to grow. Every time the two were out at a mall, which was at least once a week, they visited the mall's hobby store and seemed to always come across one or two model airplanes that interested them both, and though Avriel tried, he couldn't stop himself from purchasing them, especially with his little buddy cheering him on, and the two soon had a second hobby of collecting unopened model plane kits, until Lisa put a stop to it. When she saw the growing pile of shrink-wrapped boxes in a corner of Dewey's bedroom, she insisted they don't buy another until they had assembled the current ones... or else she would ground them both. They still bought more, but they stored those in Avriel's home office, which he was glad to have found a use for.

Then, to Dewey's delight, one afternoon after school, Avriel and his mother surprised him with a freshly painted white bedroom, and though he felt no different, Dewey soon discovered he was no longer a child when he started using the regular dishes instead of the Tupperware ones, and no longer being a child, he removed the nightlight from his bedroom and thoughtfully placed it in a socket along the hallway.

CHAPTER 17
The Early Morning Visitor

Tightly gripping the metal railing with each step, Avriel followed further and further behind Ruth and Lisa, both seemingly oblivious to him as they talked about something he failed to make out through the echoes of Dewey's laughter bouncing off the square tower's brick interior.

From the metal stairs along the opposite wall about ten feet above the adults and wearing his Spiderman pajamas, Dewey interrupted his laughing at his friend's fear of heights to yell down, "For a really, really tall person, you sure are afraid of heights!"

Avriel wanted to respond with something like, "I am twice as tall as you, so that would be twice as far for me to fall," but he couldn't. He was too scared to get the words out, and he didn't understand why he was so scared. He and Dewey had been there the week before and he wasn't as fearful then, and what fear there was, he thought he had hid well, except for Dewey telling him he was gripping his hand too tightly.

When Avriel finally joined the three at the top of the tower almost a hundred feet up and overlooking the calm waters of the Northwest Arm, Dewey was asking Ruth the same question he had asked Avriel the week before. "Why does this place have two names? The sign says Sir Sanford Fleming Park, but everyone at school calls it The Dingle." Avriel wasn't able to answer the question then, and he was surprised when his wife could.

"Dear, most people take the name of the tower, Dingle Tower, to be the name of the park. Its actual name is Sir Stanford Fleming Park, but I expect the tower was named after the area. Dingle is Gaelic for the wooded valley. I'd guess a few people started calling it Dingle Park or The Dingle because it's an easier reference and the name just caught on."

Impressed with his wife's answer, it suddenly occurred to him that she wasn't the least bit out of breath. Then realizing it was a dream, which would also explain Dewey's pajamas, he decided to go along with it and enjoy the ride, but when he tried to get back to it, he ended up dreaming of something else.

It was close to two in the morning when Sam woke. Somehow over Avriel's snoring, he could hear something at the back door. Curious, he got up, stretched his back, stretched his front legs, and then stretched each hind leg separately before jumping off the bed, and then, after taking a few seconds to scratch the carpeted cat post, he casually made his way down the stairs and into the kitchen.

Standing beneath the kitchen table, he stared at the back door, where from around the doorknob, it creaked as it bent in slightly. It did it again and was doing it a third time when, with a snap, it flew open and bounced back from its stopper. After jumping back a few inches before a chilly breeze entered the room, Sam crouched down to curiously and cautiously watch a pair of black pant legs enter the kitchen before, with a click, the outside light came on and covered it in a soft glow. Then, after quietly removing the dress shoes, another click lit up the kitchen.

Sam stepped out from under the table to get a full view of the visitor whose opened spring coat revealed his dress shirt, who carried a heavy metal bar, and who wore something black over his head that distorted his facial features, and when he used the light leaking out from the kitchen to guide his staggering way down the hall, Sam followed him. From several feet behind, Sam continued to follow him up the stairs and into the bedroom filled with snoring and partially lit by a streetlight. Crouching down near the entrance, he watched the visitor walk to the bed and raise the crowbar over his head. Then pausing, as if having second thoughts, he lowered the bar and quietly leaned it up against the bed.

Avriel woke up struggling for air. He could get some, but hardly enough. Then realizing what was happening, he found the two hands forcing down the pillow and pulled back on their wrists, and as more force pushed it down on his face, he kicked about as he beat on the arms with all of his energy, which was quickly depleting. Exhausted, he went limp and began seeing stars, a few at first and then more and more, and as he was about to pass out, he heard through the pillow a muffled scream, but it didn't concern him. He had accepted that the time had come to meet up with his wife. Then, with another muffled scream, the force on the pillow relented, and as Avriel gasped for air, he heard more screams, but this time with cursing. Weakly pushing the pillow off of his face, he looked to the side where a male figure was trying to grab at Sam, who was clinging by his teeth to the stretched nylon stocking covering the head while furiously scratching the visitor's hands and face with all four paws.

Bumping into the bedroom's doorframe, the man turned around several times, moving from the bedroom to the staircase where, with bloody hands, he worked Sam free and threw him against the wall.

Using what little energy he could muster, Avriel got out of bed and knocked over the crowbar that he then tripped over and joined on the floor.

The visitor turned to face him, and just as he made a step toward him, Sam was back on his head. Screaming and cursing again, he spun around, moving closer toward the staircase, and as Avriel got to his feet and readied the crowbar in his hand, the man pulled Sam from his head again, and with Sam hissing in his hands as he took another swipe at his nylon-covered head, he stepped back onto the stairs, and fell backward, flipping head over heels, until, with a bang and a crunch, his head slammed into the wall beside the front door.

Cautiously, and with the crowbar still in his hand, Avriel made his way down the stairs, where Sam stood proudly next to the head, his front paws resting on the bloody and torn nylon-covered face. Setting down the crowbar, Avriel picked up Sam and patted him. "It is ok. It is over now." And with Sam purring in an arm, he bent down and pulled the nylon from the head to reveal the bloody face of Paul Dixon staring up at the ceiling.

Twenty minutes later and with sirens off as requested, two police cars and an ambulance arrived.

**

Dewey would never know the full details of his father's death. He was only told they found him dead of a broken neck from a bizarre accident.

There was no formal funeral for Paul. Lisa had him cremated and together, the three drove out to Beaver Point to spread his ashes.

On a short wharf partially covered by what was left of that winter's snow, Dewey performed the ceremony. Bundled up in his winter coat and with eyes dried from the two-hour drive, he recited the words the three had worked on earlier. "Earth to ocean, ashes to sea, dust to water, Lord please deliver this man to heaven. Released from his physical body, please forgive his sins... and honor his life as You deliver him to Your Heavenly Kingdom. For Yours is the power and the glory forever and ever. Amen."

"Amen," Lisa and Avriel repeated.

Struggling to pull the top from the wooden box, Dewey gave

up and handed it to Avriel, who pulled it off and handed it back. Removing the plastic bag of gritty light-gray ashes, the boy tore a hole in the top, getting some ashes on his coat, and when he spread them from the corner of the wharf, all held their breath as they watched the wind carry them out into the harbor.

With the ceremony over, Lisa gave a quick tour of the spread-out community where Dewey got to see the small house she had grown up in, the grocery store where she had worked, the school she had attended, and the general store where they stopped and got gas, and it amazed Dewey that his mother seemed to know everyone they passed.

They ended their tour by visiting the small church's graveyard where in front of her parents' plot, she held Avriel and Dewey's hands and said, "Hi, Mom, Dad. I know it's been a while since I was here, and I'm sorry for that. I thought it was time I introduced you to your grandson, Dwight. That's right, Dad, we named him after you and gave him your nickname too. And this here is Avriel Rosen. He unofficially adopted us as daughter and grandson."

Dewey laughed but stopped when he looked up at the watery-eyed Avriel.

"Dad, you'd like him. He has your sense of humor. He's a wonderful man whom Dewey and I have come to love. Lucky for Dewey and me, we found him at the right time. He's been a big help in our lives. Oh, and Paul's not with us anymore. If you run into him up there, please say hello from all of us. And while I'm at it, if you run into Ruth Rosen, Avriel's wife, let her know we miss her and that Avriel is doing fine. She had once asked me to look out for Avriel, but please let her know he's looking out for us. Well, that's it for now. I miss you and love you, and I promise it won't be another ten years before my next visit."

On the long drive home, all were silent as Dewey, sitting between his mother and Avriel, dwelt on how strange it was that death was such a common occurrence, so common that he was already halfway to being an orphan, and that would've overwhelmed him if not for the comfort of having Avriel in his life. Eventually, he fell asleep against Avriel's side, but like magic, when they arrived home, he woke in the back seat with his head on his mother's lap.

Later, Dewey would be satisfied to learn from his mother that his father was in heaven with Mrs. Rosen, and he would be more satisfied when Avriel confirmed it.

CHAPTER 18
Av Rosen

On a cold, wet Saturday afternoon, Dewey and Avriel leaned back in their reclining chairs, Dewey watching television while holding a glass of pop between his legs and Avriel reading a book with his glasses resting halfway down his nose. With a knock on the front door, Dewey reached over and slapped his oblivious friend's arm, and when Avriel looked over at him, the boy mouthed, "The door."

Getting up, Avriel took off his glasses, handed them to Dewey, and went to the door to find a man in his mid-thirties with his medium frame tucked neatly into a well-fitted three-piece suit looking awkward as he stood almost at attention. "Gerald? Gerald Wilson? This is certainly a surprise. Come in out of this unusual cold," Avriel said in an unusually loud voice before moving out of the way so the gentleman could enter.

Then wearing Avriel's glasses with the ends of their arms sticking out half an inch beyond his small ears, Dewey twisted his body so he could better hear their conversation over the television.

"Thank you, Mr. Rosen," Mr. Wilson said, as he stepped in and moved to the side so Avriel could close the door.

"So what brings you here on a Saturday... or any day for that matter? Do not tell me the stock market crashed and I lost everything," Avriel loudly joked with his straight face.

"No... no, sir, nothing like that. I just need to talk to you about something... something less dramatic. I tried calling three times last week, but you weren't home."

"Sorry?"

Mr. Wilson raised his voice. "I just need to talk to you. I tried calling."

"One moment, please," Avriel said as he reached into each ear and pulled out rubber earplugs. "Sorry, I tend to forget I have my reading plugs in."

With Dewey laughing, Avriel went to place the earplugs into his shirt breast pocket, but there wasn't one on his Polo shirt, so he placed them in the front pocket of his new and uncomfortably rough jeans.

"Gerald, that is Dewey. Dewey, this is Mr. Wilson. I am *babysitting* Dewey in order to pay the bills."

Dewey huffed. "It's *I'm* not *I am*!" he said before turning back to the television.

"Hi, Dewey."

"Hi, Mr. Wilson," Dewey said, waving the back of his hand above the back of the recliner.

"Come, we wi... *we'll* go into the kitchen. Would you care for a coffee?" Avriel asked, hoping to impress the young man with his knowledge of coffee making.

"No, thank you. I'll only keep you a few minutes, sir," Mr. Wilson said, nervously removing his polished black loafers at the door before following the old man to the kitchen.

"Ok, what is going on?" Avriel asked, pulling out Ruth's chair for his guest and sitting down across from him just as the volume of the television dropped.

"Well, sir, it's more a question for Mrs. Rosen. May she rest in peace, but I'm hoping you can answer it. I must say, I do miss her Friday phone calls. She was always so full of life," the stockbroker said before his face reddened.

"Yes, she was. Not so much now... but she is in a better place, or so I want to believe. Anyway, Gerald, what is the question? I may be able to help, but I make no promises."

"Well, sir, Mrs. Rosen made me successful."

"Oh, I did not know she did that much trading."

"No, not in that way. Every Friday she'd call me with her buy and sell requests. She was always right on the mark. If she sold the stock, its price plummeted and if she bought it, it soared. After a time of watching her results, I started passing the information on to my other clients... after I first completed her requests, of course.

"I've quite a few clients and they all made money from your wife's actions. Whatever she did, I did the same for them. Sir, I was even the top earner in the office. Now, with her gone, may she rest in peace, I'm just an average broker and my clients who've become accustomed to their gains are losing faith in me. There's a saying: *if you want to be successful, do as the successful do*. So, Mr. Rosen, if you know how your wife got her information, I'm hoping you would be kind enough to share it with me."

Once again, Avriel was proud of his Ruthy, and he expected she would want him to help her broker, so he did it in a way she would appreciate.

"Well, Gerald, I can certainly appreciate the courage it takes to come here and ask," Avriel said, before switching to a whisper to say, "So, I will tell you the secret," and then making a gesture with his eyes as if to communicate that his kitchen was bugged, he leaned across the table and whispered again, "But I will have to tell you over dinner in a very public place." Standing up to grab a pen and a small pad of paper from the kitchen counter, he sat back down, wrote on the pad, and whispered, "How about we meet this Thursday night at five-thirty at this location? I will make the reservation, but you are paying." Tearing the piece of paper from the pad, he handed it to Mr. Wilson, and warned in another whisper, "Tell no one about this meeting, Gerald, no one."

Mr. Wilson stiffly nodded his head, awkwardly stood up, and headed to the front entrance with Avriel following behind. Sliding his feet into his loafers, he rigidly shook Avriel's hand and said, "Thank you, Mr. Rosen. Thank you, sir."

Avriel whispered into Mr. Wilson's ear, "Tell no one of the meeting, Gerald, no one," and then in a louder voice than normal said, "Well, Mr. Wilson, I'm glad you could join me for a coffee. Come again when you have more time... and bring Mildred and the kids along next time. Well, I must get back to *babysitting* Dewey."

With a loud huff coming from the boy, the unmarried and childless Mr. Wilson quickly nodded several times and said, "Thank you again, and it was nice meeting you, Dewey" and left the house as the boy replied, "Bye, Mr. Wilson."

Smiling a mischievous smile, Avriel removed his glasses from Dewey's face and sat back down in his recliner.

"What was all the whispering about?"

"This Thursday, we are all getting a free dinner at a very nice restaurant."

"Neat," Dewey said before he raised the volume on the television and Avriel squeezed his earplugs back in.

**

That coming Thursday, Dewey found himself in a black suit, which matched Avriel's, which was a step down from Lisa's formal dress she had last worn to the charity dinner.

Arriving at the restaurant, Avriel was glad to see Mr. Wilson, whom he worried he might have scared off, anxiously waiting outside the entrance, and when the two greeted each other, Mr. Wilson's face registered confusion when the old man introduced his two guests without explaining how he knew them. Then recognizing Dewey's voice as the child buried in the recliner the previous Saturday, the stockbroker smiled, and after the handshakes with the little man and his mother, he opened the restaurant's heavy wooden door for the three.

Lisa and Dewey looked around curiously. The sharp contrast

between the inviting smell of potpourri and the dark, intimidating atmosphere of the lobby confused both. In front of them sat an attractive middle-aged hostess behind a grand oak desk holding a brass lamp with a green glass shade, an antique penholder with a spot for an inkwell, an open leather-bound reservation book, and a stack of leather folders. The hostess, who appeared to recognize Avriel, seemed startled when he spoke to her about his reservation, and with an awkward half-smile, she pulled the pen from its holder, made a scribble in the reservation book, and then asked them to follow her. Picking up four folders, she led the four into the dining room and to their table.

Dewey noticed he was the only young person in the dining room and then noticed the restaurant used wood floors as walls. He didn't understand why there were several shelves placed around the room holding old leather-bound books unless some people liked to read while they ate, and he was surprised to see the only light in the dimly lit windowless room coming from the several oil lamps hanging off metal hooks sticking out from the walls. To the boy, it seemed they had gone back in time.

The group sat at their table, situated almost in the middle of the dining room, which Avriel had specifically requested when he made his reservation, and with Mr. Wilson sitting next to Dewey and across from Avriel, the four opened their folders and stared at their menus for several minutes.

"Mommy, it says it's six ninety-eight for a hamburger! That's how much a G.I. Joe costs!"

"Yes, Honey. This is a very special restaurant."

"It is a very special restaurant," Avriel nodded. "Ruthy and I would come here every Thursday evening. Our first time here was for her birthday, about twelve or thirteen years ago, and then we came here every Thursday after that, every Thursday evening... the evening before Friday."

With his hint going unnoticed, Mr. Wilson nodded with

disinterest and closed his menu, and as the four placed their orders with the waiter dressed entirely in black except for a white tie, Avriel did something he had never done: he ordered something other than the one meal he had ordered there every week since first going there.

Soon after their stiff waiter left them, they watched their salads being made on a stainless steel cart by an older gentleman in a black suit and apron, and when they were finished eating their salads, their waiter arrived balancing four large dinner plates with just one hand. A skill that impressed Dewey so much that he applauded, causing everyone at the table, including Mr. Wilson, to laugh, and the waiter to break a slight smile and bow to the little boy, and then, as if realizing where he was, he stiffened back up.

Throughout the meal, Mr. Wilson, who seemed to be purposely avoiding Lisa, questioned Dewey about his hobbies, sports, and school, and Dewey gladly answered, with Lisa reminding him several times not to talk with food in his mouth.

With their meals finished, all were silent through their desserts, until Mr. Wilson whispered, "Mr. Rosen, about the... the secret."

"Yes?" Avriel whispered back, picking up his coffee.

"When would be a good time?"

After taking a sip of his coffee, Avriel whispered, "Let's just take a moment to listen in on the conversations around us."

"Ok," Mr. Wilson whispered back, obviously trying to control his impatience with the bizarre request, and as he did as Avriel suggested, Lisa and Dewey said nothing as they too listened in on the conversations.

Two minutes later, Avriel whispered to Mr. Wilson. "The table with the two suits to your right. What are they saying?"

"Really?" Mr. Wilson asked. "You want me to listen for you? Really?"

Avriel sipped his coffee again. "Really."

"Uh... ok, let me see," Mr. Wilson said before listening for half a minute. "They're talking about... about... an oil company, an oil exploration company called... Zenev. I know about this one. Its shares are struggling." Then Mr. Wilson paused to listen some more. "They're talking about something... something about it discovering oil somewhere off Newfoundland."

"Right, now what about the table behind you?"

"Really? Again?"

"Yes."

Mr. Wilson took a deep breath, listened in for a moment, and then whispered, "They're talking about one of their sons graduating from Dalhousie."

"Right. Forget about that one. What about the one to your left?"

Continuing to humor the crazy old man, he listened for about a minute before saying, "They're talking about Warner buying Otari."

"Atari. He said Atari," Dewey corrected him before his mother hushed him.

"Right, Atari. Thank you. They're saying Atari is coming out with a TV-type game next year. It's supposed to be better than Pong. It sounds pretty stupid if you ask me, but I'm not one for TV games. Pong is a big seller though, so that could be pretty hot news if it's true."

Avriel nodded his head. "Exactly."

Mr. Wilson stared at the old man for a couple of seconds before a light seemed to come on in his head. "That's it?" he asked in a loud voice.

"That is it. That is all she did. All she ever did every Thursday evening. Now, this evening we got lucky. Some Thursday evenings it is not as free-flowing."

Then, with his face showing his excited delight, Mr. Wilson paid the bill, laid down the tip, wished the best to the three, and was off before they could get up.

"So, what do we do now?" Dewey asked.

"What do you want to do?" Avriel asked, pulling out his wallet.

"Can we go to a movie? We never went to one before, not with you anyway, ever. It could be fun."

"Lisa, would you be up to it?" Avriel asked, laying a twenty on top of Mr. Wilson's five-dollar tip.

"Sure, if that's what you two want."

"Ok, we will go to a movie on two conditions. First, you two must sit on each side of me, so no strangers are fighting for my armrests. I'd like to get the full use out of them," he said, and with a smile and a nod from Dewey, he added, "And second, you call me Av. I would like you two to call me Av."

Dropping his smile, Dewey said, "But Mrs. Rosen told me to call you Avriel."

Not expecting that response, Avriel said, "Well, yes... yes, she did," and after thinking for a moment, he added, "But we were not best buddies back then so I think... no, I *know* she would agree Av is more appropriate now."

"Best buddies?"

"Yes, best buddies. Best buddies are closer than friends and will always be there for each other... no matter what."

"Neat! I'm your best buddy!"

"And I'm your best buddy too," Lisa said with a grin.

"No! Boys can't be best buddies with girls! Mommy, he's only my best buddy!"

Smiling his then common smile, Avriel said, "Well, now let me see. I... I seem to recall reading somewhere that best buddies can be a mix of boys and girls, but I believe the limit was four per person at any one time. I read it a while back in a law book somewhere."

Then, with the boy pacified, when their waiter came by to wish them a good evening, he pointed to Avriel and said, "I'm his best buddy!"

With the waiter cracking the second smile of his shift, Avriel shook his hand and thanked him for the service, and Dewey did the same, and as they were leaving, Avriel pocketed a box of Morgan's matches, explaining to the two, "You can never know when you will need one."

That box of matches would soon become one of a kind, perhaps even a collector's item. Three and a half months later, Morgan's would burn to the ground and Mr. Wilson would spend more than a year searching for another restaurant to replace it.

The next year, the city prohibited the use of oil lanterns in restaurants.

CHAPTER 19
Saturday Morning, March 12, 1977

He was apprehensive, and he hadn't been apprehensive for some time. He would've been more apprehensive if he were going alone, but then, if he were going alone, he wouldn't be going at all. He was going because he would be with family.

Showered and in black dress pants and a half-buttoned dress shirt, with Sam watching from the toilet seat cover, Avriel stood in front of the bathroom sink with his face lathered up. Picking up a small towel from the counter, he wiped the cream from his hands, traded the towel for a straight razor, and as he had done eighteen thousand times before, give or take a few hundred, he repeatedly slid it down his left cheek, slowly working his way to the right via his chin.

Finished shaving, he wiped his face, hands, and razor with the towel and examined his mustache before picking up a small pair of scissors and trimming it.

About to button his shirt, an idea came to him, and placing an index finger over his mustache, he squinted into the mirror and turned his head from left to right. Taking a deep breath, he brought the scissors back up to it and nervously clipped the hairs from the bottom to the top, carelessly scattering them over the sink, floor, and Sam, and after lathering up what was left of his mustache of over thirty years, in less than a minute, it was gone.

After wiping his face, hands, and razor again, Avriel stared into the mirror. He looked different but familiar, like an old friend whom he had not seen in many years, and then forcing his eyes from it, he buttoned his shirt, picked up a small black yarmulke, and gave it a shake and pat before folding it over twice and sliding it into his shirt pocket.

Earlier that week, he had decided to give Dewey his ancient yarmulke, the one he wore when he was around the boy's age. It took him half of a day to find it, but seeing the delight in Dewey's eyes would be worth it. If not for his little friend that previous Sunday, he would never have accepted Thomas' invitation. Dewey's excitement with them going — he had assumed the invitation was for him too — pushed him into considering it, and in the time it took them to eat his first attempt at brisket, which was a bit tougher than he had been aiming for, it was decided he, Dewey and Lisa would meet up with Thomas at the synagogue that coming Saturday morning, this morning.

Avriel felt good knowing he wasn't going to the synagogue because he was lonely and/or bored and/or fearing death. No, he was going because of the love of his friends; friends he considered family; a family that kept him too busy to be lonely and/or bored, and too content to give death any consideration.

With the fresh bare skin beneath his nose tickling, he rubbed it and noticed how strange it felt, but he knew he would grow accustomed to it, much as he had grown accustomed to his new life, his new life with close friends, his first intimate friends in over thirty years. After spending the last thirty years avoiding people, what saved him after Ruth's death were people, her people. His life was worth living because Ruth had found herself two friends whom he had inherited.

Staring again at the clean-shaven face his wife hadn't seen in over thirty years, Avriel wished he had shaved it before she passed, and then he wished she had had more time to spend with Lisa and Dewey. She had worked hard to find friends for herself but was given little time to be with them.

Then it hit him and he froze as the pressure behind his face built up so fast that tears were running down his cheeks before he even realized it.

He had figured it out.

Avriel had finally figured out that Ruth wasn't trying to find friends for herself.

AUTHOR'S NOTES

1) Though the characters and their situations and events are fictitious, the named streets, except Gilmore Street, are true for the period of the story.

2) All the places mentioned in Halifax, except King's Bar and Rose Sons' Pharmacies, are real as of the period of the story.

3) Beaver Point is a fictitious name of the actual village described in the area of the Eastern Shore.

4) The places and events recounted during World War II, not the characters involved with them, are true and accurate.

5) The measurements of speed, distance, weight and temperature used in the book follow the Imperial System used before Canada adopted the metric system in 1977.

ABOUT THE AUTHOR

Michael Kroft is a Nova Scotian Haligonian and writes character-driven novels about the relationships between complex and lovable characters. Having almost (one book remaining) completed his first series, Herring Cove Road, he's now working on his next, The Lovelys' Family Tree.

Current Works:

The Not-so-Nuclear Family Saga Series, *Herring Cove Road*:

Volume 1) On Herring Cove Road: Mr. Rosen and His 43Lb Anxiety

Volume 2) Still on Herring Cove Road: Hickory, Dickory, Death

Volume 3) Off Herring Cove Road: The Problem Being Blue

Volume 4) Before Herring Cove Road: Ruth Goldman and the Nincompoop

Volume 5) Still Before Herring Cove Road: The War of the Rosens (Coming March 2024)

The Family Saga Series, *The Lovelys' Family Tree:*

Volume 1) Indentured Bonds: The First Generation, Circa 1715

Volume 2) Family Bonds: The Second Generation, Circa 1735 (Coming October 2023)

CPSIA information can be obtained
at www.ICGtesting.com
Printed in the USA
LVHW101115300523
748307LV00020B/72/J